Bad Guys

ELIZABETH ARTHUR

Bad Guys

ALFRED A. KNOPF New York 1986

Arthur, Elizabeth.   Bad guys.

  I. Title.
PS3551.R76B3   1986   813'.54   86-45263
ISBN 0-394-55442-6

Manufactured in the United States of America

FIRST EDITION

■

Grateful acknowledgment is made to the National
Endowment for the Arts, with whose support
the first draft of this novel was written.

PART ONE

Sometime After
the Earthquake

1

◼ SPIKE WAS WAITING patiently for the train. Patience was
a virtue he did not hold, in the abstract, in particularly high
regard—since lightning-quick decisions and instantaneous actions were the province of those he most admired—but five
years in the British Columbia Penitentiary had developed his
facility for waiting to an unfortunate degree, and although anyone looking at him as he sat on the thin-slatted green wooden
bench would have thought that here was a man who was eager
to be gone—his taut, rather feral face was held forward of his
neck in a way that seemed to anticipate movement, and his
eyes stared fixedly at a distant point in space—in fact, he felt
as relaxed as he ever could. He wore a pair of khaki army-
surplus pants, a thin gray T-shirt with a canvas jacket buttoned
over it, a pair of black jungle boots laced all the way to the top,
and an earring in his left ear. Occasionally he would stick his
left forefinger directly into that ear and leave it for a moment,
as if he were testing the temperature of the interior of his brain.
His right hand was occupied in holding his harmonica, which
he had set on the knee closest to his bench mate, where he
tapped it and turned it over, his thoughtful consideration of the
harmonica an attempt to conceal his surreptitious interest in
the man beside him.

That man had a wart on the tip of his chin, and a pair of glasses on a chain around his neck. He was as large and sodden as Spike was small and wiry, but he wore his fat apologetically, as if he were aware that some people might take bulk to be a personal affront. He had on a checked shirt in shades of brilliant red and over this he wore a seersucker suit, the combination so incongruous that Spike could not help but think the man had just been released from some institution even more sinister than a prison—although the brand-new running shoes on his feet would tend to argue against that since no institution in the world provided its members with Adidas. As Spike stared at the man, slowly forgetting to conceal his interest, his attention became fixed, not on the wart, not on the shoes, not even on the green-rimmed glasses hanging from their thick brown chain, but on the small square traveling case he held on his lap, the kind of case that victims of the Depression might have clutched as they walked the dusty roads in search of work.

To Spike everything, no matter how ordinary, appeared at times unaccountable or difficult to comprehend. A nylon jacket, a steering wheel, a lawn sprinkler, a flashing neon sign—all these had the power, at times, to catch him off guard; just the day before he had stood for five minutes or more before a supermarket cart thrust up against a curb, one wheel askew, overcome by a sensation of vertigo at its existence, and then later, after drinking water from a paper cup, had held the cup in his hand, stunned that such a cylinder of stiffened wax should be. He knew that the really great criminals—and he had been overtaken more·and more lately with the sense that he would never be one of them—were able to act as quickly and effectively as they did because of a preternatural awareness of the real significance of objects; knew that some men were able to read directives for action in any point in space. But for Spike, surfaces hid, did not reveal their meanings. A pile of cooked spinach might suddenly look so awful to him, so threatening, that the only thing to do with it was thrust it into his mouth— and to one extent or another the same technique applied to all those things that troubled his peace of mind. He had always been a grab-it-and-run man, though he had always aspired to more. He wrenched his eyes away from the suitcase and in an attempt to distract himself, spoke.

"Where ya going?" said Spike.

The man quivered a little as he shifted his sad bulk sideways, and his hands moved together toward his glasses with great effort, as if he were tugging at invisible ropes that fastened them to his knees. Before the glasses reached his face, his eyes—blue eyes—had an airiness about them, a childlike candor; but after those ponderous hands had tugged their way up to the chain and helped the glasses settle themselves on his nose, the light left his eyes and they became fixed and polite as they moved to meet Spike's.

"Onto the train," the man said. "I follow the suggestions of the world spirit, and it simply told me, 'Get onto the train.' For all I know, the train is just going to come uncoupled and sit in the yard. Then the world spirit will presumably direct me further."

"I was in Vietnam," said Spike. "You think the world spirit directed me there?"

Actually, he had not been in Vietnam, but he found it almost always a good way to direct the conversation back to himself, where he preferred to have it. If this man were normal, and not the lunatic he appeared—from this brief sample of his ideas—to be, he would have said "Anchorage" in response to Spike's first query, or named one of the smaller towns that lay on the far side of Fairbanks, and then followed that up with "What about you?" And that would have given Spike a chance to air his views on any number of things, some of them views he would have had no idea he held until he spoke them aloud—which was the whole fun, in his mind, of talking to other people at all.

Moodily, the man seemed to be wrapping and unwrapping Spike's remark in his mind.

"We're all brothers," he said at last. "Even those thin people in Asia. You didn't, by any chance, get married while you were abroad?"

"I got laid," said Spike. "I got the clap."

"No. Well, in that case—unless you were to tell me that you learned to play the harmonica while you were in Vietnam or that you lost one leg"—and here he paused to examine Spike's pants quite earnestly—"I would have to say that no, the world spirit probably did not direct you there." The man sighed.

Spike looked at his harmonica. It was a perfectly ordinary blues harp, a little dented on one side, with HOHNER HARP inscribed across the front in fancy letters. He had stolen it in the prison library one day when its owner had laid it down for a minute and he had never managed to play a real tune on it, though he had subsequently impressed his cellmate by playing random collections of notes and then giving them fancy titles like "Low Down and Dirty" or "My Baby's Busting Loose." When asked for a repeat of a particular favorite, Spike would explain haughtily that he was not a player piano, and that his range was too great for him to constantly play the same pieces. Now, lifting his right hand, he blew a few spitty notes on the instrument, then tapped it on his forearm with great vigor.

"I got the harp in the joint," he said.

He expected an animated reaction to this statement, since in his experience the one thing that excited people even more than the incorrect information that he had fought in Vietnam—sometimes he had been a Green Beret, sometimes a foot soldier, "cannon fodder," as he called himself—was the information that he had just been released from prison. Generally speaking, he had *always* just been released from prison, except when he was in prison, so this was a reliable constant in his conversational arsenal. To the best of his recollection he had never spent more than seven weeks on the outside since he was fifteen years old and first sent to the Chenega Youth Training Center—and to tell the truth, he had never really wanted to. Prison was so safe and predictable; naturally there were dangerous people to look out for, and it was true that objects could take you by surprise even there; someone would put a new poster on the wall of his cell or for some bizarre reason they would start serving stewed prunes for breakfast. But on the whole, there was little change and little chance for confusion.

"The harp," said the man, "in the joint. How rhythmic that sounds, how much like the beginning of a song of the spirit. I got the harp in the joint, the harp in the joint, oh, yeah, I got the harp in the joint. I played it for the world, I played it for the world, oh, yeah, the harp from the joint."

Spike was beginning to feel distinctly aggrieved. Nothing he said seemed to make the right impression on this fat man, and he contemplated a sudden, savage invasion of the huge expanse of chin that sat between the man's head and the top of his body, like a mezzanine floor between a lobby and a penthouse. The man did not notice the aggravation. He adjusted his glasses with both hands and said, rather diffidently, "My name's Hannah. Wesley Hannah. What's yours?"

"Jones," said Spike. "Mica Jones." He had no idea why he picked this name, out of the many that were available to him, although it was true that the rock rubble which littered the Fairbanks train yard was glinting fiercely now in the late afternoon sun. Usually he did it the other way around; the last name would be the peculiar one, the first name perfectly ordinary, since he had found it was easier for him to respond to names that were not his own when they were distinctive and preceded by a "Mister." But he liked the sound of Mica, and repeated it aloud with satisfaction, feeling that his new name, with its connotations of something that was sharp, thin, tough, and often transparent, boded well for the journey he was now engaged on, a journey to visit Chenega.

But, as usual, his bench mate's reaction was all wrong.

"Micah!" he exclaimed. "A name of powerful omen. Micah, as I'm sure you must know, was a prophet of the eighth century B.C.—the sixth book of the minor prophets in the Old Testament bears his name. If I had known your name was Micah— well, of course the world spirit directed you to Vietnam."

In disgust and some disbelief, Spike got to his feet. Picking up the duffel bag with one hand, he attempted to toss it casually over his shoulder, but he had never been a very coordinated person, even as a boy, and the duffel bag slipped and fell, narrowly missing Wesley Hannah's head in its descent. Spike picked it up again, and this time drew it into his arms; then, nodding coolly, he walked away down the train platform. At this moment the train, now almost an hour late, pulled into the south end of the station with a great hissing and screeching of brakes, and suddenly all was action, men running to and fro to switch levers, sound bells, place steps where they would be needed. For a moment, while the passengers were climbing down, Spike's attention was fixed on a pile of brown-wrapped packages which an Indian in a turban was rolling along the platform on a dolly, and Spike was forced to wonder why brown paper was the universally accepted masking device for all things, cheap and costly, and then the conductor shouted to the waiting people: the train was ready to load. Spike beat Wesley Hannah to the door by at least a minute, and had settled himself happily into a seat in the fourth car before Wesley had finished mounting the steps.

Spike loved trains. As a child in Nelson, British Columbia, he had lived right next to the train yards, in a bright blue house with a sooty picket fence around it. The house was unusually tall and thin, and stretched away from the tracks like something too susceptible to the Doppler effect; inside the rooms were all so narrow that it was hard to arrange furniture in them except facing north and south, which had always given Spike the feeling that the house itself was ready to travel, all set to just step forward one day and hook on to the back of a caboose. At night when he lay in bed awake he would listen to the sounds of the cars being coupled and uncoupled, drawn backward or forward, loaded or unloaded, and once in a while moved on their way. But he had no real desire, then, to follow the trains on their travels, and was glad, on the whole, that his house never stepped forward. It seemed to him not that the trains must be bound for marvelous places, but that they had already found one, that these trains had traveled from all over British Columbia—and from even farther away, Alberta and Saskatchewan!—just to reach his own front yard, the center of the world. They were, in a way, his personal chattels, huge and noisy and powerful, like the animals that knelt for Jesus in the manger or the lemmings that worshiped the sea.

He had left Nelson when he was twelve years old and his father moved to Alaska. Although they had abandoned everything else that they had accumulated up to that point—even Spike's collection of Superman comics had been deemed too bulky to transport from Nelson to Anchorage—they had brought with them their peculiar Canadian accents which, though apparently acceptable to his father's fellow workers in the factory, were far from acceptable to Spike's fellow teenagers; he got beaten up time after time for simply saying "Hey?" Eventually he had lost the more pronounced aspects of his foreignness, but not before his optimism too had vanished. When Chenega had been proposed, Spike's father had suggested to Spike's social worker that instead of what sounded like summer camp his only son should be sent to the state pen, and after the key had been turned in the cell door it should be ground to small bits and baked; for two years before that, every time the police telephoned, his father had shouted into the mouthpiece of the phone—so loudly that Spike, standing near the other end of the line in the police station, could hear him—"Beat the bastard to a pulp! I don't want nothing to do with him!" and then crashed the receiver down. He would relent, however, when the police actually appeared at his door with his child in tow. Then he would reach out, take Spike by the shoulder and, completely ignoring the cop standing there, ram him several times into the nearest wall.

So Spike had already had quite a record when he was sent to Chenega, and he had only gotten in at all because the program was still so young. Six breaking and enterings, one assault with a deadly weapon, two assault and batteries, one malicious damage—that was the only one of those they had caught him at—and a number of lesser offenses: shoplifting, drunk and disorderly, car theft, etc. The Chenega Board of Review had apparently had a terrible fight over whether they should take him on, some of them maintaining that he was already incorrigible, and that they should give the space to some boy for whom there was still hope, others maintaining that here was the perfect test case for the whole concept of behavior modification. The incorrigibles had lost by a thin margin, and Spike had been delivered to Chenega Island by his social worker, who told him at least thirty-five times, "This is your chance. Don't blow it."

Well, he had blown it, or had it blown for him, though for a while he had thought things might be different there. For one thing, there had been a predictability about life on Chenega that satisfied him in much the same way that prison life satisfied him later on; almost every hour of the day on the island had been filled with a set activity. The bugle had sounded at six o'clock in the morning for the five-mile run and a plunge in the ocean—and Spike still remembered the smell of the sea in the early morning sun and the fog drifting languidly on the water—and then they'd had morning work details. Industrial education, more work details, school, more running, all had given Spike an unfamiliar feeling of satisfaction; the routine, something about the routine, had made him feel he belonged.

And Chenega had even been fun. They had had big charts on the walls there, telling you how many points you could earn for doing various things, so even the simplest activities had the potential for a reward. Putting the tools back in the tool shed after you had checked them out for a special project, showing up on time for meal duty, keeping your bunk area neat; you got little prizes for everything. Spike had enjoyed studying the charts, and figuring out how many points he had already earned that week; if you earned more than three hundred a month you got a free trip to Anchorage, where they took you to a hamburger place for lunch and afterwards to a movie or a gym or a pool hall. That was the best, but even the lesser rewards—a six-pack of gum, extra time with the basketball hoop—they were pretty good, too. The idea was that—except for swearing in the dining hall—you never got punished for anything. You just got rewarded for good stuff.

But there'd been a blot on the face of Chenega, and that blot's name had been Burke. One of the six "counselors" who supervised the kids, Burke had been a big man, with huge shoulders and great thick arms, and he had greatly enjoyed picking boys up by their jackets and hanging them on a coat hook in the bunkhouse—a cliché of a bastard if Spike had ever known one, and he'd met lots of bastards since. At the slightest excuse—a misplaced shoe, a dirty look, it didn't really matter, anything would do—Burke would go into his fork-lift imitation, laughing at the boy who was hanging in front of him like a package. Sometimes he would put his fingers around the boy's throat while he hung there, so softly that the hands felt like feathers, but underneath the feathers there was a nasty little threat and the boy felt sick and helpless. Spike had *been* the boy, more often than not, and though at first he had tried to tough it out, pretending it didn't matter to him, after a while he had started to live in dread; even now, so long after, he still did.

As yet, Spike was a little uncertain why he wanted to go back to Chenega. He sometimes thought that he just wanted to drop by and pay it a visit, to show the place, if he could, the way his life had turned out. Perhaps he would stay on for a few days, talking to the boys who were presently in residence, giving them tips on how to survive in the pen once they got there, telling them stories about corrupt judges and lawyers. If he could pick up a woman to take with him to the island, that would be even better; they would ask him to sleep in the bunkhouse with them and he would refuse, implying that his nights with the woman were far too exciting for him to give up even one of them, and thus driving all the boys crazy with lust. Maybe they would even ask him to give one of those special presentations, and all the boys would cheer when he was finished, inspired by his words and his wisdom. Mostly though, it was simpler than that. He wanted to murder Burke.

Spike opened his eyes, wondering if Burke could still work there, to see Wesley Hannah walking toward him. He held the small square traveling case in one hand, now, and he was muttering to himself aloud as he moved down the aisle. "The fourth car, the fourth car," he said, and then, as he approached Spike, he leaned suddenly, dolorously, against the seat in front of him and said, "This is the fourth car, and I can only imagine, Mr. Jones, though it didn't specifically say so, that the world spirit intended that I sit here with you. Of course, if you object, I'm certain that other arrangements can be made." He studied his traveling case through his thick green plastic frames as if he half hoped other arrangements *could* be made.

To his own surprise, Spike said, "Take a seat," then added, "across the aisle, natch."

"Of course," said Wesley, lowering himself carefully into position. He held the traveling case on his lap until he was settled, and then, before the train started but while it was making preparatory rumbling noises, he unclicked the two rusty hasps that held the case shut and let the lid pop open. Inside, Spike could see a mysterious collection of roundish and squarish objects packing the case from edge to edge, all of them neatly wrapped in clean white tissue paper. Wesley's hand hovered over these objects, moving uncertainly from one to the next, until he finally settled on a round one in the far right-hand corner; he lifted it out, unwrapped the white tissue paper and revealed a large tomato. The train started with a jerk and Wesley, holding the tissue paper beneath his chin to catch the drips, bit hugely into this tomato, his eyes opening wide as his teeth met around it.

2

◼ WESLEY WAS GLAD the train was going somewhere, after all. No one could say he was a demanding man, agreeable as he had always tried to be, but sometimes he did get a little tired of the dead ends the world spirit seemed to think it amusing to lead him to. One day he had sat for over fourteen hours on a park bench in front of the Fairbanks Hilton, waiting for what he firmly expected would be a message from his daughter Amolia, and only when the sun had gone down at one in the morning had he realized that this time, too, the world spirit had been having its little joke. Another time he had gone up to the top of the Ferris wheel in the Anchorage Fair Grounds twenty-five times—not a cheap undertaking, since he was charged for five different trips—and each time the only thing he could think of to do was to get off, and get on once again.

Wesley had not always believed that he was directed by the world spirit to do things. Once, not too long ago, he had not been doing much of anything, had sat day after day behind the counter of the Recreational Vehicle Supply store where he worked, directing the customers to the proper aisles to find Porto-Toilets or spice racks that bolted to the wall and held their bottles in little metal clips that would not loosen. The recreational-vehicle supply business was a busy one in Alaska, but it required little action on Wesley's part, except when some of the larger items were called for: awnings that could be stretched in front of the RVs' doors to create instant porches, plastic picnic tables that would fold up and fit above the cab of the truck. These he had to fetch from the warehouse behind the store. But mostly he just sat and directed the whirling human traffic. The people were so anxious, with their lists, neatly checking off each item as they finally secured it, and just as neatly rushing on to the next one, a light of something like fury in their eyes. That would have been all very well, he supposed, if they had been buying something vital—food, perhaps, for their children, or woolen blankets to store against the chance of a nuclear disaster—but tipless mugs, pegboard chess sets, large plastic clothespins that stuck to the walls? It was really as if they were driven by forces beyond their control. Odd as he had then thought them, though, perhaps it had been those very customers who had first given him the idea to go on journeys himself, since really it wasn't so much that he believed he was *directed* to act by the world spirit; the world spirit was just a convenient shorthand way of explaining to other people what he felt—that he was floating, for the first time in his life, on the sea of circumstance.

Wiping imaginary sweat from his eyelids with his fingers, Wesley peered down intently at his food case and prepared to make another selection. The tomato was gone, the only evidence that it had been, a lone tomato seed riding on his jacket front just to the left of his glasses chain, and a certain tingling in his mouth as if all the taste buds had been lightly slapped awake. Another tomato would be nice, but so would a crisp green pepper—no, it was never wise to mix fruits and vegetables in the same meal, and a tomato, though most people did not know this, was a fruit. A love apple, it had been called in the long ago, when it was believed by most people to be poisonous. Wesley's grandfather, however, a Polish peasant whose name had been changed on his arrival in America—changed to one that seemed to give the Americans no trouble, though it had certainly given his daughter a little trouble, as Anna Hannah—his grandfather had believed that tomatoes were edible, and had eaten them in large quantities, much to the horror of his neighbors and friends, who had watched with grim satisfaction every time he performed this act, certain that today he would die of it.

In a rather sad family history, the tomato story was a triumph. Polish peasants who had gotten on the wrong ship in the North Sea and had landed in Japan before they finally caught a boat to Alaska, Wesley's grandparents had tried to homestead in the area south of Denali. There they had met unfortunate ends: the grandfather who loved tomatoes had been eaten by a grizzly bear when he tried to fish for salmon in the same small stream as the cretaceous beast; the grandmother had died in childbirth, giving passage to Anna Hannah's sister. The baby sister, too, had died, when she was lost accidentally off a dog-sled load and not found again for hours; only Anna Hannah and her older brother, Joe, had taken firm hold of the Great Land. Eventually they had married each other, for lack of better prospects in the two hundred thousand square miles of wilderness they called home, and Wesley had been the sole issue of their loins. At the age of ten, he'd been brought by his parents to Anchorage, where he'd lived, summer and winter, ever since, often wishing he could brave the great land beyond it. Now he was doing just that, like his grandfather before him.

Of course, he too had to be careful of animals, about whom he felt strangely ambivalent. On the one hand, he admired them greatly—they seemed so *instinctive*, as he often said to Amolia; they always knew just what they were about. On the other hand, he distrusted them, thinking it an accident of fate that had allowed mankind to become the dominant animal species, a mistake the world spirit might at any moment rectify. When he had first heard about the experiments that demonstrated rationality in chimps and gorillas—some of them were apparently not only able to use language, but to invent it—he had expressed to his daughter the sinking conviction that this was just the beginning, that they would take over the world within twenty or thirty years. Still, he did not eat meat, whatever he thought. He wanted to stay out of the conflict.

So what should he eat next? Perhaps a bit of French bread? With a little butter spread across it, it would soothe his taste buds before the next offering. He selected a long oval object wrapped in white tissue paper and a small tin canister with a screw-top lid.

He realized as he studied them that he hadn't brought a knife. Strictly speaking, a knife wasn't necessary, since he could always simply rip chunks off the bread and dip them into the butter, but he hated to have to do this, being a naturally neat man, and he glanced across the aisle at Mr. Jones. Mr. Jones looked like the sort of person who would carry a knife, who, indeed, might carry several of them, one kind for weekdays and another one for Sundays. The small weekday kind would be adequate for this occasion and Wesley leaned slightly across the armrest, which was now, along with the rest of the train, rocketing south toward Anchorage at the deceptively slow speed of thirty miles an hour. "I wonder if I might borrow a knife," he said.

He planned to go on and explain why he needed one, but at the word "knife" Mr. Jones's eyes, which had been half shut, seemed to be hit with an electric charge and they snapped in the direction of Wesley's seat, while the body beneath them tensed as if for a spring. Mr. Jones had taken off his jacket and Wesley could see now that on both of his well-muscled arms he had adorned himself with tattoos: a Ford Mustang lurked about his wrist and above it, near the elbow, there was a tiny antiaircraft range.

"I don't like to give out knives to strangers," said Mr. Jones. "I've had bad experiences that way."

"Ah," said Wesley soothingly, "but we are no longer strangers. I want to introduce you to my daughter Amolia, as soon as we reach Anchorage. Amolia is thin, like yourself."

To say that Amolia was thin was, Wesley realized, something of an understatement. Actually, she was very thin, so thin that you could see the whites all round the irises of her eyes, so thin that her shoulder bones showed beneath the flesh of her shoulders like two round knobs for opening cabinets. Presumably other of her bones were knobby as well, but it had been a long time since Wesley had seen any of them. Ever since this thinness had come upon her, Amolia had taken to wearing long-sleeved, ankle-length dresses, baggy in the middle, often dark blue or green, and tied around the waist with ropelike belts. They made her look very much like a wandering monk, except that the dresses, instead of coming closed around her neck, were for some reason pulled down off her shoulders and therefore exposed the triangular ridge of her clavicle, above which her neck drew up like Alice in Wonderland's after she had swallowed the contents of "Drink Me." Wesley had come back from more than one of his trips to discover that Amolia was in the hospital for some reason he had never quite grasped, and even there she had scarcely gained weight, though he was sure they had tried to fatten her. Wesley had often thought that if his beloved wife, Cynthia, had not been killed in the Great Earthquake, perhaps Amolia would never have grown so thin. But:

"Who said I was going to Anchorage?" asked Mr. Jones, his arms parting slightly from his sides as if he were about to plunge them to his hips in search of a matched set of pistols.

"I hope you will," said Wesley. "Otherwise you'll miss my daughter. The knife was just for spreading butter; it could be really very dull."

"Anchorage first. Then Prince William Sound," Mr. Jones said grudgingly. "Yeah, I got a knife you can use. You want a big one or a small one?"

"The weekday one will be fine." Mr. Jones handed him a Barlow, and Wesley opened his butter tin. Perhaps, after the bread, he would converse more with Micah Jones. Prince William Sound? Maybe the world spirit wanted him there too.

An hour later Wesley and Mr. Jones had become much better friends. Mr. Jones had explained that the reason he wanted to go to Prince William Sound was to "get away from civilization forever." Wesley had remarked that Prince William Sound had something to do with the place where his daughter Amolia worked, though he couldn't remember just what she did; a school for juvenile delinquents was involved, that was the only thing he was sure of. After the news about Amolia—which had interested Mr. Jones so much that Wesley really wished he could recall more of the specifics—it had been agreed between them that if things continued to go well, Wesley and Amolia just might be able to accompany Mr. Jones on his trip, to visit a place where, as he put it "rocks were really rocks." When that was decided, Wesley made his way happily to the back of the last passenger car, where he pushed open the heavy door and stepped onto the iron platform outside; the wind slapped his face, which made him smile, and he leaned the great bulk of his stomach against the iron railing. Then he laboriously lifted his glasses into place on his nose so that he could study the sandy bottom of the railroad bed.

3

■ AT CHENEGA THAT AFTERNOON things were in some disarray. The teacher had unexpectedly left five days before, just a month into the nine-month session—a development for which the boys, though in fact hurt, crowingly claimed all credit—and although Linda, the on-island director, had been substituting this week until a new teacher could be found, she had become convinced that she would never get a replacement until she went and hired one herself. So she had gone to Anchorage for the day, and the counselors who were left were taking a semiholiday. Lorne was supposed to be in charge, but Lorne would always make himself scarce, given half a chance, and Phil and Gwen, the social-work interns, were studying for their exams. With Motor running *The Reach*—a converted trawler—for Linda, only Ian was really around, and though he was stalking from place to place, he couldn't be everywhere at once.

Naturally, with this sudden windfall of freedom, the boys were all hard at work trying to get away with something. Stan, Derell, and Josh were tinkering with the lock on the gunhouse, a tiny log building set back among the trees where the camp's three firearms—a shotgun, a rifle, and a pistol—were kept. They were having a singular lack of success. Rudy, Eric, and Doug had climbed through the window of the schoolhouse into the teacher's office, where one of the island's two radio phones was bolted to the wall—the other was in *The Reach*—and they had turned it on and were listening to the open channel broadcast, although they had not yet dared to join in on any conversation. Norm was giving Arnold a haircut, with Emory looking on— not exactly getting away with something, but since he was using his woodcarving knife, when he was done Arnold's hair would look as if it had been plugged into an electrical socket. Kennie Dugan, whom no one liked enough to even break the rules with, was wandering down the beach alone, looking for small sea creatures to kill. And Harry and Jack were in the bunkhouse reading, or, more exactly, searching for words in the dictionary, words that sounded like swearwords but weren't, and that they could therefore use with both satisfaction and impunity in the dining hall, where no swearing was allowed on pain of fifty push-ups.

Right now, Harry was lost in the *m*'s. He still found diction- aries a mystery. Where he was from, the trees all looked alike, the hills all looked alike, even the houses all looked alike except for their colors, and it didn't seem possible that all these words could actually mean something different, each one a snowflake, no two of them the same. At the moment he was searching for "miasma." Neither he nor Jack was quite certain how to spell it; or rather, though Jack had been quite certain—*myasma*—he had also been quite wrong, so Harry had worked his way slowly, by the process of elimination, toward the *mi*'s, where he was now stuck on "mica," apparently a rock, though they certainly didn't come right out and say so. He moved his finger slowly up the page, past "mib"—a game of marbles—to, at last, *miasma*.

"Miasma," he read aloud to Jack. "A noxious exhalation from putrescent organic matter; poisonous effluvia or germs infecting the atmosphere." Although he knew only three of the words in this definition—poisonous, germs, and infecting—he was pretty certain that miasma was a nasty word on the basis of those three alone, and a glow of satisfaction overtook him. As it did, he started for some reason to get an erection, a phenomenon that he was by now so used to it hardly even troubled him. At first, he had thought it was awfully weird when he started to get erections with no girl in sight, no girlie magazine in sight, and no girl anywhere in the confines of his brain, but now, after almost three years of having his penis pop up like a buoy at the oddest times, he had simply stopped brooding about it. Since he was sitting cross-legged on the upper bunk, facing Jack who also sat cross-legged, the present erection, which was pushing straight out and down, did present something of a problem, having moved rapidly from pressure to pain, and he slipped his left hand into his pocket to try and ease it into his left pants leg. In order to distract Jack from this attempt, he said, "You sure that's not a swear word? It's quite a mouthful of marbles."

Jack, who had been laboriously writing the definition down, glanced up just as Harry, having failed to jar his penis loose by jiggling his pants, was reaching all the way into his crotch to ease it carefully out. Jack grinned.

"What ya doing? Playing pocket pool?" he asked.

Harry blushed. Blushing, like getting erections, was something he had absolutely no control over, and if the truth be told, it bothered him a lot more. Since Harry was half Aleut and half white, he had a rather strange face anyway; his hair was black and as thick as sheet metal, and his eyes were black as well, but his skin, rather than being a complexion to match, was very pale and revealing. When he smiled, all his teeth showed, both top and bottom, and he looked a little bit like a cheerful shark; but when he didn't smile he imagined he could look very threatening, his bangs cut sharp across his forehead like a knife. Then, of course, he would blush, the blush moving from the neck to the forehead, and brightest just around the eyebrows.

Jack took pity on him.

"Hey. Be my guest," he said, and returned to writing in his notebook. "Anyway," he added, "I'm positivo, manno. That's the great thing about dictionaries. They don't even list the swear words. You look up shit and what do you find? Shittim wood, some ancient tree."

"Shittim?" said Harry. "So write it down."

"I already used it, bro," said Jack. "But you could look up piss."

Harry and Jack were bunkmates—Harry had the lower bunk and Jack the upper—and in the month since they'd arrived on Chenega they had become real friends. Sometimes Harry found this puzzling. Jack was as white as they made them, the son of a man who had come up to Alaska to work in the North Slope oil fields; he seemed to be enamored of his own muscles more than was reasonable, and spent inordinate amounts of time combing his hair this way and that. He also added o to the ends of lots of his words and called people "bro" to whom he wasn't even remotely related, whom he didn't even like. He was constantly putting himself through "tests of valor," lying on his bunk, for instance, with his face directly below the burning lightbulb, or keeping his hand in the air for thirty or forty minutes at a time, usually when he was in school (the teacher who had just left had quickly learned to ignore this hand in preference for those few which occasionally rose into the air flopping like the wings of great birds). All of this struck Harry as peculiar, but not in an unattractive way. Jack was easy to listen to.

So Harry proceeded to look up "piss." While he was leafing toward the *pi*'s his attention was arrested by the word "pusillanimous," a long and luscious-looking word that was right at the top of the page.

"Pusillanimous," he said to Jack. "Lacking of strength or courage; fainthearted; cowardly. Proceeding from or indicating a cowardly spirit. Wouldn't that do? He wouldn't know that one, I bet."

"Ian wouldn't know any word of more than two syllables. Let's use it. But we have to find a noun to go with it."

"You noxious miasma," said Harry. "You pusillanimous ..."

Ian was at the moment the particular object of Jack and Harry's scorn because he had caught Jack saying "I sure hope we're not eating the same old shit tonight, bro," in the mud room of the dining hall—the mud room, for heaven's sake, not in the dining hall itself, and Jack had only *muttered* it anyway, just to Harry; it wasn't as if he had really said it out loud. But Ian had come in suddenly from the trailer end of the mud room and had made Jack do fifty push-ups right there on the floor. So Harry and Jack were out to get him, to trip him up with big words.

All of this counselor-baiting still seemed a bit odd to Harry. In his opinion—secret, of course, never to be revealed to any of the other guys—the counselors, except for Lorne Burke, were really pretty okay. Motor and Ian, the two industrial-training instructors—Motor taught motor repair and maintenance, as well as some plumbing and electricity, and Ian taught carpentry and general construction skills—both really knew a lot, and though Gwen and Phil, as social-work interns, weren't as skilled as the other two, at least they would stop and explain things they did understand three times before they told you to shut up; in this, they were so entirely different from the members of Harry's family that he had been pleasantly surprised. His own mother wouldn't explain anything even once before she told you to shut up; in fact, she would tell you to shut up before you even opened your mouth. His father was better, but he was rarely around, since he worked in the bush as a logger and recently had been spending more and more time with Harry's grandparents, Aleuts who lived north of Kodiak. Harry's oldest brother, Tom, was doing time in the state pen for first-degree murder, and ever since he had been sent up Harry's father had been depressed by his children. He seemed to think it was inevitable that they would all follow in their brother's footsteps, polluted by white blood and white culture as they had been, and two of them besides Tom already convicted of breaking and entering and theft.

The fifth of nine children, Harry had grown up in a five-room house that was usually pink, sometimes yellow, and once, for three months, had been bright green, but which always had black shutters on it that got loose when the wind blew hard. The wind often did blow hard on the hillside above Bear Lake, and in the winter it blew into the house through all the cracks in the walls. There wasn't much furniture inside the house, but there was a lot of bedding, and on the very coldest days the children would stay piled underneath it for hours at a time. When Harry was little, he had always tried to get the spot on the big bed right next to the wall, even though the wind was iciest there, because through the crack that ran down the corner he could see the frozen lake. He loved the water; it seemed to him like a great hole, a passage, into the center of the earth where, he always imagined, there was another world, a kind of paradise, with mountains on the horizon, big trees with rich green leaves, and enormous flowers that filled the air with perfume. Sometimes he would close his eyes and imagine that the lake was a huge whirlpool, hundreds of feet across, and he would go down through it, down and down and down, almost gliding as if he was falling through a tube perfectly fitted to his body. When he came back up from that other world he ascended in the same way, and he seemed often to bring back up with him a sense of great tranquillity.

So being on Chenega was heaven to him. In the first place, the ocean was much better than any lake could ever be, and though he did not have any longer those whirlpool fantasies which transported him to another level of the earth, the sea and its environs amazed him. Clear braided streams came rushing off the mountain in the island's center, and after crashing across the pebbled beach, buried themselves in the foam. When he had first arrived at the camp at the beginning of August, he had begun to gather things with an almost maniacal delight; not only useful things that the ocean washed up—lumber, steel, old nets—but also useless things, things to fill his pockets with, things that squished and wilted and finally broke. Everything here was scaled to a size that he had, with coming adulthood, grown unaccustomed to. The skunk cabbage were enormous. Kittywakes nested on a cliff you could dock an ocean liner at, and they filled it from top to bottom, excess birds dropping off like plaster, circling frantically in the air. The berries, the late summer flowers, the sunsets over the western islands, the whales and sea lions playing; it was all so lush, so rich, so different from the starkness of interior Alaska, and this, added to Jack, the counselors, the good food—well, he couldn't imagine a place on earth where he would have been a whole lot happier.

"Pismire," he read. "An ant."

Jack looked up. Screwing his face into a snarl, he spat out, "You pusillanimous pismire," then relaxed, grinned broadly, and said, "That's good, bro. Very good indeedo." Carefully, he wrote *pismire* on his pad, then tapped it with his pen. "We'll use that on that—that psychopath tonight."

Harry, anticipating it, sighed. Jack, he thought, didn't know what a real psychopath was, if he was able to call Ian one. But Harry knew, all too well; he'd met many genuine crazies. The first one he could remember had been a man who had lived at a neighbor's, a man rumored to be a chain-saw murderer. Accused of ripping both houses and people apart with his Husqvarna, he had been let off by the courts for a sad lack of evidence. The psychiatrist at the hospital had given him a letter saying that he was sane, and he carried this letter about with him everywhere, and every time someone said, "Oh, you're crazy, man," he got dangerously excited and yelled, "No, I'm not!" then whipped out this letter to prove it.

Harry didn't know what it was, but he seemed to attract crazies like a cow moose calls in bulls, and once called, there was nothing he could do but try to placate them somehow. Actually, he had, from long experience, gotten pretty good at this. For example, a few months before he came to Chenega, he had been in a deserted section of Anchorage one night looking for a brother who was supposed to be working in a sheet-metal plant there, and he had been approached by an absolutely enormous Asian, who had insisted on calling him "Charlie." Harry had told him at least three times—as he fled through the streets back toward the lights and the traffic—that his name was Harry, and this Asian had smiled an enormous crazy smile and said soothingly, "I know, I know, Charlie," while, whenever he was close enough, he kept reaching out to pinch Harry in the arms and thighs, as if he were testing the plumpness of a bird he was thinking of roasting. Harry had had the brilliant inspiration to ask him whether he wanted to come home with Harry and have a good turkey dinner, and the man, all six feet seven inches of him, and probably two hundred and twenty pounds, had started shaking with sobs and crying like a baby.

Harry's own brother Tom, of course, was probably the most psychopathic of the lot. Could it be true, as their father said, that bad blood was bad blood and that Harry was doomed to be a criminal like Tom? If so, it seemed a little unfair, since Harry had spent most of his life to date trying to keep Tom out of trouble. One warm December night, when he was nine years old and the snow was four feet deep, Tom, then fourteen, had taken the snowmobile out and mowed down the fence around their house, the only picket fence on the reserve. He had been drunk, of course, so drunk that after he crashed the snowmobile against the side of the house—where it had broken through into the living room—he had just lain in the snow, totally passed out, and not from the collision. All of the other kids had been too scared of their mother's fury when she found out to do anything at all, but Harry, although terrified too, had managed with an elder sister's reluctant help to drag Tom inside, take his clothes off, and get him into one of the two platform beds where the children slept. Then he had put on a pair of his father's logging boots and tramped all around the accident and across the yard to the street, leaving these huge man-sized footprints in the snow so that later he could tell his mother that a perfect stranger, a big logger, had stolen the snowmobile and then wrecked it against their house before tromping away into the night.

His brother hadn't gotten into trouble that time, but it had always been a losing battle. Once, not long before he was sent up for life, he had held a pistol to their mother's head and had threatened to kill her for "crimes against humanity." Harry had been just barely able to talk him out of it, while the oatmeal they were supposed to be having for dinner burned on the stove and the house filled with acrid smoke.

Jack closed his pad and stretched his arms over his head, and Harry shut the dictionary.

"Aren't you on dinner this afternoon?" asked Jack. "With the little kiddo, no less?"

"Oh," said Harry. "Yes. Where is Arnold, anyway?"

"I think he's getting his hair cut. Norm's doing it, with his carving knife."

But the haircut was over; the bunkhouse door opened and Norm, Arnold, and Emory walked in. Arnold looked, Harry thought, not quite as if he had been scalped, but as if someone had been thinking about scalping him while working on his head with a razor. Although he was fourteen years old, just one year younger than Harry, Arnold was still very small and he seemed like a child, not only because of his size, but because he had a face as innocent as the moon, and tender little fingers. His mother, so Harry understood, dealt drugs, and had probably fed them to him like candy at an early age, since his brain, while not exactly broken, did seem improperly connected.

"All right," Emory was saying now, "where do you *think* you left them? In the schoolroom? The sauna? Down on the beach somewhere?"

"I think, maybe . . . oh," said Arnold, drifting over to his bunk and settling himself on it as lightly as a moth. "I think . . . the schoolroom." It was obvious to Harry that he had picked one of the available options pretty much at random, but Emory said, "Okay. You stay put until Harry takes you to make dinner," and went hurrying off looking for whatever it was that Arnold had lost.

■　■　■

A little later, Harry was hard at work opening a large, industrial-size can of tuna fish—he had checked the dinner menu posted on the wall and had seen that they were having tuna casserole tonight—and Arnold was eating an apple. On his way over to the dining hall, Harry had heard the unmistakable sound of *The Reach* just rounding Chenega Point, so he knew that Linda, the grownup on dinner duty tonight, would be arriving back from Anchorage at any minute. Although he was eager to learn whether she had managed to hire another teacher—whatever they might say, most of the boys had actually liked the old one—Harry hoped she wouldn't come to the dining hall *immediately* after the boat docked, since he loved tuna fish, and he figured that if he got the cans open fast enough, he could help himself to a short snack before Linda arrived to stop him.

Arnold stood in the middle of the kitchen, his pants, too long, dangling around the tops of his sneakers, the edge of one of his cuffs absorbing water from a puddle on the floor. His eyes were fixed vacantly on a point somewhere short of the wall, and he had nibbled the skin off the apple in little bites such as a mouse might take, until the flesh was exposed all over it, as white as the inside of a chicken. Then seemingly in a trance, he got a salt shaker down from the shelf over the big gas range and salted the nibbled apple very carefully, as if he was spreading mulch. Finally, he ate the fruit, wiped his hands on his pants, and said, "Harry?"

"What?" said Harry, who had gotten both cans of tuna open and was now working furiously to empty them into a bowl.

"Are you going to run away, too?"

"Am I *what?*" said Harry, letting the fork fall into the bowl and turning to stare at Arnold.

"When the others go. Are you going with them?"

"What others?" said Harry. "Are you?"

But already his mind was working furiously and his head had started to hurt with the pressure of it. First of all, whoever "they" were, they had made a bad mistake to talk about it when Arnold was around, because Arnold was quite incapable of distinguishing between people it was all right to say things to and people it wasn't. Harry, of course, was one of those to whom it was, but not all of the guys could be trusted—Kennie Dugan, for example, had verbal diarrhea and a delight in telling on people that had already almost gotten him pulverized several times—and certainly this wasn't something you wanted to talk about in front of any of the counselors. Then, too, Harry was suddenly, sickeningly convinced that he would be asked, eventually, to participate in the escape attempt and that he would have to agree to go, even though he had no desire at all to leave Chenega. His only chance to get out of running away lay in avoiding contact with all the other guys in any situation which might lead to a confidence, and that was much harder than it sounded. If he wanted to go to the bathroom in the middle of the night, for example, how was he to be certain that he wouldn't meet someone at the outhouse, someone who would whisper to him out of the darkness, "Hey, Harry, you want to run away with us?"

"Well," Arnold said, "Norm and —"

"No," said Harry instantly, regretting that he had ever asked. "Don't tell me! I don't want to know who they are. And whatever you do, don't talk about it to *anybody* else, anybody at all, you understand me? And move out of that puddle. Your pants are getting wet."

"I'll peel the carrots, I guess, can I, Harry?" Arnold responded, and happily started strewing shavings about the kitchen. One landed in his hair and hung above his ear like a bright orange ornament.

Just then, the door from the mud room opened, and Linda, who had apparently headed straight up after the boat docked, came into the dining hall, smoking a cigarette. Harry liked Linda—he had nicknamed her Stovepipe—and even on a regular night he would have been happy to have dinner duty with her instead of with someone else. This afternoon, he was especially glad they were working together, since it put him in an ideal position to find out all about her recent trip to Anchorage before she had time to get tired of telling about it. But when he asked his usual opening question, "Hey, Stovepipe, how much those boots cost?"—asking how much something cost was his main conversational gambit—she just glared at him, as if she was already tired of talking. That, coupled with Harry's lingering uneasiness about the proposed escape attempt, made him reluctant to move on from his gambit to more genuinely interesting material. So, while Linda threw down her magazine and ground out her cigarette, tossing her two entirely inappropriate pigtails back over her shoulders several times, Harry kept working assiduously on the tuna casserole—unhappily, Arnold's revelation had prevented him from eating any tuna before the Stovepipe's arrival—and he just nodded and grunted when she said, bitchily, "Ah, the deadly duo. The ptomaine twosome. We might as well leave for the hospital right away."

Arnold looked at her in surprise.

"The idea, Arnold, is to get the parings in the sink, put the carrots on the cutting board. And you don't pare them till they're toothpicks." She took the vegetable parer out of his hand and demonstrated, whipping furiously away at a fresh carrot until it was just about as well pared as Arnold's.

"There," she said. "Like that."

Everyone worked in silence for a while. Harry got out noodles to toss into the water when it boiled, and Linda heated cans of mushroom soup. Arnold kept working on the carrots. Every once in a while he paused to wipe the vegetable parer on his leg when a carrot slice had gotten stuck in it, but most of the time he stayed as busy as could be. When she was finished heating the soup, Linda said, "What possesses you kids, anyway, to get yourselves in such trouble?"

For a moment, Harry thought she was accusing him of some recent misdemeanor; then he decided her query was more general. He would have been happier to answer her question if he had not been brooding about it already today—although the worst thing he had ever done, really, was his forty-fifth breaking and entering. That, he had to admit, had been pretty damn stupid, as indeed had been the forty-four before it. Part of the reason he did b and e's was because it was fun to see other people's houses and part of the reason was because his friends, who were on the whole (he was sorry to say) even stupider than he was, would otherwise probably have wrecked the houses, while he just liked to explore them. But this was not the first time, after all, that he had been sent up, it was just the best time; once, he had spent six months vegging at Napier Prison when the juvenile detention farm had been full and they had rented the nearby prison for the overflow. Even though it had been turned off, the place actually had a siren that would wail if it saw anyone trying to escape, and big concrete walls, and a spotlight. That had been no fun at all, and yet as soon as he got back home he had started breaking and entering again. There was just nothing else to *do* out in the sticks where he lived—or maybe his father was right, and his blood really was polluted.

But Arnold was staring at Linda, clearly puzzled. Obviously—for this was how his mind worked, when it worked at all—he had put together Linda's last two remarks, the one about the ptomaine and the one about the trouble, and was trying to find a way to make them fit somehow, like the final two pieces of a puzzle. "Ptomaine twosome"; "possesses you kids"; "leave for the hospital"; "such trouble." Jam them as he might, he couldn't, apparently, find a way to unite them; at last he asked, "Why should we go to the hospital?"

Harry would have laughed, if he had not been brooding again. "Arnold," he said instead, "what the Stovepipe meant— why did you deal drugs?"

"I don't know," said Arnold. "Because they wanted them."

Linda snorted and turned to Harry.

"You got a good reason like that too?" she said.

"What's bugging you?" he asked. "You have a lot of trouble in the city?"

"Oh *no*," said Linda." I *loved* having to go after a new teacher. I'd just like to see some changes around here, kiddos.

I'd just like to be able to trust someone for once." She lifted a bag of Kool-Aid from a cupboard and slammed it so hard on the counter that it burst.

"Yeah," said Harry. "So how much those boots cost anyway?"

"Ninety-five dollars," said Linda. "Trust, that's what we need," and for a moment, as Harry thought about what she had said—ninety-five dollars; that was a lot!—he imagined that her mood had changed for the better. But a little while later she disappeared into the storeroom, emerging again with four loaves of white bread in large plastic bags full of air, and as she started to lay slices out on the counter, she delivered a final pronouncement.

"No wonder," she said, "we're all dying."

4

■ LINDA WAS STILL in a rotten mood when the staff meeting began after supper. She sat at a table in the dining trailer, scowling fiercely at her knitting and waiting for the others to straggle in. The trip to Anchorage had reminded her—if she had needed any reminding—that not only was she saddled with a staff of counselors here who would make a bunch of ditch diggers look smart, but Rob, her nemesis in Anchorage—they called him an Educational Facilitator but it was Linda's opinion that if he were told to define the word "facilitator" or die, the firing squad would get him—was totally unwilling to do anything about it, even at the best of times. Now, although he had absolutely promised to have the new teacher out to Chenega before darkness fell tonight—in the summer that would have given him until about one o'clock in the morning to keep his word, but now, at the beginning of September, he only had a couple more hours—she still wasn't sure she should believe him.

And to top it off, Rob had taken the opportunity afforded by today's confrontation to tell her he was going to be sending a Survival Expert out in about a week, no doubt another in a seemingly endless series of anything-but-expert know-it-alls. You'd think, that as the director of Chenega, she would be allowed to decide for herself what programs to have on the island, but three years of dealing with the Alaskan government had proved conclusively that this was not so; if she wanted the place to keep getting funded, she had to put up with madmen. A survival expert. She could just imagine what that meant. How to boil water in a baseball cap.

At the moment, her agitation over all these issues was being translated into mistakes in her socks, which were bright blue, shot with red, and marked with a fine double purl stitch up the middle. These socks were for Harry, one of her favorites among the present crop of boys, and he had particularly admired the purl stitch, which had started, she saw now, to wander. If she decided to reconstruct it, she would lose an hour of work. Not that there was any particular time she had set to complete her socks, but—although she used her knitting as a kind of therapy, her needles two strong leashes she whipped around the ankles of her nervous energy—once she was well started on a project she would go into overdrive until it was finished. Working faster and faster, more and more furiously, when a pair of socks was nearing completion she might stay up for hours past lights out to work toward their ending, and when she finally crept into the bunkhouse, it might be one or two in the morning. If she was lucky, all the boys would be asleep—since they already had taken to attributing her absences to wild sexual activities—but last night when she had entered, Jack's head had popped out from under the covers where he had been reading, his flashlight had stabbed her, and he'd said, "Greato! Another pair of socks, bro?"

What a madhouse this place was. She hardly knew why she stayed. If appearances could be trusted, she was the only human being in the entire state of Alaska who still believed you should do something with juvenile delinquents other than toss them into prison for life, the only one who had faith in the program at Chenega; and she couldn't carry the place by herself, no matter how much she would like to. Founded in 1970, the work camp was, in the minds of too many government officials, an expensive, undesirable anachronism, a relic of dogooding liberals. Chenega Island lay about twenty miles out from the small port town of Whittier and had been taken over by the government after the earthquake, when the Aleuts who originally lived there had abandoned it. Even in *The Reach* it took almost an hour to get to the mainland on bad days, and then there was still a two-hour train trip before arriving in Anchorage, so if anyone was ill or seriously hurt—and such was the active imagination of most of the boys that there was almost always someone ill or seriously hurt—the camp had to call in a rescue helicopter on the radio phone. Not only did it have this huge and remote physical setting "against" it—though of course it was the very strangeness of the setting, the rawness and difficulty of the life here, that helped create conditions favorable to change—but the student-staff ratio was two to one or better. All of this cost money, naturally, lots of money, and each year when Linda traveled to Juneau to present her arguments for spending it, she was met, it seemed, with more resistance. Aggressive and determined as she was—here she ground out her cigarette, and, deciding she might as well do her best for Harry (who called her, charmingly, Stovepipe, with that menacing half-smile of his), started to rip out fifteen rows of sock—she had been quite unable to get it through those legislators' thick skulls that with a success rate of thirty percent or better—thirty percent of the kids who graduated from Chenega never committed another crime—they were doing *terrifically*, twice as well, or better, than regular institutions for JDs. With twelve kids in every camp year, that meant they saved an extra kid and a half every nine months. A kid and a half! But try and tell that to Juneau.

There. The fifteen rows were out and she was back to the

heel, a tangle of slightly bent yarn on her lap. For a moment she sat and studied it, her nervous hands, fine-boned and heavily veined—oddly so for a woman not yet thirty—still for a moment as they rested on the labyrinth of red and blue, her braids two glum ropes that grazed her shoulders, holding her brown, lightly freckled face between them. Linda had always thought that of all her bodily attributes, only her eyes could be called genuinely attractive, dark green eyes shot with silky threads of lightness, black lashes startling in that freckled face. Actually, her cheekbones were not so bad either, and her mouth was generous and full, but she was too skinny, and she didn't have any breasts to speak of, and her nose and chin were too pointy for her taste. She envied Gwen, the only other woman who worked on the island at the moment, for her dark honeyed skin and soft, subtle bones.

Gwen, of course, was what was holding the meeting up, since Gwen was always late to everything. At first, when she and Phil had been assigned to Chenega as interns, Linda had been delighted at the prospect of another woman on the island. Then, when she had met her, with her gorgeous skin and her perfect parts, Linda had been afraid that (1) Gwen would last about three minutes at the job and (2) before she left she would wreak havoc among the male staff. But neither of these things had happened. There was an inconclusive quality to Gwen that was mystifying rather than annoying. Her looseness was a looseness of direction and purpose, a sort of drifting, what-the-hell quality which revolved around her location and her attitude rather than her relationships.

The sound of a boat rounding Chenega Point brought Linda to her feet. Maybe the teacher would be getting here after all. But when she looked hopefully through the nearest window to see if the boat would be docking, disgorging a teacher of unknown sex and type, she was disappointed to see it was just another trawler, seining for salmon in the waters of the bay.

By now, Gwen had drifted into the dining trailer, and Ian

was tapping on his glass with a spoon, to call the meeting to order. He was taking over the staff meeting this evening, since, no matter how much Linda might disapprove of her staff, she believed fiercely in democracy and in giving everyone a chance. Ian, actually, wasn't so bad, though he certainly looked peculiar. He had an enormous upper body, but his lower body was relatively small, and he had a childish way of sitting on a table. Swinging his legs and peering through his thick glasses at his hands he would spit out his words as if they were being released from an inner compression tank, like popcorn popping. In spare moments in the bunkhouse, he told the boys an endless stream of stories about his own prowess, often prefaced by "You won't believe this . . ." and it was true, they usually didn't.

Ian, however, for all his absurdity, was basically a good-hearted man, which was more than could be said for Lorne, whom Linda really disliked. Lorne always wore a fine-combed woolen shirt, gray, well cut, and whenever he talked his hand would go up and down in simple, jerky motions, and he'd tug at his combed red beard with a thumb and a bent forefinger. His beard, his plump lips, his eyebrows going up and down in monotonous emphasis—for him, everything was simple: he was wonderful and the rest of the human race sucked. After spending most of his life till now planting trees, which was about what he could be trusted with, he had applied for this job early the year before and Rob, the brilliant Educational Facilitator, had given it to him. Linda fervently hoped that Rob had done better with the teacher. If he'd actually gotten one at all.

When Ian started tapping smartly with his spoon, Lorne was already silent. But Gwen and Phil, who were consulting with each other, Linda supposed, about their upcoming exams, which they would be going to Fairbanks for in a couple of weeks, kept talking as if Ian had not moved, and Motor, the most mechanically adept and easily amazed of the counselors, was staring out the window in astonishment. Linda followed his gaze, once more hoping for a teacher, but saw instead a great whale, probably a humpback, frolicking in the ocean two hundred yards or so offshore. For a moment, her bad mood lightened as she watched, but Ian kept tapping his glass.

At last, he had everyone's attention. First, of course, they discussed the minutes from last week, which Gwen had kept carelessly, if at all, and which were therefore perfectly absurd, which everyone politely pretended not to know. They then moved on to the day's agenda, which began with Stan Crow's running; this was as weak as Gwen's minute-keeping, but allowed more room for discussion. Whereas Arnold, the other very weak runner in the current crop of kids, always managed to lace his shoes either too loosely, so that they fell off, or so tightly that his heels stuck out of them, it was possible that Stan had a genuine physical problem. Genuine physical problems were very popular among the counselors, few of whom were adequately trained to cope with the genuine psychological problems that composed ninety-nine percent of the camp's human difficulties, and who were therefore absolutely delighted whenever it seemed possible that a boy was actually sick, or, better, had a congenital condition that had not yet been diagnosed and that was at the root of all the fuss.

"The kids are teasing him a lot," said Gwen. "I've kind of— you know—noticed that."

"He's only losing run points, though," said Ian. "Everything else, he's working like a beaver. I mean, you gotta give the guy credit."

"So what do you think it is?" asked Phil. "Maybe something in his knees, like calcium?"

"I think he's eating the wrong foods, and it's making him sluggish," said Linda. "He seems to be very sensitive about his weight."

Ian groaned, as Linda had known he would, but she had had to say it anyway. Yes, she had a concern with eating properly, was always trying to improve the camp diet—given the inadequate food budget she worked with—but it was true also that ever since this camp session started, Stan had been eating even more badly than the diet required. He had refused all fruits and vegetables, whether cooked or uncooked, and had stuffed himself on meat and eggs, with a little cheese thrown in.

"How can any food be the *wrong* food?" asked Motor, genuinely interested, but Linda didn't bother to respond.

"Meat," she said. "Meat. That's what Stan's up to."

"Well, for crying out loud, he's an Eskimo, Linda," said Ian. "I mean, those guys *lived* on meat."

"The Aleuts lived on meat in the winter," said Linda. "In the summer they ate berries. This is barely September, in case you hadn't noticed."

"Well," Lorne interjected. "I guess we're agreed that Stan may have some physical problem. What do we do about it?"

"Why not just give him automatic run points for now?" asked Phil. "On cleanliness, morning alert, everything else, he automatically earns."

"Any objections? No? Okay," said Ian, writing something on a pad of yellow paper.

The discussion now turned to Emory and Arnold. For all the moaning and groaning that generally preceded staff meetings, this was the one time out of the week when the counselors got to discuss the personalities of the kids to their heart's content, and it was a rare week when they didn't manage to talk about each and every one of them. There was likely to be less of that now, of course, so close to the beginning of the session, than there would be later on in the year, when the boys were getting on their nerves more. Ian pointed out now, though, that Emory certainly lost his temper easily, but Gwen countered that by saying it was very easy to get him back in a good humor just by talking to him, and that, in fact, Emory had put himself in charge of Arnold's shoes and socks—which were now almost always where they were supposed to be when they weren't on Arnold's feet. Phil suggested that Arnold had been doing better in the last day or two, but no one seemed to agree with him. Then Ian brought up Norm. Everyone, it seemed, had had it up to here with Norm.

Norman was a big, dangerous-looking guy with acne who had brought his own set of carving tools to the camp, but had not used them to carve anything and who might or might not really be a sullen bastard. Linda had not yet decided. He sat off by himself as much as he could, talked only when someone asked him a question, and often not even then.

"He really busts my balls," said Ian.

"Has he done anything wrong?" asked Phil.

"*He*'s wrong," said Lorne righteously. "He thinks just because he's Haida he shits vanilla ice cream."

"That's not a crime," said Linda. "And I think someone should check out his acne."

"Looks real to me," said Ian, and everyone but Linda laughed.

It wasn't that she wanted to be a grump, or to put down other people. And it wasn't that she thought *she* was so great, because she really didn't. It was that . . . well, somebody had to take things seriously, and very few people seemed to want to. Here they were at the start of a new session, with a whole new crop of boys, and why had she gone to Fairbanks for social work if not to do *social work*? Okay, she had a relatively untrained staff, okay, she had Rob to contend with, but she had the island and she had the kids and somehow she had to do better. For all that she might say in Juneau about saving an extra kid and a half every camp year, the sad truth of the matter was that seven out of ten of the boys who came to Chenega went on, in spite of everything they tried here to avert it, to live out their lives as criminals, and it seemed to her there must be some way, not yet discovered, to make more of them turn out straight. No matter how much evidence she got to the contrary, it was impossible for Linda to believe that kids could be ruined for good by the time they were sixteen. She herself had been a hoodlum of sorts, after all, and she had turned out all right. Besides, she liked these kids, on the average, better than the straight ones she ran into; they were so full of life, of curiosity, of mischief. They were just seriously confused about what to do with all that, and then most of them were tossed right back to their rotten families after Chenega, like tiny fish to sharks, so time was short, which was why she got impatient with these discussions, whether Arnold laced his shoes too tight, whether Norm was really a bastard. It was the whole conception of the place that needed to be talked about, the feelings, the intangibles.

"What I want to talk about today," said Linda, taking a deep breath and wishing that she had thought out beforehand just what it was she did want to talk about, "what I want to talk about is the whole emphasis on tasks that we have here. On the physical, you understand, on doing physical things."

"What other kinds of things are there?" asked Motor.

"I mean," Linda went on, "these kids have spent their whole lives doing physical things—breaking and entering, blowing up ammunition, arson, car theft, purse snatching, you name it—but here all they can earn points for is doing *different* physical things. Putting away their shoes, and so on. What about the intangibles?"

"The intangibles?" said Ian. "What's your particular point?"

"My point," said Linda, picking up her knitting needles and jabbing them into her knee, "my point is that we have to work with the psychology of the *individual* more. My point—" But here she was interrupted, not only by everyone's starting to talk at once—most of them trying strenuously to say the same thing at the same time, which was, what *was* behavior modification if it wasn't psychology, what *was* it, huh, huh?—but also by the sound, this time closer than before, of another big boat. And, to Linda's delight, this one turned toward them. Hardly pausing to excuse herself, or to try and placate the irate staff, she told Ian to carry on, and bolted out the door.

Brief as her walk down to the water was, it provided her with time to imagine at least five different thoroughly unacceptable figures emerging in succession from the trawler, and as she grabbed the rope the captain flung her, she braced herself for the worst. But the man who came out of the cabin surprised her by looking interesting and smart. He was not a particularly handsome man, but he had a rangy grace as he clambered down from the boat deck, a grace that was accentuated by the earnestness with which he seemed to be leaning forward into life. Well over six feet tall, he had to tip forward and peer down as he reached out with long expressive fingers to clasp Linda's outstretched hand. He wore a pair of docksiders over large bare feet, and a pair of blue-striped canvas overalls on top of a blue chambray shirt; his light brown hair, which was quite short, had been curled by the sea air into ringlets. He introduced himself as Trent and as Linda said all the appropriate things about how glad she was to see him, and how much she appreciated his coming on such short notice, she found to her amazement that she meant every one of them and more. Although she knew it was a little early to be making such judgments, as they unloaded luggage that included, among other things, a clarinet case and a pet turtle, and as she took Trent on an initial tour of the camp, showing him the private cabin to which he was entitled as the teacher—the teachers' union insisted that private housing be provided to teachers in the bush—she couldn't help but feel that here was someone she might finally be able to talk to about the things she really thought. In fact, before they had been together five minutes, and as she was leading him toward the dining trailer to introduce him to the rest of the staff, she found herself saying, "I mean, behavior modification is all very well. But we need to teach these kids *trust*. Trust and kindness and thinking about others. You can't put those things on charts." Trent looked a little surprised at all this, but not actually bored, though he covered one eye with the palm of his hand, as if he was having trouble focusing.

5

◼ AMOLIA HAD NOT gone to meet her father's train from Fairbanks. Although she had intended to, the unexpected visit of Chenega's on-island director to the Youth Training Society's Anchorage office had entirely disrupted the events of the day, and while Amolia had enjoyed seeing Rob, her boss, discomfited by the impatience and sardonic directness of the woman's manner, the sudden flurry of activity that had followed her arrival— and the subsequent and sudden hiring of a new teacher, by phone—had delayed her in her regular duties. So she was working late, trying to get caught up, and actually she rather welcomed the excuse to postpone for a time the inevitable meeting with whomever her father had picked up on *this* trip, the confrontation with the next of those strays that he somehow acquired like lint. Amolia had always been fond of her father, but she was not fond of this new life of his, this life of wandering which he had taken to like a bird, going on the first of his remarkable journeys at about the same time she stopped desiring food. Disarray disturbed her, and though she managed the trip from her house to work every day, and once a week a well-planned trip to the grocery store, the thought of larger locomotions filled her with fear, likely as they were to expose her to crowds and disarrangements. She sometimes wondered how much this had to do with her father's bizarre propensities.

He had been different when she was very young. Actually Amolia had been just three years old when her mother died in the Great Alaskan Earthquake, so she couldn't judge how much her father had been changed by this event, but according to his friends—whom she had, when she was old enough, pumped for information about his early life—he had undergone a transformation so complete as to be almost incredible. Before his wife's death he had been reserved, slim, rather elegant, a man who lived to care for his wife and child, and who was so protective of them that sometimes Amolia's mother, laughing tenderly, would say, "Oh, Wesley, I don't need air in a jug." Afterwards he had relaxed, expanded, become voluble and loquacious, almost as if the earthquake, which he too had lived through, had loosened the well-knit seams of his being until he oozed out of them in several directions at once. He had still, of course, cared for his daughter, loved her dearly as he said, but he no longer made any effort to protect her from the small accidents of existence; whatever happened to her, or seemed likely to happen, he would say, "Well, well . . ." letting the second "well" trail off pensively, as if half of him had flown off that day to consult with a specialist in Seattle on just this subject, but the half that was left was ill-equipped even to think about it. He simply would not take charge, and as soon as Amolia was old enough she had started to clean the house and cook, taking a powerful grip on existence. Ever since she had graduated from high school she had earned most of the money for both her father and herself; she had chosen not to go to college from a clear intuition that at college she might meet people who made her feel like a part of things, and one of her delights in life was feeling always like an outsider. For that reason, as well, she never liked to keep a job long; her present job was one she had worked at for a little over a month.

The phone rang in the inner office and Amolia picked it up. "Chenega Youth Training Society," she said. "Can I help you?"

"Hannah? This is Rob. I forgot to ask you if that man at the Survival Place has called in yet to confirm?"

"No," said Amolia. "He hasn't."

"Would you please call him, then?"

She would. She said goodbye.

Amolia did not like Rob at all. Not only did he have the irritating habit of calling people by their surnames—a particularly irritating habit in her case, since her last name happened to be a woman's first name—but he had a small mouth, small fleshy eyes, thin eyebrows, and a small patch of hair on his chin, all of which contrasted weirdly with his rather paunchy stomach. Apparently he had been in a bar one night in downtown Juneau, where he had gone with Linda to assist her—halfheartedly, no doubt—in her efforts to get more funding for Chenega, and he had struck up a conversation with this guy Joe Wilson, who ran what he called "The Survival Place." Somehow, the man had managed to persuade Rob to invite him to Chenega to give a special lecture to the boys about survival, and to pay him more for that than Amolia made in a week. Rob was convinced that the JDs needed special training, but in what he wasn't at all sure; Amolia herself had no opinion on the matter. She had never been to Chenega and though she sometimes thought that it would be nice to get away from it all, and to live off in the woods for a while with the animals, she did not think she wanted those animals to be teenage boys.

As she located the number for the Survival Place, and proceeded to dial it, she wondered about why that might be, that she could find a whole sex so offensive. Not her father, of course; although she sometimes got exasperated with him and often even angry, she never doubted his good intentions and his warmth toward herself. But most men—she found them so messy. It was difficult to keep them clean. Just when you thought you had everything all organized, your room, your life, your brain, along would come a man to dirty it all up, to bring dust and chaos into order. When she was a child, Amolia had often played a game she called "cleaning my mind," in which, as she lay in bed at night, she would start at the very top of her mind and work downward with her best cleaning implements, a nice little straw broom and a beautiful chamois dust cloth; sometimes it took her hours to do the job thoroughly, to empty out and straighten all the nice wooden cabinets, to polish all the surfaces and sweep in all the corners. Her mind, as she had discovered, was divided into four major compartments; in one of them she kept her words, in another one she kept her numbers, in a third she kept her feelings, and in the fourth she kept her memories. Her favorite compartment was the one that held the numbers—big gleaming crystal 5s and small crisp 9s, bold steel multiplication signs and those pastrylike long divisions.

But men had a way of intruding on your brain, as she had learned when she was still young. While she lay in bed with her cleaning implements—sometimes before she started she would take her little straw broom and pretend that she was going to go for a ride on it, feeling very wicked and a tiny bit scared—a boy from her class at school would pop in and inhabit the numbers compartment. He certainly didn't belong there; if he belonged anywhere it was in the feeling compartment, but in any case he should have been tiny and naked, small enough to fit neatly into one of the wooden drawers, and instead he was huge and clothed and kept bumping his head on the ceiling. When he bumped it, all the numbers would shake in their drawers, and the ones that were stacked neatly on shelves or hung on racks on the walls would tremble, sometimes falling down and once or twice even breaking, so that she had to go shopping for new ones. She had lost a very elegant six that way, a lovely sapphire color with perfect curves, and the replacement six, when she had found it, had been small and a plain brown color. At school she had tried very hard to ignore the boy entirely, and had succeeded—as far as she could tell he did not even know she was alive—but then again at night there he'd be, just when she was almost done cleaning.

The phone at the Survival Place was ringing, and a gruff voice with a very peculiar accent came on the line.

"The Survival Place!" it said jovially. "You want to live, we tell you how. You want to die, sorry, we can't help you!" It laughed and then said, "This is Joe Wilson. Can I help you?"

Amolia couldn't have said just why, but something in his voice seemed significant. Hearty, jovial people normally disturbed her almost as much as dust, since they managed to embody in their manner the same kind of certainty that the wind embodied in its debris. They never appeared to doubt that they were *empowered* or that they had a right to tell you what to do, and that made Amolia actively angry—though of course she never let on. But in this case it was easy to be civil to the man, and that seemed slightly portentous; delicately she set the phone back in its cradle, wondering what it might portend.

Then she continued with her interrupted work. It was time for the Chenega Youth Training Society to send its first monthly report to the social workers of all the boys presently in residence on the island, and she had received the rough drafts the day before. Normally, as she understood it, the camp's director reviewed and corrected these reports before sending them on, but as the woman—Linda—had explained in an appended note to Rob, she had been substitute teaching this week, and although she could *hardly wait* (these words heavily underlined) to get back to her regular schedule, until she got a teacher out there, things were going to hell in a handbasket. Amolia found that most of the reports were relatively coherent in any case, but one set was almost illiterate, the set signed by a man named Motor.

"Harry Dance is emproving all the time," one of these ran, "because we think he wants creddit for his effort." Not only did this contain execrable spelling, but it made no sense whatsoever. Amolia's job, as far as she understood it, was to clean up whatever monstrosities the reports contained so that the social workers, when they received the monthly letters, might continue to think that Chenega was a worthwhile institution.

"Harry Dance is adjusting well to life at Chenega," she typed. "He must certainly be given credit for his efforts." Although that meant almost nothing either, at least it was well organized.

An hour or more passed quite swiftly, as Amolia typed up the reports. She had not eaten lunch that day, and of course she would hardly be eating dinner, either, but at about six o'clock she stopped and took a break for some tea. Tea was one of the small pleasures she still allowed herself. Sometimes she even added a noncaloric sweetener to it. Tonight she did not—

she had had dry toast for breakfast—but she took her mug of tea to the mirror, and watched herself drink it down. There was an indescribable delight to be gained from watching herself eat and drink; when she was finished she smoothed down her hair till not a strand was out of place. She didn't have that much hair anymore, but what she did have she loved to keep neat, in much the same way that she loved to keep her mind neat, polishing confusion out of existence. The last time she had been in the hospital she hadn't been allowed a mirror; before, they had put one in her room so that she could see "how starved she looked" but she had simply used it to assess those areas of her body which still looked ugly and bulgy and to work especially hard on them in the hospital gym. So this time they had taken the mirror away from her, and for weeks she had been able to keep track of her progress only in stolen moments in the public bathroom, and from studying herself under the sheet. Then, as she "got better"—and she had finally seen that in order to be released at all she would have to make herself eat, temporarily—she hadn't even wanted to see herself. Now, though dressed in her street clothes, a gorgeous blue dress of thick woven cotton belted around the waist with a lovely piece of gray satin, she was happy with the mirror again. How beautiful the veins in her neck were, blue and bulging slightly with the blood that flowed so close now to the surface. The pretty triangular ridge of her collar bone rode beneath them like a clipper ship.

As she turned away from the mirror, she heard her father's step in the hall. He must have gone home and, discovering that she was not there, come right down to the office to find her. It was funny, but since she had grown thin her sense of hearing had improved, and she could identify almost everyone she knew just by the sound of his shoes. Her father's step, of course, was so distinctive that she could have recognized it even in her fat days; a loud, soft step, it sounded as squishy as his stomach, muffled by the sneakers that he habitually wore. But with him today there was another set of steps, a sharp, staccato gait, and

Amolia, who had been just about to go strolling out to greet Wesley, paused in resignation at this evidence of a stray. Before she could recover, Wesley entered the room and right after him a man with an earring in his ear.

"Amolia," said Wesley. "Darling daughter. You look very well, very well indeed, though still perhaps just a little . . . ah. And that dress, so charming, so monklike, a real contribution, I would say, to our trip. Amolia, I want you to meet Mr. Micah Jones, who will be accompanying us to Prince William Sound. Mr. Jones, my daughter Amolia."

But before Mr. Jones would look at her, he looked intently around the office. He studied the map of the Gulf of Alaska, with Chenega Island marked in red, and he studied the lists and charts on the walls, and the nameplate on Rob's desk. Then, tearing his attention away with what seemed like difficulty, he stuck his finger in his ear, chewed on his lower lip, and said to Amolia, "Pleased to meet you."

"Pleased to meet you too," she said.

The moment she'd said this, she was sorry it sounded so weak, but the truth of it was she suddenly felt weak, weak and a little bit dazzled. When he finally did turn to look at her, Mr. Jones had fixed her with an unwinking stare and he had not yet once, as far as she could tell, moved his eyes away. Although Amolia was not usually much impressed by the people her father picked up on his travels, this man seemed very intense somehow, as if he had just delivered a speech. He had an air about him of absolute certainty very different from her father's air of befuddlement, and different, to tell the truth, from that of most men she had known. And it wasn't the same kind of certainty that she objected to in hearty, jovial people; no, it was something else, something more, something rooted more deeply in need. He riveted her with his gaze, pinned her down, and she felt a great sweeping sense of anticipation, as if for a moment she had long been awaiting. Even as she entered the moment, now, she felt that it was fixed forever under glass, preserved like the snowfall in a glass paperweight, and that she would always have it to come back to when she needed it; more, that her life, both future and past, would radiate outward from this point now—along with two or three other moments of vital meaning—like light radiating forever from a star, which is both fixed and moving, energy and matter.

"But I didn't know, Wesley," she added, adjusting her satin belt, "that you were taking a trip to Prince William Sound."

"Well, not at once, of course, not at once. But Mr. Jones here has an idea that he would like to move out to the Gulf of Alaska, far from any other people, where rocks are really rocks, you know, and I thought perhaps it might be interesting to go along with him and generally help him get settled. That is to say, the world spirit directed me to sit in the fourth car this morning, and Mr. Jones . . ."

"Mica," Mr. Jones interrupted. "Or Spike. Most people make it Spike."

"And Micah was there, and—"

"Yes," said Amolia. "I see."

6

■ WESLEY DIDN'T KNOW why it was, but his daughter always had the power to render him inarticulate, and now, just when it was most important that he impress upon her the marvelous opportunity that the world spirit and Micah together had arranged for the Hannahs, he found that he couldn't formulate the words. Micah and Amolia were staring at one another in a very peculiar way, both of them peaked and jutting forward and Micah—who had been so unexpectedly talkative on the train once he had gotten on to the subject of his experiences in South Africa—had suddenly clammed up again. It was probably just because this building was so depressing, full of sterile cabinets and forms and typewriters that looked like they could walk. But really, just a half hour before, as they had carried their bags from the train station, Micah had been describing in loving detail the kind of cabin he wanted to build on the Gulf, a nice little cabin with skins on its log walls and gun slits instead of windows and smoke curling up from its big stone chimney. Wesley had almost felt as if he were there, so minutely had Micah described it, and although it struck him as strange that anyone would want to live entirely without other human beings, there was no doubt in his mind that this was a chance he and Amolia couldn't pass up. Mr. Jones—Micah—said that the best way to get to the Sound from here would be to take the train, and Wesley loved trains, and when they got to the ocean they would have to take a boat, of course, and then, who knew what, maybe a raft, to actually get *out* there to where, as Micah put it, "the trees will tell you their secrets." And here was Amolia looking both very interested in Micah and very disapproving of Wesley—it was hard to tell whether she was excited by the idea of traveling at all.

Somehow, he got them all out of the CYTS building. Despite Wesley's warm desire to provide whatever care his daughter needed, Micah did not allow him to carry Amolia's briefcase as he wanted to, insisting that he himself was both stronger and more agile. Wesley got to carry his own empty traveling case while Micah took the rubber grips on Amolia's briefcase and squeezed them as if they were pistols. And Amolia, who was generally too dignified to move fast, actually smiled and hurried a bit when Micah strode down the street. Sadly, Wesley trudged along behind.

But by the time they all arrived at home Wesley had cheered up again. He still thought it remarkable that he had been able to persuade Micah to allow the Hannahs to come along with him to the ocean, and besides, he was always very pleased when he was able to entertain someone in his home. He would bustle about the kitchen making tea and putting fruit and cheese out on the huge platter that looked like a fish biting its tail; he would lift towels out of the linen closet, a big towel, a littler towel, and the littlest one of all, and lay them invitingly on the bed in the spare room. If it was summer, as it was now—oh, well, it was really more like fall, but it *seemed* like summer, it was still so warm and sunny—he would go out into the garden and pick the largest assortment of fresh flowers they could spare, thrusting them all into a huge copper jug which he would set on the floor of the living room. Then he would sit back to enjoy the visit, while Amolia took care of anything else that needed doing, cleaned the things that needed cleaning, cooked the foods that needed cooking, and so on—though not entirely as if she, too, enjoyed it.

This time, however, this time she was enjoying it, Wesley was sure of that. And instead of feeling upset, as he had a little at first, he saw now that this was wonderful, all to the good. If there was anything about Amolia that had troubled him in the years she was growing up, it was that she didn't seem to enjoy anything, didn't seem to take the pleasure in just being alive that she should; she was always worrying about something, always trying to make something come out right, when it was fairly clear to any sane person in this world that you had no control, absolutely no control, over how things finally turned out. When Cynthia, his beloved wife, had been killed . . . well, that had just gone to show him, to prove his point, and it was funny that Amolia hadn't seen it too.

"And this is your room, Micah," he said proudly, leading the way down the hall of the little bungalow to the third bedroom, the one that looked out, unfortunately, at the least amount of garden, but on the other hand got the darkest at night in the summer. It had a double bed in it—the bed Wesley had shared with Cynthia—and curtains that Amolia had made herself.

"Very nice, very nice indeed," said Micah. "Though the windows aren't quite gun slits, are they?"

"You can draw the curtains, if you want," said Wesley. "I'm afraid you don't have much garden, anyway." He tried to be helpful by drawing the curtains, but Micah stopped him.

"No, I like to see what's happening behind me," he said.

"Don't want anyone to sneak up when I'm not looking." He tossed his duffel bag on the bed, which was covered by an antique lace bedspread from Cynthia's family, Victorian in style, slightly yellowed in color.

"Of course," said Wesley. "Though you know, Micah ... that is, I have observed that it is terribly hard to keep things from sneaking up behind you if they want to—if they really want to, I mean. I have always thought, perhaps, this was the world spirit's way of—"

"Whatever," said Micah. "Whatever." And Wesley left him alone.

When Micah emerged from the bedroom ten minutes later, he had changed his clothes. His jungle outfit had been replaced by blue jeans and a shirt with a zipper down the front, a green shirt with large flowers printed on it; but he still retained his jungle boots, which he must have taken off and then put on again. He was smoking a cigarette but was otherwise bare-handed. He wore a knife, however, on his belt. Amolia, as soon as they arrived home, had disappeared into the kitchen, where the banging of cupboard doors and the clatter of cutlery indicated that a cooked meal was in progress.

"Got a pad of paper?" asked Micah. "And a pen? It's time to make some lists."

"Some lists? I ... that is ... of course." Wesley went into the kitchen to consult.

"Amolia," he said. "Do we have a pad of paper somewhere? And a pen? Micah wants to make some lists."

"In the third drawer down," Amolia said, "the cabinet next to the door." Wesley himself had no reason to remember this, since he had stopped writing when he gave up his job at the recreational-vehicle supply store. Writing was something that, in his opinion, acted as a kind of Lomotil in the bowel system of the world, inhibiting the natural flow of events, not completely, of course, because nothing could do that, but partially. If it weren't for writing, there would be no complicated analyses of economic trends across the globe; it would be hard for generals and so on to get messages to one another in times of war; it would be more difficult to suggest to people what they should be thinking and feeling; and there would be every excuse, as well, for a daily trip to the vegetable market. But he knew his duties as host, and so he supplied Micah with the necessary implements for writing without even hinting that he disapproved.

Micah had settled down in the large easy chair next to the fireplace, his feet up on the coffee table in front of him. He received the pad of paper and the pen, wrote at the top of the paper in large letters TO GET and then mused, the pen poised above the paper much higher than it needed to be.

"What do you think, Wes, old man?" he said. "What should we take to the Gulf of Alaska?"

Wesley, if he had been going alone, wouldn't have taken anything but a suitcase full of food, but he tried hard to think what he might take if he were Micah.

"Clothes, I suppose," he said vaguely. "And, well, food . . . and heat."

"Heat?" said Micah, looking up sharply.

"Heat. Like, well, I don't know, like matches, I imagine, aren't those supposed to be the three essentials of human survival, clothes, food, and heat?" As he said this, it struck him as a little wrong, somehow—after all, clothes provided heat themselves, at least in the winter and in the summer, too, when you didn't much want them to, but he couldn't think, then, what the third thing could be. Micah, however, seemed to get great satisfaction from his suggestions, and grinning to himself, wrote HEAT in large letters on his paper under TO GET.

"Heat," he said. "That's absolutely right."

7

■ SINCE TRENT HAD arrived, the week before, he had felt somewhat less than grounded. He still wasn't quite sure how he had ended up on Chenega; when he'd left California he had been heading for a job in Fairbanks, and the process by which he had been sidetracked—traded, really, in a deal between two school systems—had been one which had caught him by surprise. Luckily, his disassociation had not hurt his appetite any; now, at dinner, he devoured his hamburger casserole and munched on his neatly trimmed carrot sticks, wondering again how he could find the food on Chenega so good while all the counselors seemed to think it was so bad. In the brief moments when his mouth was empty, he tried to convince Harry and Jack and Emory and some of the other boys to help him work on the fireplace that evening.

He had started the fireplace the day after he arrived on the island, from an impulse to do something simple with his hands— an impulse he had sometimes had when he lived with his ex- wife, but had never followed up on. For all her craziness, Rae was very ept, and she had done all the practical stuff, unless it involved sawdust, which she was allergic to. With one twist of her slim arm she had started outboard engines; if a lightbulb needed changing she had unscrewed the globe to get to it. When the furnace went off one freezing January night Trent had rushed around the house wringing his hands and moaning, riffling frantically through the telephone book to find the num- ber of the appropriate repairman—and what *was* the appropri- ate repairman, anyway, a plumber or an electrician? Neither of them seemed to have very much to do with furnaces—but Rae had gone down to the basement and found they were out of oil, then had returned, taken the phone book out of his hand,

and looked up 24 HOUR OIL SERVICE. Well, when you were married to a woman who was that competent, how much room did it leave you to learn things like rock laying?

But now, perhaps that could start changing. Familiar only with "camps" that had names like Winnihaha, and half expecting that on Chenega they would sing rousing songs by the campfire in the evening, he had been amazed to discover there weren't even cookouts, and had resolved to do something about it. He found that he liked laying rocks, that the simplicity of the activity was in inverse proportion to the satisfaction it gave him; choosing and fitting, tapping and smoothing, all took his mind off his troubles. Today, he had been afraid that he might not be able to work, since it had been raining on and off all afternoon, and the rain had accentuated his depression, a depression brought on mainly by the memory of the ill-advised and ill-fated phone call he had made to Rae just before leaving Anchorage. The main reason he had agreed to take this job on Chenega, in fact, given both the extremely short notice and the foreign nature of the wilderness, was because here he would at least be entirely away from telephones—only in the absence of telephones could he be certain that he would not be tempted to call Rae up yet again and beg her to reconsider (even someone as desperate as himself was not likely to pour his heart out over the radio phone's open-broadcast channels to twenty or thirty hard-boiled Alaskan fishermen). He had almost bypassed the telephone booth in Anchorage too, but like a mouth it seemed to call out to him, and he had been drawn inexorably into its seductive maw, only to be chewed up and spat out once again.

"Oh, Jesus, Trent, when are you going to grow up?" Rae had said. "You can't indulge your feelings like this." He wondered what else she thought you could do with your feelings—punish them?—and started crying against the glass of the phone booth. A drunken Indian staggered by and looked in at him, goofily registering astonishment and Trent just cried some more, his heart pounding a mile a minute, his chest getting damp with tears.

"But I *love* you," he had said in answer, and Rae had just sighed, exasperated.

Trent finished his dinner and went to rinse his plate, bumping into Arnold by the sink. Not even bothering to admonish him for wiping his salad bowl with his cuff, which he was doing with a look of concentration so intense you might have thought he was taking the SATs, Trent took the bowl away from him and rinsed it along with his own. Above the sink a small window faced the sea, and Trent stared through this as he rinsed, hoping that the rain had stopped for good. Large white clouds shoved their way across the sky far above, though in the northeast an ominous-looking line of gray and black rose steadily above the horizon. Some seals were airing themselves on the lower reaches of the next island over—Mummy Island, it was called, because a mummy had once been found in a cave there—and in the trees some cormorants were drying their wings. One stood on the topmost spire of a dead spruce; the others were much lower on the trunk. They all held their wings open like pieces of broken umbrellas and they swayed drunkenly in gusts of wind. Their bodies were a hideous dark brown, but they seemed perfectly unconcerned about their looks, almost like windvanes molded of wrought iron and set upon the tree by some delirious joker. In fact, maybe they *were*—no, that was impossible. Ah, they looked more like birds now.

Without realizing it, Trent had set the plates on the drain board and covered his right eye with the palm of his hand. Taking it down restored the birds to normal. He lifted his hand again—though not against his eye—and stared at it. The covering of his right eye was a newly acquired habit and one he had no particular explanation for. Ever since Rae had left him, he had found it soothing to keep one eye covered in moments of repose and that was certainly odd, since without the use of both his eyes his depth perception was thrown off. He would catch sight of a group of people sitting together around a table and he would think, for a second, that they were made of papier-mâché, and would just have time to marvel at the patience of the artist who had put all those strips of glue-covered paper one on top of another before they moved and he realized they really were people after all. Or he would look at a building, perhaps abandoned, with a gas pump in front of it covered with weeds, and he would think, "What an enormous Edward Hopper painting! And what's it doing *here?*" before he took his hand down and let the building pop back out. He had even taken to titling such works of art in his mind. "Windvanes Drying Their Wings in the Breeze." "Papier-Mâché Figures Confer About Dinner."

The thing was, he still couldn't understand how it had happened. One day they had been together, Rae neither more nor less crazy than usual, and the next day, through a series of machinations that even when they were happening left him dazed by their complexity, she had moved to San Francisco, "just for a little while," and had proceeded to find an apartment so small that when he came to visit he could hardly drag his little suitcase through the door and once inside could find no place to settle it except in the bathtub, where it was still very much in the way, since he showered every morning and Rae— so severe was her allergy to dirt—showered twice a day and sometimes three times. While they showered, the suitcase went back out to the kitchen and had to stay there until the bathtub had dried out, so really the only time both Trent and the suitcase were quite comfortable was in the middle of the night when Trent was fast asleep.

Not long after his third visit, Rae had called him one night, quite hysterical, and said that she had just been talking to her therapist, a woman who belonged to the Sun Bear tribe and who claimed to be a shaman, and the therapist had told her that her latest bout of allergic reactions was probably due to her repressed feelings about the marriage, since she, the shaman, could find nothing organically wrong with Rae when she

"journeyed to the lower kingdom." No snakes, frogs, pterodac-
tyls, or other symbolic reptiles had made themselves known to
her. So, Rae said, she couldn't risk her health any longer, she
had to tell him—she was leaving. Despite the tiny apartment
and the suitcase in the bathtub Trent had really believed Rae
when she said she wanted to go to San Francisco for just a little
while; being a freelance journalist she could easily pick up some
work there, while Trent, as a teacher, was pretty well stuck in
Sacramento for the nonce. It took him the longest time to understand what she was saying.

"You mean you want to come back home right away?" he
said at first, and she screamed, "No, no, not leaving *here*, leaving *you*," and he said in response to that, "But you already left
me. Three months ago." Finally he had gotten it straight—what
she meant by leaving him was that she didn't want him to come
see her anymore, now or for the indefinite future. "Probably
forever," she said. "I think I'm allergic to you."

Well, that certainly shouldn't have surprised him. She was
allergic to almost everything else. Once, when they had just
made love and he was still lying languorously back on the sheets,
one arm beneath his head, the other beneath her shoulder, she
had suddenly sat bolt upright and started scratching her inner
thighs furiously. By the time he roused himself to find out what
was wrong, she had already raised three or four huge red welts,
and when he asked about it, quite solicitously, she said, matter-
of-factly and not at all like a crazy person—indeed she was as
cool and calm as anyone can be who is trying to tear the flesh
off her thighs with her fingernails—"Your semen. I'm allergic
to your semen. I read an article about it." When asked why she
had never noticed this before in five years of marriage she said,
"Your body can only take so much of any allergen. Finally the
toxin builds to a critical level and you react. We finally hit critical." Trent had lain back down, utterly bemused. His penis still
had a drop of semen on it and while Rae went off to the bathroom to shower he shook it gently, watching the drop fall
dreamily down to the sheet. Then he dipped his fingertip in

the drop and brought it up to his eyes. It looked the same as ever, maybe a little whiter. He sniffed it. It smelled the same as ever; maybe a little more eggy? He licked it. It tasted the same as ever; awfully bitter really. He sighed.

Now, thinking about it, he sighed again, as Stan and Norm pushed past him; the kids had all finished dinner and were muscling their way toward dessert. Trent helped himself to a rather large portion of the banana-apple cobbler, a substance that on the outside somewhat resembled the dark brown seaweed that anchored the sand in place off Chenega Point, and inside looked like yellow oatmeal, but certainly smelled delicious.

"Come on," Trent said to Emory, who stood beside him spooning some up, "you could help with the fireplace for just ten minutes."

"Sorry, mon," said Emory kindly. "I'm writing my mother tonight." From nearby, Motor, who had just tasted the cobbler, said approvingly, "Sparkplugs!" which was his general all-purpose word for both approbation and its opposite.

"Lemme taste that," said Derell, whizzing by Trent toward the kitchen with his spoon outstretched, and plunging it into Trent's bowl to lift an enormous bite from it. "All *right*," he said, and kept on going.

Trent carried his cobbler to the table, musing on the subject of food. When they had first been together Rae hadn't realized the extent of her allergies and she had eaten anything she wanted, which had the effect of making her hyper, or hysterical, or depressed. Then, gradually, she had begun to cut the allergenic foods out of her diet, first dairy products, and then eggs, and wheat, and finally lettuce and other innocent vegetables, by which time his life, their life, had been turned entirely upside down because if you can't eat eggs or bread or muffins or milk or cheese or yoghurt, what *can* you eat? and Trent had, like a good mate, gone right along with her almost up to the end, cutting each food from his diet as she cut it from hers. No wonder he liked the food here, actually. It was the first he'd eaten in five years.

■ ■ ■

A little while later, Trent was at the fireplace site and Harry and Jack were with him. While Trent mixed up a big batch of mortar in a metal tub that he had discovered behind the gun-house, Jack and Harry went off to get rocks, cursing colorfully all the while as if this were the worst punishment in the world. Trent didn't mind getting rocks himself, but it was much more fun to lay them; as long as he could wangle some helpers he didn't see why he shouldn't. He stirred the mortar, adding water in large uneven spurts until gradually it turned viscous, a beaded bubbling gray, and by the time Jack and Harry returned, he was ready to use their stones.

"You pusillanimous pismire," said Jack. "This is hard work, bro."

"What's this fireplace for, anyway, mon?" asked Harry. "To roast Christians in or something?"

"Kennie Dugan, bro," said Jack.

"To have cookouts," Trent said enthusiastically. "To overcome dejection."

"There's a lot better stuff than rocks around here for that," said Harry, but he pushed off once more to the woods.

As he started the soothing process of laying rocks, Trent's thoughts went back once more to Rae, why he'd needed her, why he missed her, what he would do without her. Trent had grown up in a single-parent household; his father had died when he was seven. He remembered his father as a bluff, hearty man, a pediatrician who thought the best approach to take with children was jocularity, who believed that they were perhaps a little dangerous. Trent's mother had been different. She was a high school teacher at a tough city school in Sacramento and, worn down both by the necessity of raising her two sons alone and by the need for constant vigilance at her job, she had always treated Trent as a grownup, in a tired, dutiful, way. Trent was the elder of the two boys, but he had never been able to feel the special smugness which is normally the privilege of the elder, since his mother's treatment of both her sons was always exactly the same. He sometimes thought that if he had known his mother, too, was going to die young, he wouldn't ever have become a teacher at all; he had done it mostly to please her. But Trent had been in his senior year of college when she got cancer, and he was too stunned then to change his plans, even if he'd known what else he could do. Until he met Rae, there'd been a cavern in his life. So now there was one again.

As Trent was laying his third layer of rocks, Linda approached from the dining room. Today, she had somehow ended up on both cook and cleanup crews and she was tapping her hands furiously against her buttocks as she walked, as if in outrage at this occurrence—which was funny, if true, since she herself had devised the assignments. Behind her trailed what appeared at first to be a miscellaneous collection of boys, come to see what was going on, boys who gestured and grimaced, clucked their teeth and tapped their heads, trying generally to be as obtrusive as possible, and to distract Jack and Harry, who were still bringing in rocks, from "sucking up to the teacher." When Trent looked up long enough to study the boys, he saw that they were Rudy, Eric, and Doug, not a deadly combination, though not a particularly appealing one either. Rudy, a very quiet boy who was at Chenega for incessant truancy and for running away from home, had, like many quiet adolescents, a sly streak in him which made it seem as if he were only half there, while the other half was off somewhere scouting. Eric, on the other hand, was rambunctious, though at such unexpected times and with such little logic that he seemed almost demented; just as everyone had finally settled down for the night, for example, and soft snores were wafting from the blankets, he would leap out of bed with a great whooping noise, and say, "Oh, boy, maybe there'll be a shooting star tonight!" He was at Chenega for purse snatching, a habit he was having a lot of trouble breaking, and which certainly suited his impulsive nature. And Doug—Doug was just a stupid kid. Trent was doing remedial reading work with him, along with Arnold and Josh, and naturally, Doug was the one who, at the moment, was being most vocal in his bitterness about "people who are teacher's pets," while Eric was shaking his arms like an ape and making grunting noises.

Linda told them all to shut up and go away, which they didn't, so she told them again in a louder voice and then sat down on a chunk of wood. If she had really wanted them to go away, Trent had no doubt that she would have achieved it, but she seemed less concerned with the boys at the moment than she did with talking to him about the Survival Expert who was scheduled to come the next day—"as if individual survival was the point of anything!"—flapping her braids vigorously back over her shoulders for emphasis, evidently delighted to have an audience that wasn't interrupting.

"But," she said, directing an icy glare at Eric as he skipped and danced around her in a circle, making little darting motions with his hands, "I'm going to do something about it. When I was making dinner tonight, trying to keep Josh from slicing off his fingers at the palm, I had a sudden brainwave. When I took an Outward Bound course in Colorado years ago we did something called trust games, where you all get together in a meadow and fall off rocks and things so that everyone else can save you, and I've decided that that's *exactly* what these kids need here. Cooperation, that's what they need. Getting things done *together*. Look, get lost. *You*, take them away." These last remarks were to Rudy.

Trent nodded sagely, as if in profound approval, but the truth of it was that he had hardly heard her. He was struggling to situate the last rock of the evening, a huge piece of green-veined quartz that Jack had found, and though there was a place that was just perfect for it, a semitriangular opening right at the corner of the firebox itself, a tiny little bump on the rock beneath it was keeping it from lying flat. Suddenly, he had an inspiration. "Excuse me," he muttered, and, leaping to his feet, he ran to the toolshed, where he found a claw-footed hammer that looked pretty tough; then he ran back to the fireplace, poised the hammer and smashed the bump to oblivion. Looking with satisfaction at the now flat rock, he tried to remember what Linda had been talking about and, as if for the first time, heard it. A Survival Expert was coming, eh? That was just terrific, really great. He'd always wanted to know how to fry an egg on a paper bag.

8

■ SPECIAL ACTIVITIES HAD quickly become Harry's favorite thing about Chenega and probably everyone else's as well, so the next day as the boys gathered in the bunkhouse there was a lot of excitement in the ranks. Even when the special activities were just movies about drug abuse and alcohol abuse or the perils of driving under the influence, the guys all attended to them raptly, watching the neat little diagrams about the correlation between alcohol consumption and impaired motor reflexes move across the screen with stunned fascination. They had no television on Chenega, of course, and no real movies, so the special-interest horror flicks they saw—the bodies of five teenagers sprawled out of the wreckage of two automobiles, blood all over them; the Indian kid with the headband twitching as he died of a heroin overdose—got A-1 ratings by default.

And now they were about to enjoy what sounded like the most exciting special activity yet—a lesson in survival from an Expert. Rob—whom the boys had only met once before, on the first day of the session—had brought the man out personally from the city, but before introducing him he felt compelled, for some reason, to review the Point System for the kids, who lived with it, Harry thought, a lot more intimately than Rob did. Harry noticed that Linda looked annoyed as Rob said in his rather soporific voice, "You can never *lose* a point, you can only fail to gain one," and then went on to enumerate, at some length, the things the kids were *not* to do. They were *not* to cut the handles off the brooms to make kung-fu sticks, they were *not* to play basketball in the rec room. In the midst of all these *not*s Harry, who had climbed onto the upper bunk with Jack, suddenly interrupted Rob to ask the Expert—a bulky man with an enormous black beard that looked as if it had never been combed and big bushy eyebrows that stuck out an inch from his head: "Hey, mon, how much that shirt cost?"

Rob tried to silence Harry with a glare, but the Expert laughed and said, "Fifty-four dollars. Why, you want one?"

At that, Rob apparently gave up, since he said, pointing toward the beard, "Um, Wilson here is an expert in survival and I would like to see you all paying strict attention because, well, someday your life may depend on it." Then he faded into the background, letting "Wilson"—"Call me Joe"—take over. Joe looked a little like a cartoon character Harry had watched when he was small, a know-it-all called Sourdough Sam, but he didn't talk like Sourdough Sam, since he had an Australian accent.

"I'm from Australia, mates," he said right off. "We got to survive there, too." For a while after that, Harry had some trouble paying attention because Jack, who was sitting right next to him, kept poking him in the side and saying, "Now, pay attention, bro, righto? This is the stuff we're going to need when we run for it."

As Harry had feared, he had gotten dragged into the escape plot. Once Jack was involved, there was no way that Harry was going to stay clean, particularly because Jack was more excited about running away than Harry had ever seen him be about anything. Last Tuesday during free period Jack had been approached by Norm and Stan—which was odd, when you thought about it, since Norm hated whites, but then it turned out that Derell, who was also white, was in on it too—and so now five of the twelve kids were active on the escape list and at least two more—Arnold and Emory—knew about it. This, as anyone could have told them, was far too many people aware of the plot; eventually, Harry had no doubt, the remaining guys would be approached by somebody, the blabber-mouthed Kennie Dugan would talk about it to the counselors, and it would all be over except for the fights about who was to blame for what. Harry would have felt even more depressed about the prospect of being forced to leave Chenega if he had not been so certain that the escape plan would fail, but as it was he just said as little as possible on the subject to anybody, and listened patiently when Jack talked about it, so animated by the idea of running away that he even forgot to add "o" to the ends of his words.

Now, though, Jack at last shut up, and Harry could give his full attention to the Expert, who was pacing about the front of the room, gesticulating with his hands and doing little dance steps from time to time as a form of visual punctuation.

"So you know what, mates?" he said triumphantly, executing a kind of waltz. "There *is* no expert on survival. *You're* the only expert on your own survival. 'Cause what's good for you isn't worth the powder to blow it to hell for me." And he went on to tell a story that illustrated just that point.

"Once, there were two Indians who went out for a day of fishing. A storm came up and their canoe sank in the lake, and they just barely made it, swimming, to shore. They managed to drag their canoe with them, so they had some supplies, and one of the Indians said to the other, 'Listen, don't worry, it's okay. I heard about what to do when this happens. You just shoot off three shots, one after the other, and that means you need help. It's a universal distress signal, you see what I mean?' So the other Indian started firing off shots, all excited about being rescued. He fired off three shots, then three more, and so on and so on, all day long. But nobody came, and finally, exhausted, the second Indian said, 'Nobody's coming.'

" 'Hey, mate,' said the first Indian, 'this *always* works. I heard it in a lecture on survival. Come on, fire off another three rounds.'

" 'I can't, man. I'm all out of arrows.' "

Everyone laughed at this except Norman, who had been

glaring at Mr. Survival from a crouch in the corner. Now he muttered something, slamming one fist into the palm of his hand, obviously in a bad temper because the intelligence of Indians had been insulted.

"Look out for Norman!" Jack said to the air. "Look out he don't scalp you."

"You son-of-a-bitch," said Norman angrily and for a while there was almost a fight. Jack showed off his muscles and Norman made threatening gestures until Linda got to her feet.

"Cool it," she said. "Bundle it up. You guys got a long way to go."

Though Harry had laughed at the joke good-naturedly, and had even, for a second, thought it was funny, now that things had settled down, he thought it was really pretty weak. He hoped that the Expert would get on to more serious stuff soon, real information that people might use, not while they were running away from Chenega—especially since, with any luck, it would never come to that—but just generally, in life, in later years. There was so much stuff that Harry really wanted to know; most of it, he realized as he considered the question, had to do with how to survive the psychopaths with which his life had been filled. That was what survival was all about, when you came right down to it: learning to talk your older brother out of it when he was drunk and threatening to shoot your mother, learning to soothe the chain-saw murderers when they whipped out their Sanity Testaments, learning to invite fat Asians home for dinner when they pinched you in the thigh as if you were a fowl. But so far Harry had managed all this without any conscious plan, and he would have felt a lot better about his future prospects if he had had some more global idea of the methodology.

But the man at the front of the room didn't seem to want to give him one, because now, to contradict Harry's thoughts, he said:

"Survival is learning to live with *you*."

And then he was off on another story, this one about a pilot in the Air Force who was supposed to know everything there was to know about the Alaskan wilderness and who, forty-five minutes after he had to crash-land his plane on the Barrens, shot himself through the mouth and splattered his brains all over the tundra. The back-up plane got there in an hour, but by then it was too late—the guy had just lost his head.

"What do you mean, he lost his head?" asked Derell truculently. Harry sighed, both at Derell's obdurate refusal to see the very obvious pun and at Joe's insistence on telling these stupid stories to begin with.

"He went nuts."

"And he was an expert, kinda like?"

"He was an expert on the wilderness, but not on his own survival."

How to identify a really dangerous guy—that was what Harry wanted. What arguments were most effective in defusing him. But now Derell had subsided and the Expert was moving on, giving them simple rules to remember in case they ever got lost in the wilderness.

"So what you say to yourself," said the Expert, "you say to yourself as you sit there freezing, 'Stop, Sit, and Think, and Keep It Simple, Stupid.' That's right, 'Stop, Sit, and Think, and Keep It Simple, Stupid.' And you know why you say that, mates, aside from that it's true? Because it's easy to *remember*. All you got to remember is SSAT and KISS, just like the kiss you're wishing you were giving your girlfriends right now."

And then, leaving behind twelve very befuddled brains, he was off again, talking about how when our ancestors ran around wearing furs and carrying clubs, they were eating! And there wasn't any Safeway to buy food at. When someone chopped their leg off—chop chop chop!—they died, or they put on a tourniquet.

When the meeting broke up, Harry took his time leaving. Although the Expert had turned out to be very little use, and, on top of that, really not as entertaining as the movies about drunken driving, Trent was now talking to him respectfully, and Harry wanted to talk to Trent. He went up and stood behind the two men, Joe still jovial and loud, Trent leaning forward, almost whispering his query.

"Can I ask you a question?" he said to Joe. "Where would you go to take a course if you were me? I mean, just a basic course in how to build shelters out of brush and how to fry an egg on a paper bag and all that stuff?"

"If I were you, I'd come to my school. The Survival Place, I call it," Joe said, then took a pad of paper from his pocket, scribbled something on it, and ripped the top sheet off to hand to Trent.

"Edible fruits, too? How to light a fire by rubbing two sticks together?" Trent pressed him.

"Edible fruits, too," said Joe.

"Well, thank you very much—Joe," said Trent. "I'll certainly be in touch."

"Hey," said Harry. "Hey, mon. You think I could talk to you for a minute?"

"Edible fruits!" said Trent. "I could probably eat shark too, and whale blubber . . ."

"Yeah," said Harry, interrupting. "Even the food they serve here. Listen, man, do you think . . ."

"Oh, sure, of course, you mean privately? Come on over to the school." He thanked the Expert again and then led the way to the schoolhouse while Harry followed, trying not to look guilty; he was almost certain, however, that he saw Jack giving him a slightly suspicious look. Well, he'd just have to think up a good cover story, that was all.

Trent's office was at the back of the school, along the northern side. It was one of the few places on the island with a lock on its door. The lock was rendered relatively useless by the window, which also provided easy access to the room, but since there was nothing in it worth stealing except for the radio phone, and that was bolted to the wall, the room had never been damaged. Trent unlocked the door, flicked on the light, then settled Harry into one of the two chairs, and leaning forward again, his long hands comfortably on his knees, said, "What's up, Harry? You look guilty."

Guilty! Well, that certainly tore it. Harry, who had been planning to ask for Trent's advice about the escape plan—not only did he like him, but he figured that Trent, who had only been there a week, would be the safest person to approach, as the least likely to already have a grudge against some or all of the boys who were planning to run for it—felt, now, that he couldn't possibly. Not that he had been going to say anything direct anyway; he had just intended to say, "What would you do if you had a friend who wanted to do something you knew he shouldn't do, but you knew it was no good telling him he shouldn't do it, even though the reason he shouldn't do it was mainly because it wouldn't work and it would just get him into big trouble? Would you try to make it impossible for him to do it somehow, like telling someone else about it privately? And how would you keep him from finding out it was you who told?" But now that it came to it, Harry could see that such a speech would be disastrous, because Trent would keep saying that he couldn't give any advice until he knew more about the nature of the plan, and in the end would weasel something out of him, and anyway there was nothing anybody could do if the kids wanted to try and run away, so why was Harry even here?

"Guilty!" he said indignantly. "Well, I like that! I come in here to ask you a simple question and I get accused of looking guilty. You noxious miasma! You piece of shittim wood! I ..."

"All right, all right," said Trent. "You don't look guilty. So?"

"So I was just wondering. I mean, I wanted to know if you would like, be willing to, not that I really expect you to, but anyway, it was just a thought, maybe you could ..." Here Harry paused for a gulp of air and to look around desperately in search of inspiration, "like, maybe, teach me to play the clarinet?"

Trent looked stunned. He uncoiled his arms from his knees, raised his eyebrows incredulously, and then immediately lowered them again, attempting to get his face arranged in an expression of calm interest. While he struggled, Harry stood up, and said in a hurt tone of voice hoping against hope that a little display of injured feelings would be enough to get him out of this mess: "Hey, so forget it. I never really wanted to learn to play, anyway. I just thought *you* might want to teach someone, that's all . . ."

Trent grabbed his arm and shoved him back into the chair.

"Sit down, kiddo. Of course I'll teach you. When do you want to start? Right now?"

So, a few minutes later, Harry found himself getting his first instructions in the care and maintenance of a clarinet. Trent had decided that the dining hall would be the best place for the lessons, since it was, except at mealtime, the least used of the buildings and they would be least likely there to disturb the other residents of the island. But his caution did not, at least initially, yield results, because almost every boy on the island followed Harry and Trent to the dining hall and, even after Trent had firmly kicked them out, they clustered around the windows, cupping their hands around their faces and peering in to examine this new perversity. Harry had blushed terribly when Trent told the other kids what he was up to, but embarrassing as it had been, at least it had made the suspicious look on Jack's face yield to one of happy derision. Jack stayed on at the window long after the other guys had left and he was still there when, after a long series of explanations about wetting the reed, and pursing the mouth, and covering the entire hole with his finger, Harry got to blow his first ridiculous note.

9

■ THE SURVIVAL EXPERT had been everything Linda had expected, and more, a dyed-in-the-wool macho pig from Australia where, as Linda had once heard a comic point out, the men liked to get the women pregnant just to kill a rabbit. When it was so obvious to her that what was wrong with American society today was that people didn't ever learn to cooperate and depend on one another, that what was wrong with American society was that it was just heading for the logical outcome of a belief in the free-enterprise system—in fact, the logical outcome of a belief in the free-enterprise system was a place where kids of fifteen managed forty breaking and enterings—why wasn't it obvious to everyone else? But here were these kids, in an absolutely perfect position to learn to rely on one another and not on themselves, being told that "survival is learning to live with you!" Well, she would do her best to counteract that advice by taking the kids over to Bear Hill Meadow for an afternoon and doing some trust games with them. What a brilliant idea that had been. Trent had seemed to think so too.

Linda was sitting in the outhouse, leafing through a copy of *Hustler* magazine. She often came here when she wanted to be completely alone; sometime in the dim past the Chenega management had decided that the women counselors should have their own, separate outhouse, and had built this one and painted it a sickening pink and white, even going to the extent of installing a little box to keep the toilet paper in and lining the box with a scrap of flowered wallpaper. Then one of the counselors, who had been, Linda did not doubt, a dreamer of the first degree, had decided to build a little shelf to keep candles on, so that in the evening when the women used the outhouse they could do so by the soft yellow light of burning paraffin, and the same counselor had provided a small bucket with dirt in it, so that everyone could sprinkle her own waste products with dirt instead of all the products together waiting for the lime of Morning Cleanup. Finally she had put a small chart on the wall, a chart surrounded by a border of flowers that attempted to match the wallpaper, and listed in chronological order all the steps that each person should take when she sat down to use the outhouse. Or almost all. Point number five was

"Burn A Match To Dissipate Other Odors." Point number six was "Sprinkle Some Dirt Into The Pit."

But Linda was not here to use the outhouse; she had come merely to think. Although it was almost time for the afternoon run and the boys were struggling, or hurrying, into their running shoes and clothes, she was already dressed and could listen for the bell from here. On the way up the hill she had made the dubious decision to stop in at the men's outhouse, which was much closer to the bunkhouse than the women's, either because it was assumed that men, if given half a chance, would simply pee in the bushes, or because it was assumed they would, instead, peer in at the women if ditto. There she had picked up, at random, one of the ten or twelve tattered magazines that provided the men with reading material. These were all copies of *Playboy*, *Hustler*, and *Penthouse*, most of them at least a year old but still, from what Linda could tell, fairly topical. The particular magazine she was looking at seemed to have a fondness for shots of two women making it together in a variety of odd places: on a banquet table laden with fruit, at the bottom of a powerful and one would think dangerous waterfall, in a bathtub with old-fashioned HOT and COLD faucets. It always amazed Linda that men could be as perverse as they so obviously were and still seem, to all appearances, like decent human beings. Undoubtedly even Trent had, at times, studied such pictures with fascination and yet he seemed like a nice guy. And what *was* that woman doing with her tongue? Linda wondered if she should bring the issue of the magazines up at the next staff meeting, pointing out that they inculcated in young minds the damaging idea that women were not human beings in their own right, but simply objects to be . . . Even as she thought this, she yawned, indicating to herself with fair accuracy what the reaction to such a speech would be. She set the magazine aside.

What she had really come here to think about was her life. Before Trent had arrived on the island, she had been toying pretty seriously with the idea of leaving Chenega, of getting out from under Rob and the whole system, which didn't really work. After all, not only did she feel hamstrung by the way Chenega was administered, but she had already been here, to her own amazement, three solid years, and she had never in her life stayed that long anywhere before, not since she had lived at home. When she had left, at seventeen, her one desire had been to *move*, and for a couple of years after her precipitate departure she had done just that, never staying long anywhere she landed.

Linda was originally from Seattle. She had grown up in a small house near a power station, and the constant hum of the wires at the station had filled her life with the only excitement it provided. Though her parents both had jobs—her father was a policeman and her mother worked for a florist—and the family could presumably at some point have moved to a larger house, they had stayed right next to the power station with a kind of grim inertia. The house had only two bedrooms, and Linda had been forced to share a room with her two sisters, one older and one younger, and both very different from her. When Linda was thirteen, both Janice and Eileen had already acquired breasts, hips, brassieres, tampons, and an uneasy fascination with sex, while she still had a flat chest, no hips, and the usual assortment of undershirts. The family doctor had said there was nothing to be concerned about, her hormones were just a little late in moving into production, and that she should go ahead and enjoy her "childhood" for as long as it happened to last. But the family doctor had not had to share a room with two sisters who smelled like a perfume factory, and one day when she could stand it no longer she had moved down into the basement. There, she had set up her bed between the furnace and a concrete wall, and had taped to the wall pictures of motorcycles, which were her earliest heroes. The basement had three small windows, well above eye level, and as Linda lay in bed at night, listening to her two sisters giggle over her head, she would stare through these windows at the lowering sky, and dream about Harley-Davidsons.

Her parents hadn't liked all this, and they had let her know it. As time passed and her body stayed the same, the situation worsened. She had started hanging around with boys, all right, but not the kind that Janice and Eileen favored; no, these were the local band of bikers, the only boys who would stand for it. They thought it was a kick, since she was the daughter of a policeman; she became a kind of mascot to them, finally acquiring someone's discarded leather jacket and leather pants, though not a Harley-Davidson. When she tried, just once, to explain to her parents the thrill of riding fast—even on someone else's bike—she was told in no uncertain terms that good girls didn't feel that way, and that she was, dismayingly, bad. The fact that her father was a policeman probably exacerbated the seriousness with which she felt this charge; when he came into the house and hung up his gun, she saw it as a reproach. As soon as she graduated from high school she left, making her way first to Oregon, where she managed to finagle a job as a bucker, trimming the branches off downed trees at a logging operation, and then to Colorado, where she got a job on a ranch. It was while she was working at the Double O that she had taken the Outward Bound course that had had the trust games, and she'd set off to Alaska afterwards in search of serious adventure. So now, even after college and three years of a responsible job, she still had a bit of trouble seeing *herself* as an authority figure. But the truth of it was, she didn't want to leave Chenega yet. Especially now that Trent had arrived.

Yes, that was true, she was interested in Trent. She would like something to happen with him. It had been over two years since she had had a relationship with anyone, and she had recovered enough from the typical disastrous ending of that one to be ready to think about the next. Two summers ago she had decided to take a job as a cook on a fishing boat during her vacation—more for the change of pace it would give her than from any other motive—and she had made the mistake—it was always a mistake—of getting involved with one of the fishermen. He was a good bit younger than she was, just out of high school, in fact, and had been taken on because he was the younger brother of the boat's captain. He knew nothing whatsoever about fishing and he didn't seem all that eager to learn, but he had an enchanting smile and very large pectoral muscles, which had immediately taken Linda's fancy, particularly because—in an effort, he said, to prevent his skin from absorbing the odor of fish—he had always greased them with baby oil. These days large pectorals were enough to give Linda a mild case of nausea, but at the time she had not yet been through a relationship with a pair of them. The boy—his name, disgustingly, had been Tony—had come on to her one night when everyone else was sleeping, or trying to sleep. His opening remark had been, "Did anyone ever tell you you have beautiful eyes?" She should have known right then that this worm was to be avoided at all costs, but instead, she had melted. No one ever *had* told her she had beautiful eyes, even though she had always secretly believed that she had, and she chose to think that Tony, instead of being blind to everything but the shine of his pectorals in her irises, had actually seen her with clarity. "Is that a proposition?" she had said and he had responded, winningly, "It would mean a lot to me to sleep with you."

In bed, Tony had turned out to be dull, and there was something so hunklike about him that it was hard to overcome the inertia generated by his dullness. Instead, she had become dull herself, and after a while she felt she was participating in a highly choreographed mating ritual between two rather stupid birds, like grouse. But she refused to admit to herself, even then, that Tony simply wasn't very deep, didn't have a whole lot of soul, and had insisted on imagining, as she always could, that he was capable of great things. When the voyage ended, he disappeared without a trace and it took weeks for it to sink in that he probably wouldn't even remember her name if she met him again on the street.

But now almost two years had passed and Linda had recovered. She thought she had learned an important lesson, which was never to have a relationship with someone less neurotic than yourself. Even then, it probably wouldn't work out, but at least you wouldn't be embarrassed about acting as nutso as you were, and there was always a chance that two people with that much in common could actually make a go of it. And now, after a perfect horde of well adjusted, self-centered, and self-confident males, a real neurotic had somehow landed on Chenega, and he was, from what Linda had seen of him, per- fect—intelligent, loyal, unhappy, insecure. She supposed she should be considering the question of whether she, as the camp director, should get involved with one of the staff, but somehow she couldn't take that very seriously, especially since Trent was the teacher, not a counselor; the question she was more con- cerned with was whether he would want to get involved with her. She knew, of course, that his wife had recently left him, much against his wishes, and that was something that always made men uneasy for quite a while. He was probably still in love with his ex-wife, and dreamed about her at night, and . . . but there was no telling until she looked into it, and the ques- tion about that was how?

Linda stood up and stretched. From the schoolroom came the tortured sounds of a bugle on which Ian, who was the duty counselor, was playing the call to run, and shouts and whoops from miscellaneous boys indicated that they were gathering. Tightening the drawstring on her running pants—her hips were so small that there was always a danger her pants would fall off when she ran—Linda dropped *Hustler* into the pit, thinking that here was at least one magazine all those young minds would never be exposed to again, and started down the hill toward the school.

The boys, she found when she arrived, were still talking about the survival man. Emory, the best runner in the bunch, a graceful Aleut with gentle eyes and a shock of hair that con- tinually fell across them, was wearing, as he did in most weather, a pair of cut-off denim shorts and a pair of denim running shoes, the latter of which he treasured as if they were made of solid gold; it was said that his girlfriend back home, whom he planned to marry, had given them to him as a going-away present. Now he was kneeling at Arnold's feet, urging Arnold to lift them.

"Come on, Arnold," he said, "the heel's still out," and he carefully plucked at the laces again, undoing them. There was no haste whatever in his action, although all around him the other boys were pounding on their thighs, leaping into the air, punching the palms of their hands, and so on, and the minute the run began, Emory would be away like the wind.

"I don't know why they won't go in right," said Arnold, gazing down at his feet as if he had never noticed them before. "*Sometimes* they do," he added.

"Oho," said Derell, an awkward youth from a wealthy Anchorage family who had been caught stealing stereo speakers, a yellow Ford Bronco, and an electronic typewriter, on three separate occasions, "*sometimes* they do. You, Arnold, would *never* survive. Never in a million zillion years."

"Come on, bro, let's get goingo," said Jack, punching the air in front of him. "Today I want to win." At that, everyone laughed.

"Emory wins, you know that, mon," said Harry, as kindly as he could.

"Hey, kiddo," said Linda to Harry, "I hear you're learning to play the clarinet, is that right?"

"Yeah, that was me," said Harry, starting to blush, and moving in front of Linda abruptly, so abruptly that he—accidentally? on purpose?—brushed his elbow over her breasts. Then he blushed harder and, probably to cover his embarrassment, stared down into the bay to where a family of sea otters was playing. Linda watched them, too, until one of them, almost as if he felt the human eyes upon him, detached himself from the rest and, lying on his back, paddled closer to shore, his back paws moving against the water, his front paws tucked together on his chest. Linda felt somehow akin to the otter, which darted glances at the humans out of half-averted eyes, like a tourist sunning himself on a raft and eager for a sight of the newest arrival. At the last moment, as he moved south, past the camp, he looked back over his shoulder for one more glimpse, leaned too far, and rolled over onto his stomach with a splash. He righted himself immediately and paddled away, as if he had intended all along to do just that.

"All right, all right, we're off," said Ian, just as Trent and Lorne and Phil pulled in. "Five miles this afternoon, we'll take the sea route, watch your feet and don't break a leg," and even before he finished speaking, the group was off, Emory falling forward into action almost literally like something thrown from a spring, Jack furiously behind him, the rest pouring after them like a thick wave, heading down to the beach where the path began. Linda generally brought up the rear for the first mile or two, until the campers began to tire, and now she waited until the rest were on their way before she started off, breathing great gulps of sea air. She tossed her braids back over her shoulders and ran, the steady thump, thump, thump of her feet on the uneven surface of the beach a reminder of the way she had spent much of her life, scurrying, bustling, dashing, scrambling from one place to another, one job to another, running and running in a feverish attempt to precipitate wisdom, which continued, she was afraid, to stay suspended.

About a mile into the run some of the campers began to fall back, and Linda grunted as she started to gain on them. She loved being alone on these runs: the smell of the sea, the sound of the wind, the rush of the eagles searching for fish, all of them made her feel at once important and insignificant, made her feel, joyously, that she didn't matter, her life didn't matter, not even man himself mattered. She tried to run more slowly so as to avoid catching up to the laggards and then she noticed that Trent was with them, and that he seemed to be favoring his ankle. He fell back more and more and finally stopped altogether just as Linda came alongside him; so what the hell, she stopped too. It was the first time they'd been alone.

"What's wrong?" she asked unnecessarily, trying to slow the beating of her heart.

"I twisted my ankle, can you believe it? Not badly, but I

think I'd better stop." And Linda, as she studied Trent's brown curls—more tightly packed together than ever from the sweat and the sea air blowing through them—and his arms—tan still from California and bare beneath his coveralls—thought that if she had tried to do it on purpose, she could not have arranged a better meeting.

The lower beach was wet, since the tide was going out, and even as she listened to Trent discussing his ex-wife, Linda could hear the water making a tinkling noise as it ran back over the pebbles. It had taken very little questioning on her part to arrive at the fascinating subject of Rae, and once arrived, Trent had proved anything but reticent.

"It just didn't compute," he was saying now. "Oh, I know I was very demanding, expected Rae to be all people to me, was constantly asking her to pat me on the back, approve of what I did. I was just a child, really—she did all my clothes, all the shopping, she protected me completely from the world. But even so, it was just a total shock." He glanced tentatively at Linda.

Linda didn't respond. She wanted him to get it all out, and anything she said now might make him aware that he was telling his life story to a perfect—almost—stranger. So she tugged on her braids, and then, lightly chewing on the end of one, shook her head in dismal sympathy. Trent went on.

This was really better than anything she could have hoped for. It wasn't that she was a ghoul or anything, that she loved to hear about the tragedies of other people's relationships— although it was true there was something warming about the complete mess Trent had made of his marriage—and it wasn't that she actively wanted to hear all the gruesome details about a woman she had never met (Trent had now moved on to the year Rae became allergic to his semen), but Trent's willingness to open up and reveal himself seemed to Linda like an extraordinary departure from the men she had known, who wouldn't admit to feelings if you poked them with a cattle prod. Perhaps

Alaska—which she really loved; its fierce winters, its storms, its exaggerated nights and exaggerated days suited her character perfectly—perhaps Alaska was nonetheless the wrong place for her to live, since here, if anywhere, she supposed, you were likely to run into men who still believed that they should be strong, silent, and utterly without need. But California, where Trent was from, well, it seemed as if they were developing a different breed down there.

"And the suitcase was always a little damp," Trent was saying now, "because we couldn't completely wipe the bathtub each time we took a shower." And then, a little later, "So I wasn't sure I should come here. I thought I would just prove to myself what a klutz I was." He glanced at her again, as if asking to be contradicted, then bent down to pick up a green Japanese glass float, which he tucked down the front of his overalls. Suddenly he looked six months pregnant.

"Don't trip," said Linda, then realized her mistake in light of his recent statement and added: "You're not a klutz. Aren't you building that great fireplace?"

Before Trent had time to do more than beam, ridiculously pleased, they heard shouting and whooping behind them. The fastest runners had returned along the high woods trail and, Emory leading easily, of course, were loping toward the beach. At the end of the afternoon run, they all jumped into the ocean to cool off before they got ready to start on the evening chores, but certain of the boys who had a fear of water still had to be thrown in almost every night. The shouting, it turned out, seemed to be mostly from Lorne, who was breaking his usual rule of staying as uninvolved with the boys as possible by yelling at Stan that if he didn't get his ass in the water, he, Lorne, was going to personally whip it off. Linda, fascinated as she was by Trent's narrative, felt she had to intervene, and so she nodded Trent a goodbye, called out firmly, "I've got him," then shepherded Stan into the sea. She let him leave some of his running clothes on—indeed, she could not have gotten him to strip, short of tearing his clothes off herself, so embarrassed was he by the configurations of his body—and while he was walking, terrified, into the water, and she was standing by making encouraging noises, she took the opportunity to remark once again about all the meat he was eating. Stan glowered at her, miserably unhappy, but she hardly noticed as she pulled off her own clothes to dive in.

She thought that Trent was on sauna fire tonight and she was on bunkhouse cleanup, but though that meant they wouldn't see each other again until supper, it didn't matter. Things had started off very well indeed, and, in a way, the runners' interruption had come at a propitious time. She had noticed that, at first—before they got addicted to her charms—men tended to like her best in small doses, and she was certain that she'd gotten Trent at least curious. She dunked beneath the surface of the ocean and shot out again, exuberant and lean.

10

■ THE WHOLE ENCOUNTER left Trent feeling puzzled as he went off to round up his crew. Though he had, of course, noticed Linda before this afternoon—principally the previous evening, when she had sat and watched him while he worked on his fireplace—it had only been in the most abstract kind of way, as one of the papier-mâché people who figured so prominently in some of his artistic illusions. She had seemed rather attractive, certainly, with her long blond braids and her sparkling broken-marble eyes, but she had also seemed, like a lot of things these days, to have nothing to do with him. He had assumed that she had a boyfriend somewhere off in the Real World—he, like the rest of Chenega's inhabitants, had already labeled it thus, not because it was any realer than theirs but because it was polite to pretend so—and she seemed like the competent kind of woman who would have everything worked out to her satisfaction before she was twenty-one. She reminded him, in fact, a little of his competent Rae; certainly Linda, too, would know what to do if the oil burner ran out of oil.

So why had she wanted to talk to him at such length, or, rather, listen to him talk about his life? Her questions had been remarkably frank and straightforward—"Why did you and your wife break up? Have you started to get over it yet?"—and their central concern had certainly been the present state of his heart. To tell the truth, he had gotten the distinct feeling that she was interested in him, although his past experience with women had proved to him that ninety-nine point nine percent of those he met wanted to be "just friends," and he spent most of the time he imagined other men spent seducing women in sympathizing with them about their cruel and hateful men, men whom—after he had dried the last of their tears and patted their shoulders—they shot straight off to again like bullets out of a rifle.

"So who's on sauna fire with you?" Lorne startled him by asking, but he didn't wait for Trent's answer as he went to round up his own crew of firewood carriers. Jack and Arnold were on sauna fire, Trent remembered now, but he thought Arnold hadn't gotten back yet from running. Oh, no, there they were, both of them coming toward him down the hill. Trent started to meet them, calling out as he did so, "There you are. You guys all set?"

"Hey, bro," Jack called back, swinging his arms up to muscle position and pausing for a moment to hold the pose. "Time for the gigantico fire? Beat those little suckers till their fannies glow?"

"I just saw a toad," said Arnold happily. "It had a big body, all swelled up, and it couldn't seem to move and then it did. They cure warts." He put his finger to his mouth. "Or do they give warts? I . . ."

"I told the little mother not to touch it," said Jack.

"I'm sure you won't get warts," said Trent.

"But I already have them. See?" Arnold held out his knee where, sure enough, a little wart family, all clustered around a central hearth, was squatting.

"But not on your hands. Did you pick up a toad with your knee?"

"I might have kneeled on one once." Thoughtfully, Arnold stared at his knee as if it had just landed from the moon.

"I'm sure it'll be okay," said Trent. "For now, let's think about the sauna. Arnold, you sweep down the floor and the benches and get any clothing out of there. Jack, you start chopping wood. I'll haul some water to fill the tank."

"Oh ho, the counselor takes the easy job," said Jack.

"Oh ho," echoed Arnold.

Nonetheless Trent grabbed the two metal buckets from their hook underneath the ceiling of the porch and made his way over to where the stream, rushing hysterically toward the ocean, had been dammed to provide a pool of clean, and freezing cold, water. He thrust the buckets under its surface, his hands growing numb in the short time it took to fill them up, then, trying to avoid dripping on his legs, he awkwardly carried the buckets into the sauna. On top of the great potbellied stove in the far right-hand corner sat a five-gallon tub of galvanized steel, which provided steam to the air and ladlefuls of hot water to throw on the hot rocks. He made three more trips to the stream before the tub was full, and each time he came into the sauna Arnold, tongue clenched with unqualified commitment between his teeth, was sweeping the same bench. He would reach into the far back corner and draw all the bristles toward him, managing to almost separate them as he drew so that instead of a broom he seemed to be holding in his hand an army of straw, marching in close formation. Then again into the same corner, and again, long after any dirt that might once have been there had changed its residence. It was as if the kid were in the final stages of a speed jag.

"You're looking good, Arnold," said Trent. "Why not do another bench now?"

Outside, Jack was furiously at work on the firewood. His muscles bulging, the sweat gleaming on his forehead, he stacked a piece on the chopping block and whack, whack, it was shattered, four pieces falling like the sections of a grapefruit neatly around the block onto the chip-littered ground. He wiped the sweat from his forehead with his sleeve and when Trent came out again, said, "How come Arnold never has to do any choppingo, bro? This stuff is a real bitch."

From inside the sauna, surprisingly, came Arnold's reedy voice.

"Yeah, how come I never get to do any chopping? It's always so dark and stuffy in here."

Trent looked from Jack to the sauna and back again. He was sure that letting Arnold near an ax would be tantamount to signing the kid's death warrant, but it occurred to him that this was probably the way Rae had always felt whenever *he* had wanted to do something for a change. Maybe if he just let Arnold take one or two chops, the kid would get tired of it, and his ego would not, thus, be permanently damaged.

"Hey," said Trent. "It's fine with me. You can do anything you want, as far as I'm concerned." Before he had even finished speaking, Jack had sunk the ax into the chopping block so hard that it would take King Arthur himself to get it out, and Arnold, with a merry clatter, had wrenched open the door and come out, blinking, into the sunshine.

Then they all three stood looking at the chopping block. Jack loosened the ax in the block, glanced doubtfully at Arnold, and said, "Well, wait a minute, bro . . ." but Arnold interrupted him by picking up the ax. He could hardly lift it and he had to put it down again to grip it nearer to the head. When he had done that, however, the head was unfortunately upside down and both Jack and Trent started to talk at once, attempting to explain exactly how one went about splitting wood without killing oneself. While they were doing this Arnold stared at them dumbly, one finger to the corner of his mouth. Trent began to get the feeling that he had been right in the first place, and that if he wanted to avert some dreadful catastrophe the only thing to do was to move swiftly, and to move now, but his tongue was still tangled in explanations, and Jack was moving in close to Arnold to demonstrate the technique, and by the time Trent found it in him simply to shout, "Stop! Not that way!" Arnold had gotten impatient and was giving the ax a mighty heave; it poised at the top of its arc and then it was falling, falling backward totally out of control and right toward the spot where Jack was standing, and though at the last minute Jack saw his danger and tried to wrench his body out of the parabola of the ax, it was too late, the blade hit him in the shoulder and disappeared inside him. A wall of blood rose like a wave and then surged over the beach head of Jack's chest, and Jack fell to the ground, where he rolled over, trying to scream in agony, but instead just contorting his face into a frightful mask of pain, and making small grunting noises that went *uuuuh, uuuuuh, uuuuuh,* and every once in a while *ooooooooohhhhhh.*

Trent lost only a second watching all this, though it seemed to him much longer. The whole world had suddenly brightened for him, as if a flashbulb had gone off, and surprisingly, in this well-lit, slow-motion world, he could see just what had to be done.

"Arnold," he said. "Go find the first counselor you see. Tell him to call a helicopter. And move!"

Then he ripped off his shirt and started systematically to tear it into strips, effortlessly managing the rips even at heavy seams, his usually tentative fingers full of a sudden surge of force. He left half the shirt intact and wadded it into a ball and then, holding Jack's right arm down with his own, and pulling the blade of the ax away, he shoved the wad of cloth between the open lips of the wound. Here Jack did scream, finally managing to translate all those *uuuuuhs* and *ooooohhhs* into a strangled shriek of pain, but Trent hardly heard it as he began to tie the wadded shirt in place with the strips he had prepared. Already the bandage was soaked with blood but the blood itself would help to stop the flow beneath it. He managed somehow to get four strips tied and knotted before the first of the running figures appeared at the top of the hill.

The flow of blood had definitely been cut in half, perhaps more, and as he waited for the others, Trent pressed his palm down on the bloody bandage, which stopped it altogether. He was by now in a rather peculiar state. His heart was whanging away from somewhere halfway between his clavicle and his chin, and his mouth was dry with fear. As he had watched the accident occur and then, like someone standing at a distance, watched his own reaction to it, it was as if a door had opened for him into another, clearer world. He, Arnold, Jack, the ax— they were all just faces of a single branching whole. Every blade of grass, every shard of wood, every chip of rock, was defined for him and distinct, and every sound, no matter how involved with other sounds, emerged as identifiable and discrete.

Lorne was the first to reach him, not because he was running faster than anyone else, but because he had already been on his way to the sauna with a load of wood when Arnold ran by him, and even in his state of near-hysteria decided to move on and find a different counselor. He stopped at Trent's side, tugged at his beard with his thumb and a bent forefinger, and said, "I knew Jack would do this to himself sometime. He thinks a good deal too much of his own prowess."

"Oh, fuck off!" snapped Trent.

Before he had a chance to be astonished at his outburst and before, too, Lorne had a chance to reply to it, about ten more people arrived simultaneously on the scene. The boys started saying "Jesus Christ on a cross," and "Bloody shit, man," in hushed tones, and the counselors, who had had a first-aid course as part of their otherwise rather sketchy training for this job, started offering good advice, all at once.

"Elevate his feet!"

"Keep the blood at his head!"

"Make sure to keep him warm!"

"Someone go get some soup!"

Trent half heard them and half did not. Or, rather, he heard them clearly enough, but since the sounds seemed to pop out of nowhere and since there was no clear way, in the universe where all things were one, for him to identify one piece of advice as more or less important than the rest, all the comments just sat there, unprocessed, while he continued to press on Jack's wound.

"Do you want someone to spell you?"

"Shock is the most dangerous thing."

"The chopper is on its way."

"I thought you said you were a klutz."

This last was Linda. He looked up to find her standing on the edge of the group, her knitting bag held, but idly, in her hands. The sock she was working on was draped over her shoulder as if she had not even stopped to set it down but simply flung it over her shoulder as she ran. Her cheeks were pink from the run and beads of sweat had dampened the bangs that grazed her eyebrows. While they waited for the helicopter to arrive she managed to clear the accident site of most of the counselors and boys, send one of them for paper and a pen, and start to fill out an accident report to send with Jack.

Jack was still conscious, although he was very weak, and Harry, almost as pale as his friend, was now kneeling at his side saying "Hey, mon, don't worry, you're going to be all right," betraying with every word he spoke that he actually believed the opposite. He took Jack's good hand and squeezed it, then dropped it in some embarrassment, then defiantly picked it up again; then set it gently on Jack's chest. Jack's pupils were huge, every now and then he let out a moan, though he managed for the most part to keep his lips closed. Arnold had tried a number of times to apologize to Jack, but each time, before he got beyond "Oh, Jack, I'm so sorr'—" Jack had cut him off and said, "Forget it, bro," and once, "Forget it, bro, I'm getting *out* of here, righto?" After a while, he seemed too weak to talk, and since Arnold had been repeatedly shut up, Harry was the only one of the boys still capable of carrying on a conversation. He talked about other accidents he had seen, and how they had all had happy endings; he talked about how good the Anchorage hospital was, and how much fun it would be in the helicopter. Trent noticed that several times he leaned forward across his knees as if the sight of blood, or something else, made him faint, but each time he pulled himself together again and kept talking. Then the helicopter arrived, like a delicate green and yellow bug in the distance, and when it had landed and disgorged its EMCs and they had loaded Jack onto a stretcher and strapped him aboard, Harry went right up and spoke a few words to him that no one else could hear. And then whir whir whir the helicopter kicked up a great many wood chips and, shooting them around like darts, lifted into the air and veered away. Trent watched it go, first covering his right eye with the palm of his hand and then impatiently taking it down.

He noticed that he was covered with blood, on his face, on his pants, on his chest. Wonderingly, he touched the stuff, which had not yet really dried. Linda volunteered to light the sauna fire so he could get clean, but though he thanked her and went down toward the ocean, the blood made him feel strangely marvelous. The sea didn't seem as cold now as it had after the run, just an hour or so before, and he waded up to his knees in the salty water, then stood looking out toward the west. A pod of killer whales was surging by, three trawlers were dawdling in the distance and in the sky not far above him a seagull was chasing a bald eagle. At Trent's feet there was a dark rock almost covered with anemones, light green in color except where cranberry-colored tentacles fringed the opening in their centers, and bending down, he touched one with his finger, near the donut hole with a bottom. It started to contract, curling all its pink tendrils inward toward the center.

When the sauna was thoroughly heated, the whole camp piled into it in shifts. Trent was on the first shift tonight, along with

most of the counselors and a few of the boys. You were supposed to wear a bathing suit in the sauna—a rule handed down,
like the wallpaper for the toilet-paper box in the women's outhouse, from some previous regime—but it was a rule that was
not enforced, and generally people wore as much or as little in
the sauna as they wanted. Stan always wore a baggy bathing
suit and a T-shirt, and Kennie, too, was seedily clothed. Ian,
who probably thought that the sight of his godlike body completely naked would be too much for his fellow mortals, wore a
small bikini brief, and Motor was clearly too chagrined by Linda's presence even to dream of disrobing completely. But Harry
stripped to the skin as he would in a sweat lodge and Linda, of
course, was defiantly naked. Before tonight, Trent had worn a
bathing suit—he had always been an almost painfully modest
man, careful never to walk around his own house naked for fear
someone passing on the street might see him through the windows—but now he felt like revealing himself, like letting his
body be seen.

The sauna smelled sweet, of spruce and pine and sea salt.
Already it was very hot inside; the tub of rocks that sat on top
of the stove along with the tub of water captured and emitted
heat in great dry waves, and a soothing warmth immediately
spread through Trent, who climbed up to the top bench and
sat beside Kennie Dugan. Kennie was still quite dry, but Trent
was already starting to pour with sweat and he rubbed his hands
over his slippery body, amazed by the amount of pink dirt that
was pouring off him even after his dip in the sea. He leaned
over, wet a spruce branch in the bucket and splashed water on
top of the stones. Steam hissed from them as they darkened,
then lightened again.

Very rarely did anyone talk in the sauna, but tonight it
seemed everyone wanted to. Arnold kept trying to explain that
it had been an accident, and with unusual patience, they heard
him out. Derell remarked at least three times on the *blood* that
had come out of Jack, and asked the sauna at large how one
man could spare so much. Everyone agreed it was lucky the

helicopter had come so quickly, because when you came right down to it, Chenega was very *far* from anywhere else. Linda said sarcastically that it was really a pity Joe Wilson had had to leave so early. Then there was silence for a while, while they all rubbed their bodies until they were thoroughly sweating, and, at their own pace, went outside, soaped up, and poured cold buckets of water over themselves.

When everyone was back inside for the final sweat, Kennie Dugan seemed to think it was his turn. Once Kennie got started, it was almost impossible to get him to stop, and his scripture today was the accident that had happened to Jack. Kennie's family was fundamentalist Christian, and he had picked up from them, along with his fondness for telling outrageous lies, a complete mishmash of doctrine, with which he could drive the whole camp crazy.

"Jack is lucky he didn't die," Kennie said. "Because he would of died in sin. And when you die in sin you go down this tube into hell. Satan's down there. He tried to rule the heavens and God kicked him out with one boot. God will raise all the dead up with one hand—there's a great black book and he writes your name in it. My minister says man will destroy the earth. There'll be nowhere to hide. You walk down the street with your flesh peeling off and—"

"Shut up, Kennie," said Trent. "Nobody wants to hear that crap." And in the amazed silence that followed this remark, he wondered what on earth was happening to him.

PART TWO

Out Where the Rocks Are Rocks

11

■ A M O L I A   H A D   B E E N persuaded to quit her job, and she was going down that morning to give notice. Actually, since "giving notice" implied that she would give CYTS a reasonable period of time to find someone to take over for her, she was not giving notice—she was just quitting. Spike, and as a consequence, of course, her father too, wanted to leave as soon as possible now for the Gulf of Alaska, and although it had taken them over a week to convince Amolia that she should go with them, Wesley waxing poetic time and time again about a place where "rocks were really rocks," she had finally decided to do just that—she wasn't at all sure why. Certainly not because rocks were rocks out there; even if they were, that seemed to Amolia like an enormous expenditure of nature's energy on something that was too intransigent to appreciate it. No, it really had to do with Spike, who was obviously a criminal—which Amolia would have figured out even if her father had not reported proudly when he first brought Spike home that Spike had been "in the joint"—and yet who didn't take everything he wanted exactly when he wanted it. For example, he had tried to kiss her once, and she had pushed him firmly away, but he had not made any kind of a fuss, just looked at her intensely and said, "You're not a kisser, eh, Molia?" and when she answered, "Not anymore," he hadn't pressed her, had just whistled a few bars of "I'm Going to Ride That West Wind Down," and changed the subject. Nor had he pressed her to empty her savings account; she had decided to do that herself.

Spike was coming with her this morning to the CYTS building while Wesley went shopping for food. Wesley had discovered, he told her, an emporium in the newly renovated part of downtown Anchorage where food was treated as an "elemental spirit," and he had urged her, twice, to come with him. He claimed to have noticed that she was getting thin lately, had been *too* thin even when she went into the hospital the last time—he had never really understood, of course, the connection between Amolia's "sickness" and her "thinness," had never understood that her thinness *was* her sickness. The first time she had been taken to the hospital, he had been off somewhere in the Kenai Peninsula, and it had been a perfect stranger who had picked her up when she fainted in front of the First Alaskan Bank, and who had taken her to Emergency. The hospital had gotten in touch with Wesley—Amolia had been only thirteen when she decided to call her father Wesley, an idea that he took to with surprising pleasure, asserting that the word "Dad" had always struck him as wrong for a man of his bulk and gait—and he had returned as fast as he could, and left again almost as quickly. He said it disturbed him to see her all hooked up to tubes and pumps, that they appeared to be new and skinnier limbs she had grown to supplement her own, and that although he was a tolerant man, he didn't want a spider for a daughter. It was the closest Amolia had ever seen him come to getting upset at anything.

But she was not going with him to the food store, and he trundled off without her. Spike had already gone downtown, to shop for some last supplies, and Amolia was supposed to meet him at the Denali Theatre before going on to CYTS. Unfortunately, to get to the Denali she had to walk three blocks from the bus; that meant passing J. C. Penney on the corner of Fifth and D streets, and that meant seeing the earthquake once again.

By now, after so many years of rerunning it in her mind, it was no longer frightening to her; it was more like an old movie than a real event in which her life had been changed forever. Stepping down from the curb on D Street, she almost crushed a tiny orange butterfly resting on the concrete, and then she was back on the third floor of the store with her mother, wearing a blue dress with flowers on the sleeves, and black patent leather shoes. Her mother was shopping for some sheets in the Easter sale; pre-Easter, it was Good Friday. Amolia was looking at some pink and green glass elephants, tiny ones with curly trunks, on a shelf all by themselves. The elephants started suddenly to dance, as if they were alive. Spellbound, Amolia cried, "Oh, Mother, look!" Then her mother appeared at her side, and without taking a single glance at the elephants grabbed Amolia's hand and started dragging her, as if she had done something terribly wrong, off toward the escalator. Now the floor was bucking so hard it was difficult to walk, and Amolia, in her confusion, thought that this too was a punishment for whatever she had done wrong—and then all the lights went out and it was totally dark and Amolia's mother was shouting, "Cover your head with your arms!" which she had already done, because things were falling down all around them in the darkness. Then she was down on the first floor, which was better, because there was light, but it was still like walking on a field of Jell-O, and her mother—for some reason that even now Amolia couldn't imagine—let go of her hand and went first out the door and disappeared under a great concrete slab which came down like the blade of a guillotine.

This time, the earthquake hardly distracted her from her contemplation of the future to come. Spike was waiting, as he had said he would be, at the Denali Theatre, one leg on the concrete wall behind him, his shirt unzipped to the waist. The moment Amolia caught sight of him leaning there she felt—as she had when she first saw him—as if all her senses had awakened; everything around her seemed to be much sharper in outline, much brighter in color, than it had ever been before. Love at first sight was something that Amolia had never either believed or not believed possible; as with many phenomena, she had had no opinion one way or the other about its likelihood. Now she wondered whether perhaps she had not misunderstood all along the meaning of the phrase. What she felt for Spike bore no relation to images of love; rather, it was as if she had suddenly remembered the answer to a question on a test and just knew, with every bone in her body, that it was the correct answer; as if she had tried on a pair of pants which, for once, fit her perfectly, even in length. Not good or bad or wrong or right. Just an amazing fit. And now, on top of that, she was quitting her job—it made her feel quite lightheaded.

Despite her elation and sensual excitement, she noticed that Spike seemed bemused. When he took her arm as they headed toward the CYTS office, shifting the bags of packages from his right arm to his left to do so, he gripped her elbow more lightly than usual, half his attention elsewhere, and when they got to the steps of the building on F Street he paused and stared, stupefied, at the ground. Only when Amolia said, "Spike? Spike?" and then added "Micah?" did he raise his head and shake it slightly as if he had gotten water into his brain, and then he nodded assertively at her, said, "It's okay, Mole, it's okay," and strode up the steps two at a time, his feet slapping hard on the concrete.

In the office Rob was at work talking on the telephone. When Amolia followed Spike in—now that he had shaken off what seemed to have been a state of indecision, no one could have been more decisive or more determined than he—Rob gave them one furtive look out of the corner of his eye and then returned his attention to whomever he was talking to. While Spike strolled over to study the maps and charts on the walls, as confidently as if he were the director of Chenega and Rob his underling, Amolia listened to Rob's conversation, which seemed to involve an accident.

"Yes, yes," he was saying now, "but how long do you think

he'll be in the hospital? The director wants to know whether we should get another boy to take his place." Then, "Oh, I see, it's a matter of physical therapy. Well, of course, he can do that on the island." Finally, "All right, all right. Yes. Thank you." He hung up and turned reluctantly to Amolia.

But before she could speak Spike pointed to the map, then said, "You run Chenega, is that right?"

"Not exactly," said Rob, with a bitter expression. "But I just returned from the island."

"You know anybody out there name of Burke?" asked Spike, thrusting his right foot forward and then on second thought drawing it back.

"Burke? Yes, he's a counselor. How do you, um, know Burke?"

"Friend of a friend. Friend of a friend of a friend, actually, see?"

"At the Survival Place," said Rob, "they tell you you don't need any friends."

"Excuse me," said Amolia, "but I think you better know that I'm quitting. Today."

"Quitting?" asked Rob as if the word was unfamiliar to him, but Spike was drawing his leg forward again and, leaving it there this time, he said, "So this friend of a friend asked me, if I came to Anchorage, to just look up this Burke and see if he was still working at the island. And he is, so I guess that's that."

"Who should I say said hello?" asked Rob. "Quitting?"

Spike looked dumbfounded, then answered, "Wesley Hannah."

Amolia stared at him and so did Rob, who was making a slow connect in his brain, it seemed.

"Hannah?" he asked. "Then you're related to . . . that is, Amolia . . ."

"Right," said Spike. "A cousin."

"Oh," said Rob, and turned his attention back to the quitting.

It took another twenty minutes, but at last Amolia got a

paycheck. She went to collect the few personal effects she had left in her desk, feeling decidedly relieved and also decidedly puzzled. Spike's use of her father's name, his lame excuse about the friend of a friend of a friend, his air of bemusement before they had ever arrived at the office—all of it added up to the fact that he knew a lot more about Chenega than he had let on. But although Amolia was curious, her curiosity was the kind that is better left unsatisfied, for it promised great things ahead; she couldn't have said just how, but she knew that her life was on the verge of an enormous alteration, that she was about to become something new, something odd, and that—like a cloud blowing quickly beyond the horizon—her old life was already drifting away from her. What puzzled her most of all—more than Spike's use of her father's name, more than that excuse about the friend of a friend, more even than her own decision to quit—was that she *liked* this feeling, liked it more than anything she had yet known, this sense of elation and lightness, as if a burden had been dropped. She picked up her makeup case, a hairbrush, and a mug with small elephants on it and let them all plummet into her handbag.

The morning had been sunny, but the afternoon was overcast, and as they wandered through downtown Anchorage the sky got darker. There was a big construction project on Sixth Avenue, so they had to walk along the edge of the sidewalk there, and after Spike made a point of stepping around her so that he would be on the outside of the sidewalk, he explained to Amolia that this was a traditional position for a man, since there he could best protect the lady from the mud or water that might be flung up by the vehicles going by. There was no mud or water in the street today, and the inside position, when you got right down to it, was probably the more dangerous one near a construction project, but at his words Amolia's senses seemed to get even more anxious and eager to work for her. When she passed an old one-ton flatbed truck, the bed constructed of wood that had been warped and splintered, it appeared to her that each splinter and curve of the wood was as well defined as if it had been designed by a sculptor; in the rear curb wheel, which had a rusty rim, heavy black oil had been spilled and hundreds of tiny white flower petals had stuck to it lightly, without marring their whiteness, which glistened as sharply as the black that held it. Amolia pointed this out to Spike, who said, "Far out." They kept on walking, their path in the general direction of the sea.

The salt and fish smell grew stronger. A construction worker on a scaffolding high over their heads called out, "Bounce 'em, baby!" and Spike turned as if he were going to kill the man, but the man was looking in quite a different direction, and in any case Spike must have noticed that Amolia didn't have that much to bounce. When they got to the ocean they went right to the end of the pier and stood there, side by side, staring out to the west.

Oil slicks glistened on the water in rainbow colors, and the boats bobbed among these oil slicks gaily. For years after the earthquake, Amolia hadn't wanted to get into boats, which moved irresponsibly beneath her feet, and even now she wasn't wild about the idea, which was, in her mind, the least appealing aspect of the plan to go to the Sound. But here the sea stretched so endlessly before them, and the smell of tar was so friendly, like licorice, that even the boats seemed a pleasant sight and Amolia laughed aloud. A man in a yellow slicker looked up from splicing a tiny piece of rope on a wharf nearby. He grinned at them. Three little boys sat on the edge of the pier dangling their legs over the side and talking. A blond one said, excitedly, to a dark one, "Are you an Indian?" Then, at a muttered response, said, "My foster brother's one, too. He scalps me every week. That's why my hair's so short, ha ha."

Sea gulls wheeled and shrieked overhead. White-wing scoters floated like decoys on the water. Some kittiwakes, huge and disdainful, unconcerned about humans, walked by, holding their chins up smugly, placing their feet carefully in front of them. On a sudden impulse Amolia moved toward them, waving her arms and saying "Boo!" and, beady eyes alarmed, they squawked, moved, then rose into the air, the whole group flapping and swaying as if in response to some unseen wind. Spike laughed—and Amolia, as she brought her arms back to her sides, looked wonderingly at him. She took a deep breath of the sea air, and then realized she was hungry.

This sensation was so unfamiliar that it took her a moment to identify it: at first she thought she must be feeling sick, perhaps from the smell of the tar, then, for just a moment, she thought something had fallen down the front of her dress and come to lodge in the space between her belly and her underpants, pressing her from the outside. But she didn't have a necklace on, and no one else had been near her, and gradually it dawned on her that the pressure was inside, not out. She stared at her stomach, a puzzled frown on her face, and Spike, aware that something was wrong, stared at her.

"What's up, Mole? You lost a shoelace?"

"I'm hungry," she said.

Spike did not act shocked. He just said, "All right, Mole, what'll it be? Fish and chips? We passed a nice little place couple of blocks ago."

"Fish and chips," Amolia said. "All right."

12

■ SPIKE SAT AND STARED at Amolia as she ate, wondering if he should ask her to marry him. Now that they were almost ready to leave for Chenega—just about everything on his list had been neatly checked off, even the books, which Amolia had selected, books on edible mushrooms, books on flora and fauna, books on how to build a cabin in the woods—Spike still had the feeling there was something more he should do before they actually went. He thought this something had to do with Amolia, but whether he was supposed to marry her or abandon her he wasn't quite sure, he just felt that he should do *something*. He had never been married before, so it sounded interesting to him, as far as it went—though he had certainly never intended to take on such baggage for his great escape from civilization. But meeting her had been like fate; from the moment Wesley had first told him about her on the train to the moment he had walked into the office and seen that enormous map of Prince William Sound he had felt in the hands of something bigger than himself.

Spike had a real belief in fate—in his own fate, if no one else's. Everything that he couldn't account for by his own intelligence and perspicacity, everything that he hadn't planned, seemed to him the result of this inevitable destiny. When he had gotten on the train in Fairbanks he hadn't been sure exactly what he wanted at Chenega, and he had been half serious when he convinced Amolia's father that he was going out to the Sound to build a cabin there and live in isolation from humankind. But then, when it turned out that Wesley's daughter worked for the place—well, that was fate, no doubt about it, and it told him what he had to do. Yes, he might still talk to the boys who were presently in residence there, giving them tips on how to survive in the pen and all that—but first he would execute some justice. First he would kill Burke dead. Fate was helping him to be *organized* this time, to discover in advance that Burke still worked on the island; and Amolia had helped, had been an instrument, somehow. That was why he was thinking of marrying her.

It was not the only reason, of course. Another reason had to do with her. When he saw her brush her hair, looking, with an absorbed expression, into the little mirror she always carried, or when she pointed to something in a store window, her forefinger drooping heavily at the tip, the corporeality of the actions reflected back on him. When she smoothed her dress down around her waist, he was somehow realer—more substantial—than when he was alone. Then, too, the unexpectedness of her movements was stimulating; like a wind-up toy so complex you never knew what it was going to do next, she surprised and delighted him, and her eyes lifted a weight of uncertainty from his shoulders whenever they touched him. That was remarkable, because if the truth were told, he had never had all that much interest in women.

Oh, he had spent time with them, and made certain that whenever he was out of the pen he slept with one of them, if not more. Some of them he had actually liked, in a halfhearted sort of way; it was never any pain to him, however, to make his last goodbyes. He much preferred his male partners, and though even with them he had never found sex to be the dynamite experience it was cracked up to be, at least they always understood his jokes, and knew when to leave him alone. But Amolia showed no interest at all in sex, at least not in sex with him, and therefore it was possible to imagine that she might be an interesting wife. Certainly if he spent any time at all out on the ocean—as he fully intended to, after he was finished at Chenega—it would be pretty lonely if there weren't someone around to keep him company. And he had the feeling that Amolia would be loyal—almost fanatical. If he could teach her to shoot . . . and she already knew how to cook . . . but then, really, there was no need to marry her, she was coming with him anyway. She didn't know, of course, any more than her father did, that they were actually heading for Chenega.

As Amolia put the last chip into her mouth, Spike made his decision. No, he wouldn't marry her. But at least he would buy her a gun. Although she had helped him to compose their supply list for the trip, especially when it came to the nonvegetable food items, she had never asked him about the first entry: HEAT, in capital letters. Now, he pulled the list out of his pocket and chuckling aloud, pointed the word out as he held the paper before her.

"Got any ideas on where to find this one, Molia?" he said, and then, before she could answer, went on with, "Oh, never mind, never mind, we'll find some," and got to his feet to leave.

They walked, this time, along Fourth Street, where drunks
fought with invisible enemies and where a great many rather
cluttered stores and pawn shops lined the dirty sidewalks. Spike
looked in at the windows and up at the signs. FURS, one said.
Another read BADGES. SWORDS. MILITARY ITEMS. ALASKA TRADING
POST. LOANS. But when Spike cupped his hands around his eyes
and peered intently through the windows of that shop, he did
not find what he was looking for, and passed on down the street.
The next pawn shop they came to, however, was definitely what
he wanted: in its window, propped in the midst of binoculars,
fishing tackle, knives, and cameras, was a cardboard sign, hand-
lettered, that read GUNS BOUGHT AND SOLD. Spike pushed open
the thick wooden door and paused while a bell rang in the back
room and a lank man, pale and a little stiff, came out wiping
his hands on the brown apron that guarded his stomach. Amolia
followed Spike in, and it was she who said calmly to the man,
"Good afternoon."

"Good afternoon," he said. "What can I help you with today?" His voice was tinged with irony, as if he was certain in
advance that his politeness would be wasted on whatever customers found their way into his shop.

Spike moved forward until he stood in front of the counter,
then placed both hands carefully on its edge. Leaning forward
slightly, he stared down into the glass case, then, after a moment, glanced up at the man behind it and, still without an-
swering, looked back into the case. There were three pistols in
the case, and though he didn't want pistols, he liked to contem-
plate them; there was nothing wrong with knives or rifles, but
you got a special thrill from a handgun. He savored the moment, ran his hand thoughtfully down his cheekbone, then said,
"I'm looking for some rifles."

The man's expression of ironic politeness did not change.

"Yes?" he enquired. "What kind?"

"Semiautomatic." Spike glanced around the shop for a moment, noting the big oak mirror leaning against the wall, the

miscellany of old toasters and lamps, the overstuffed easy chairs with the arms rubbed raw and open. Then he whipped his face back to the shopkeeper, trying to catch him off guard.

"I have six or seven semiautomatics." The shopkeeper polished the glass countertop with the edge of his apron.

"Show them to me," said Spike.

The man unlocked a wooden cabinet on the back wall. The open door revealed a rack of rifles. He picked the top one off its brackets and laid it down on the counter in front of Spike.

"Here's a nice one," he said. "A Browning 30.06."

But Spike, after a desultory glance at the Browning, looked back to the cabinet, where two identical guns hung, huge clips thrust into their bottoms like armories. The man traced his gaze.

"Those are .22s," he said. "The big clip hides a little one. Special job someone had done. They just look like M-16s."

Spike's flood of disappointment at this news converted itself quickly into satisfaction, as he treated his feelings with the firm hand they required. So what if they were .22s? It would be easier to get ammunition for them, and no cop could give you a hard time for possession. And besides, they didn't look it. You could scare somebody really well with those mock-up jobs. They weren't actually fake. They were more like something disguised.

"Well, they look real nice, anyway," said Spike.

The shopkeeper lifted the top one down from its rack and laid it on the counter. Spike picked it up, noting the heaviness of the barrel, the impressive size of the butt. And really, even if you looked right down the bore, you couldn't tell the difference; the bore size was the same for a .22 and an M-16. He hefted the gun to his shoulder, squinted through the sights and held it there for a moment. He didn't see anything out of the sights, but out of the corner of his eye he glimpsed himself in the oak mirror by the door, a mean-looking man with a gun. The gun had a nice look, really nice—and to top it off, there were two of them.

"How about it, Molia?" he asked. "Would you like one for yourself?"

"Why not?" she said, and Spike suddenly had a vision of her dressed, for once, not in her long monk's robes, but in pants, tight pants that showed off her skinniness for all to see, her hip bones apparently small handballs she was carrying in her pockets, her chest flat as a board under a form-fitting cotton shirt, and slung across the chest this rifle, the only adornment to simplicity.

And Spike said to the shopkeeper, "Both of them."

The man pulled out a looseleaf notebook with some yellow sheets of Firearms Transactions Records prominent in the front. Spike flipped open a wallet he had lifted from a drunk in a bar one night to reveal a little plastic window with a driver's license inside. The man carefully copied the number on the driver's license, but did not look either at the picture or at Spike's face, and then started running down the questions.

"Have you ever been convicted in any court of a crime punishable by imprisonment for a term exceeding a year?"

"No." Spike smiled inside; in a way it was true. He'd been convicted not in *any* court but in lots of courts. He tapped his finger on the counter.

When the list of questions was complete, Spike signed his name to the declaration—Thomas McFarland the drunk had been—and shoved over a hundred and fifty dollars in crisp new cash. Then he suddenly realized that Wesley would need a gun as well, so he bought the Browning, too, turning over another hundred dollars for that. The man put the guns in a large brown paper bag, added a few boxes of ammunition gratis, and then said, not quite sincerely, "It's been a real pleasure doing business with you, Mr. McFarland. And ... Mrs. McFarland?" he added, smiling. "Use your rifles wisely."

Spike stepped back to allow Amolia to go out the door first and as she left he caught sight of her unexpectedly in the mirror—a tall, gaunt, peaked woman, her lips folded tightly together, her eyes wide. She looked as if she'd never seen herself before.

■   ■   ■

Early the next morning Spike and Amolia were packing up their gear while Wesley wandered around the house humming. They were catching the 9:40 train to Whittier, so they were in something of a rush, and whereas Spike had originally planned to divide everything neatly into categories, food in one duffel bag, clothing in another, guns, knives, and books in a third—that was an amorphous category, something like "power and knowledge"—now they were just thrusting everything, willy-nilly, into one of the three duffels, first separating it from the paper bags and cellophane packages it had been carried home in. Amolia, at Spike's suggestion, had put on a pair of the army surplus pants Spike had bought for all of them, and a cotton shirt that clung tightly to her chest. Right now she was playing with her gun, hanging it by the strap around her neck, pointing it at various objects in the room.

"Bang," she said. "Bang bang."

"No, no," said Spike. "Bang-bang-bang-bang-bang! That's a semiautomatic. You can get off rounds as fast as you can pull the trigger."

"You really think we'll need these?"

"Oh, we might, we might," said Spike vaguely. "Whales, you know, sharks, that kind of thing, out there it's pretty wild. Bears. I mean, you wouldn't want to use these little bullets on a bear or a whale, actually, but they make a nice noise, and if you ever had to scare somebody—something—well, we'll be ready."

"Are there a lot of other people out there?"

"There might be a few, sure. People like us, though. Explorers, fishermen, that sort of thing. Here, you want to see how to load it?"

When Amolia had loaded and unloaded the gun three times, he told her she was a pro, and that they'd practice shooting once they hit the ocean. That would be a good idea, Spike thought, even if Amolia hadn't looked so sexy holding the gun, because the truth of it was that it was dangerous to have a loaded rifle in the hands of a companion who didn't know exactly how to use it. Along with target practice, Amolia would have to be exposed to the cardinal rule of gun use—if you pull a gun you have to be ready to use it, and if you use it you have to shoot to kill. Otherwise, it'll just end up getting you hurt, because nothing is more dangerous than a wounded opponent. The storekeeper he had shot in Vancouver—it had been a clear-cut case of self-defense, of course—had managed, even with a bullet in him, to shoot back at Spike and wing him, which was why Spike had been caught at all. In the trial, in his wheelchair, the man had sworn that Spike had been trying to kill him, which was, Spike had sworn back, a complete fabrication—if he had been trying to kill him, he *would* have killed him, that was what he maintained. But the truth of it was that Spike had just gotten off a bad shot, and if there was that much chance of things going wrong even when you were expert and willing—well, you could just imagine what might happen if you were only pussy-footing around.

"Hey!" he said to Amolia. "Hey, hey! Just be careful where you point that thing."

Wesley came into the room, a bunch of flowers in his hand, just as Spike was recovering the rifle and laying it carefully aside.

"I guess we'll be gone for at least a week," Wesley remarked questioningly. "These flowers, I imagine, will die before we return? I think I'll just take them over to the neighbor's house then. Mrs. Williams will have a use for them."

"She has a whole garden of her own, Wesley," said Amolia. "Why don't you just throw them in the garbage?"

"Oh, Amolia, I couldn't do that." And he wandered out the side door.

Spike wondered if he should change his mind about marrying Amolia. There was still probably time to ask her. Her father was out of the house, they were almost packed, and they were leaving for the train in just a little while. For a moment, he was filled with an overwhelming urge to just do it, to take action, to say, "Amolia, will you be my wife?" Right now, her lips pressed together still, she was drawing the rope cinch on the last duffel bag, her toes tucked beneath her feet as she kneeled on the floor. She looked as she always did, intense, brooding, filled with some sort of dark purpose that Spike could not understand. Her eyes, huge in her face, were like smudges, and the veins on the backs of her hands were like labyrinthine signals, passages marked on a map to an underground cavern. With a twist of her wrist she secured the rope and then set the duffel bag aside, looking up suddenly to meet his watching eyes, so suddenly that he was overcome by the familiar sensation of vertigo. He smiled, quickly, and slickly, and said, "All ready, Mole? Then let's go round up that father of yours," and got to his feet with a careless shrug. Attendant on his movement was the fleeting thought that perhaps he had at last met his match, but since he didn't know whether to be delighted or appalled he shoved the thought aside, and clapping Amolia on the back, walked out the French doors into the sunshine. An hour later he was sitting beneath the three duffel bags on a train bound for Whittier, Amolia beside him and Wesley across the aisle. He pulled out his harmonica before the train started and played a little tune on it, bright and jazzy, with a breathy trill at the end. When Amolia asked him what it was called, he was ready:

" 'Victory Just Before Dawn,' baby," he said. " 'Victory Just Before Dawn.' "

13

■ THE TRAIN RIDE WAS as train rides always were, a happy experience for Wesley. Although he did not admit it to either of his companions, he had been on the Portage-Whittier train many times before, a fact they might have suspected if they had listened to the conductor say to him, "Nice to see you again, Mr. Hannah," which they did not, because they were staring at each other again. This time, though, rather than standing on the baggage landing in Whittier for ten minutes while all the crates and barrels of other people's lives were thrown willy-nilly to the ground and then tramping heavily back aboard the train while it screamed a warning to the wind, he would be able to stay on the ground, and journey onward, get to where rocks were rocks. He thought of this as, in habitual fashion, he made his way to the last passenger car and pushed open the heavy door at the back. They had already left the outskirts of the city behind, and the warm smells of earth and berry, tree and flower, were pushed to him by the breeze. Clickety-clack, clickety-clack, the train unrolled a bed of rails behind it like a carpet and Wesley stared into the air pocket created by its passage as if he were staring into the past, rocketing backward into the future.

But when the future arrived, well, things got a little confusing. When the world spirit had directed him to take up with Micah Jones and introduce him to his darling Amolia, it had not bothered to inform him that from now on all directives for action were going to be coming through a new distributor, a complicated and rather enigmatic distributor which seemed to be made up of a mixture of Amolia's peculiarly intense stares and Micah's, "Oh, I get ya, I get ya, Mole." When the train stopped in Whittier, they got down and walked toward the Sportsman's Inn, the town's one restaurant. On the beach below it, a very old Eskimo wearing a blue baseball cap above his brown and wrinkled face was carrying one end of a red canoe up the shingle. A little Eskimo boy carried the other, heavier end. Wesley and Amolia and Micah had passed above them just as they stopped for a rest, and though Amolia and Micah went on, Wesley also stopped, puffing. The old man stood still, resting in place, making no unnecessary movements—no wiping of his face with his sleeve, no shaking of his head from side to side. He smiled at Wesley and said, slowly and clearly, "Mosquitoes not so bad now."

Wesley, who excluded insects from his affectionate alarm about the animal kingdom, said, "No. But you know, I have always found that mosquitoes . . . bugs in general, perhaps . . . are not as heinous as their reputation paints them."

The old man replied with a giggle, "You have never been to the Barrens. There, a man will be driven crazy." He giggled again and then nodded to the boy at his side.

Wesley hurried to catch up with his daughter and Micah, who had already disappeared inside the Sportsman's Inn. A long wooden staircase led up from the beach to its lobby, and Wesley had to pause a number of times before he made it to the top and then, in the lobby, had to sit down immediately, on something long and gray and grainy. He puffed contentedly for a while and then heaved his glasses on for a closer look at this bench. It seemed . . . well, it really did seem . . . yes, Wesley was almost certain it was the rib of a great whale. And that was almost, well, prophetic. After all, they were about to embark on a long journey across the ocean and what creature knew about such journeys better than a great whale? But before he had time to turn the whale rib into a directive, Amolia appeared in the lobby looking for him. Firmly, she indicated that it was time for him to get up and he lumbered to his feet and followed her into the restaurant. Here, the bare formica table tops, the smell of grease, the fluorescent lights and the synthetic gold curtains that hung in the windows—all of them filled him with a most unreasonable joy.

But then the trouble started. As the three of them sat and ate lunch—Wesley had three egg-salad sandwiches, and the others hamburgers and fries, and, just as one more sign of how well things were going, Wesley noticed that Amolia ate almost half of her hamburger and at least seven French fries with *ketchup*—they discussed what their next move was going to be. Wesley's original fantasy had been that they would take a ferry, and then perhaps a rowboat, and finally a raft, but the ferry idea was squelched out of hand, since the only ferries from Whittier went straight to Valdez—not at all where Micah and Amolia wanted to go. It seemed they had to get a boat *now*, and there was no possibility of paying for it, since even with all the money from Amolia's savings account they didn't have any too much, and therefore the best idea would undoubtedly be to borrow a boat for the time being, until someday they could afford one. But, as Micah said, they didn't want to borrow a *big* boat right from the port here, since it would probably take him a second or two to catch on how to run it; they could get a big boat later, when they had more privacy somewhere. Soooo— and all this time Amolia was just staring at Micah with large eyes while she inserted the very tip of a French fry into the smallest dabble of ketchup and then guided it toward her lips— sooooo, they should probably take a little boat, like maybe that red canoe there. Wesley peered out the window to follow Micah's pointing finger. *That* red canoe! Why, he even knew who owned it.

"Oh, that would be a *very* good one, I'm sure," he said, "because I just now met its owner, a wonderful-looking old Eskimo man and his little grandson, and we struck up a conversation and I'm sure that if there's any way they can spare it, they'll be glad to lend us their canoe. We talked about mosquitoes up on the Barrens," he added.

"Well, now," said Micah. "Well, now, I'm sure that's very nice. But the way I see it is this, old man, the way I see it is this. If we ask them, see, whether they can spare their canoe, why they might say no, they might have plans to take it for a little spin this evening, while if we *don't* ask, well, then, they *can't* say no, and there it is, we've got it. So what I suggest is that just as soon as we're done here we meander on down to that canoe and take it out for a spin ourselves, while the owners are occupied elsewhere."

"That would be stealing," said Amolia.

"Stealing? No. Just borrowing. We'll bring it back soon, practically before they know it's gone. And we'll be on our way."

Amolia stared at him, and after a few moments Micah said, "Oh, I get ya, I get ya, Mole. You want to wait until dark. Well, if we wait until dark we'll get lost on the ocean, and that's not very smart." There was another silence and Micah said, "Good, so that's settled," and then finished eating, which Wesley noticed he did with a curiously impersonal air, stuffing the food into his mouth as if he were stoking a furnace. Wesley understood from this that they were to go down right after their meal and climb into the red canoe, and that was what confused him, because it wasn't the kind of thing the world spirit normally directed him to do.

When they had paid, and had gone down to the beach again, a light mist had started to gather; through it the trees looked very dark, bristly, all of the same height. After setting their duffel bags on the shingle, Micah and Amolia flipped the canoe over together and carried it to the water where it bobbed plashily at the tideline. Wesley kept expecting to see the old Eskimo approach them, but he was nowhere in sight, and Micah stowed all their duffel bags inside and made Amolia and Wesley put on the life jackets. Wesley's didn't really fit him; the string was just barely long enough to reach around his middle, but the sides of the vest did not begin to, and while he was trying to tie the string his glasses got mixed up in the knot. At that point, Micah said impatiently, "Come on, old man," and Amolia came and helped him get disentangled and settled into the canoe. Then she climbed in and Micah pushed off, and, as the canoe was now very heavy—so heavy, in fact, that Wesley was surprised it floated at all—it made a terrible grating noise.

But no one came. And although, by accident, both Amolia and Wesley—who was sitting in the middle and therefore couldn't be too much help as a paddler, though he was certainly willing to try—repeatedly hit the side of the canoe with the edge of their paddles, sending loud reports out into the early afternoon, still no one came. For some reason Wesley's heart was thumping in his chest rather loudly and at one point he asked Amolia, "Dearest, can you hear my heart beat? It's very peculiar, but I can hear it next to my shoulder."

She said no, however, so he supposed it was nothing to worry about. The canoe continued to slip through the water, sometimes very fast, sometimes slowly, but always unwieldy and overloaded. Still, in less time than he would have thought possible they had rounded the point at the head of the inlet and gained a broader expanse of open sea. Now Wesley began to feel quite elated; *this* was the kind of thing the world spirit was always telling him to do. To have adventures, that was what it came down to, and this was certainly an adventure.

But several hours later they were still paddling, and it wasn't nearly so much fun anymore. For one thing, it had started to rain a little, a misty rain that was making them all rather damp. Also, Wesley's hands hurt from holding the paddle, but he couldn't stop because Micah had told him that he and Amolia together were producing the equivalent of one good stroke and without his contribution the canoe would go off course. When he looked at his palms, they were an angry pink, and his back ached too, and his bottom, from sitting on it for so long. He thought that probably they had gone ten miles by now, though he had never had much of a sense of distance, and he knew they were lucky the sea was so calm that they hadn't turned over. Across the water he counted four fishing boats—big boats which, although they moved slowly, seemed to dwarf the canoe. But the men on the boats waved when they saw the canoe and Wesley waved gaily back, happy as always to meet new people, even if only at a distance.

When at last they stopped for the night, Wesley was a little surprised. The pebbly beach Micah chose for them was no different, to Wesley's eyes, from a hundred beaches they had already passed. Somehow, he had imagined that they were heading for something really different, a glorious white sand beach, perhaps, with its own little slice of the sunset or—and here his imagination went wild—a beach with an archway built on its edge that led down to a kingdom in the sea. Mermaids, big friendly lions, and his dead wife all waved to him as he peered through the arch. But no. The trees had a moist, tangly look to them, although the rain seemed to have stopped for the moment; the canoe ground on the pebbles and when it came to a halt Wesley stood up and stepped right out into the water.

His feet got very wet and they made squishing noises as he walked up the beach.

"Are we here?" he asked. "Are these the rocks?"

"We're checking it out, Wesley old sport, just checking it out. This is the place I picked on the map, but the map can't tell you everything. It's the man on the spot who sees the real situation," Micah said.

"This is no place to build a cabin," said Amolia. "Still, we'd better camp here, I suppose. We'll put up the tent. Wesley, why don't you go and find some wood?"

"Ahh, yes, wood," said Wesley. "What kind, though, in particular?"

"Dry wood," said Amolia.

"Of course." Wesley trudged toward the trees in his squishy running shoes, determined not to ask any more questions. He had never collected wood before, but he had certainly collected plenty of flowers and the principle must be exactly the same, to pick the prettiest, sweetest-smelling ones. In the woods, once he arrived there, he would surely find some clues. The woods ended in a very definite line, just like the wall of a house, and when he walked on the other side of the wall it was suddenly much blacker, and the sweet smell of the sea was buried in the dark, wet smell of earth and vegetation. Nothing was moving, and he felt, somehow, that nothing ever moved here, except for plants and falling water. He knew that there must be animals about, but he could not sense them, not directly; it was almost eerie, and for just a moment he was certain he was being directed to move his feet up and down as fast as he could, heading in the opposite direction.

But Amolia would certainly be disappointed if he came back woodless. Also, he had to pee. He didn't really relish the idea of doing it in this dim and motionless forest, where the smell of earth was so intense it was almost like the smell of death, but he relished even less the idea of doing it back on the beach, where his daughter and Micah could see him. Slowly, he reached his hand down to his zipper—the top of which he often had trouble locating underneath the lip of flesh that hung down over his belt at just that spot—and when he found it he tugged it slowly, too, using just his right hand. He eased his penis out, looking sideways to catch a glimpse of its purply veined surface and feeling the mild astonishment he always felt at the sight of the normally hidden parts of his anatomy. Then he peed, finding as he did so that the slightly gloomy mood that had come over him seemed to lessen with every spurt of his bladder, and by the time the bladder was quite empty, he felt again like his old, happy self. Completely forgetting about the wood, he inserted his penis carefully back into place, zipped himself up, and squished back out to the beach again.

He saw that Amolia and Micah had almost gotten the tent up. Although it sagged a little in the middle and the pole that had been propped up on the pebbles to tie the forward end to seemed shaky, it was definitely a magnificent shelter, a shelter that had grown out of nothing. Amolia was carrying gear up the beach from the canoe; Wesley waved to her and she waved back. A sharp crack under his right foot made him glance down then and he saw a lovely stick of wood, quite a special flower, about three feet long and as thick as his thumb. Glancing further, he saw more—there were many such sticks scattered haphazardly about, all without bark, smooth and white as a baby's chest and apparently untouched by the rain. Wesley began to collect them, laying each one carefully into his left arm.

Later, they sat by the fire after dinner, the tent firmly guarding their backs. It wasn't that they were scared, Wesley thought— after all, he himself had decided long ago, when his beloved wife had been pressed as flat as a pancake by part of J. C. Penney's storefront, never to be scared of anything again—but that they were, in sitting thus, asserting their humanity in a strangely nonhuman world. Micah had loaded the guns and set them against the wall of the tent for protection during the night, had done this while they were still eating dinner, in fact—two cans of baked beans for Wesley and hot dogs for the others, with coffee. Now, Micah checked the guns again and then told Amolia and Wesley that these woods were really not any good for building a cabin.

"Too dense," he said. "Dense and wet. Tangled. Not the thing at all. I can see it's going to take some looking, some real hard looking, to find the right spot."

Amolia said nothing.

Micah pulled out a cigarette and tried to light it with a twig burning on the edge of the circle of fire. The twig went out as soon as he lifted it, so he used a match instead. Inhaling deeply, he said, "Oh, I get ya, I get ya, Mole. You think we should find a deserted cabin to live in for a while, right?"

"Oh?" said Amolia.

"You know, place like this, a lot of rich people have summer cabins," Micah agreed. "It's a waste, that's what it is, a criminal waste, all those houses empty! Besides, the law of the wilderness says anyone who needs a cabin can stay in it. Well, we need a place to live in while we look around, right?"

Amolia didn't answer.

Wesley felt, for the second or third time since this strange day had begun, extremely befuddled. He had thought that they were coming out here to build a cabin, and get Micah settled in it, and then go home, and he had assumed, as he thought this, that Micah had some idea where he wanted to build this cabin and how to go about it. Now he was getting the distinct feeling that Micah wasn't entirely sure how to build a cabin, and didn't even know where he wanted to try and do it, and first he had borrowed that nice man's canoe, and now he planned to borrow a house. The confusion would have been possible for him to bear if he could have asked Amolia to explain it all to him, but she didn't *want* to explain it all to him, that much he could sense. He didn't think she knew exactly what she did want, though he noticed that for the second time that day she had eaten a real meal, a whole hotdog and a small cup of beans, and as far as it went that seemed a hopeful sign. The sun was setting over the sea, and in the far distance, a black blot against the sky, Wesley could see a whale leaping, turning its flipper and kicking it. Amolia and Micah were sitting now in absolute silence, side by side like two statues carved in soapstone, and so Wesley raised himself to his feet and trundled off down the beach to get a closer look at that leaping whale.

14

◼ HARRY SAT A long time over lunch, wanting to delay its ending. He nodded when Ian told him to hurry up, but he couldn't bring himself to actually do it, so he pushed his salad around with his fork and made a great display of chewing. For at least three days he had been asking the counselors if he could call Jack up and talk to him in the hospital, and now that he had finally gotten permission, he found that he was scared. The word had come back that a tendon in Jack's shoulder had been cut, and though no one had even implied to Harry that Jack might never be able to use his arm properly again, Harry, ever since he had learned about the tendon, had kept thinking morosely about the way Jack slicked his hair back with his comb and the way he hefted barbells until his muscles bulged like apples. So what was he going to say to Jack? Sorry your life might be ruined?

Harry in any case had a weak stomach; he hated even *hearing* about injuries. When he was ten his older sister Susan had fallen off the roof of the house where she had climbed in a game of hide and seek, and she had broken both her legs. One of the breaks had been a compound fracture, and when Harry saw that bit of bone sticking up out of the skin of her calf, the wound already proud around it, he had felt so dizzy he had had to sit down on the ground, and while he was on the ground he had lost consciousness for a moment. In the confusion no one had noticed—they had thought, if they saw Harry at all, that for some reason he had decided to lie down on his back—and in fact he had not blacked out but redded out; he remembered the moment just before as a rapidly expanding pool of red that he was leaning into. When other kids had scraped their knees, cut their fingers, been hit by flying hardballs, or bitten by dogs, he had never been able to stay around to see the injury itself, and later, when he was running with a crowd that was likely to suffer more dangerous injuries, the one thing he had assiduously to conceal from them was his terrible infirmity. When his friend David had gotten knifed, not in the guts but in the fleshy part of the chest, he had fainted again, and only by explaining that he had been clobbered on the head by the same miscreant who had inflicted the knife wound on David had he been able to get away with his reputation intact. Certainly his behavior when Jack was hurt had been far and away the best he had ever managed, since he had succeeded in staying with Jack and talking to him right up to the time the helicopter had shut its flimsy-looking door. But another long-standing problem was having an even worse effect on him at the moment. He felt sad, terribly sad, when anyone around him was diseased or deformed—he felt sad, now, just looking at his lettuce.

"Listen, Harry, shit or get off the pot," said Ian from his place by the sink, where he was reprimanding the dirty dishes, and Harry pushed himself away from the table. He thought fleetingly of suggesting that Ian do fifty push-ups for using a swear word in the dining hall, but without someone there to enjoy it with him there wasn't really any point.

Phil was supposed to meet him at the schoolroom and help him place the call. On the way across the compound Harry dragged his feet, kicking at small stones and sending them shooting across the hard-packed earth, bending over to pick up a piece of foil and crumple it into a ball. He stopped by Trent's fireplace as well—almost done, this monolithic structure looked like an entry in the Bigger Is Better school of industrial construction—and managed to find at least two stones in the back wall that he distinctly remembered gathering himself. Between

Trent's fireplace and Linda's trust games, Harry was beginning to think the whole place was crazy.

He continued on up toward the schoolroom, thinking about those trust games. Poor Stovepipe was in for a rude surprise when her pet project actually came off. It had been raining intermittently for over a week—it seemed that the long run of gorgeous summer weather was over—and so she wasn't making any promises, but as soon as it cleared she was taking all the boys over to Bear Hill Meadow. At the same time, so rumor had it, Motor was going to be running the big boat down to the lower dock to tune the engine; he liked working on the boat there better than at the upper wharf, since the waters were quieter and more predictable around the north side of the bay. Bear Hill Meadow was just a five-minute walk from the lower dock, and Stan and Norm and Derell had decided that if they had tried to arrange this on purpose to serve their escape plan, they couldn't have done any better. Sometime during the trust games the three of them would slip away, head for the boat, overpower Motor, and sail to freedom. About the only good thing about Jack getting hurt was that Harry wouldn't have to go with them.

Scuffing one last rock with his sneaker, Harry dragged up the schoolroom steps. Some of the boys had already gathered there for school, and Phil was waiting as well. There was no putting the call off any longer, though he still didn't know what he'd say. But when Phil had made the call for him, and he had settled himself in the hard chair in Trent's office and found the right button to push so he could listen and the right button to push so he could talk, and when he had figured out how far to hold the mouthpiece from his face and a hospital worker had taken the call and fetched Jack and Jack's voice had emerged from the speaker, surprisingly strong, saying "Hey, bro!" it was no longer any real problem to find something to tell him, and Harry grew quite loquacious reporting on events that had occurred at camp since Jack's departure. Jack kept saying, "Oh, bro!" as he narrated each minor development—Emory's precious shoes had been misplaced, they were doing evolution in school now, Eric had fallen through a window in the bunkhouse, they were going to play trust games when the weather cleared.

"Hey, bro," said Jack then, too casually. "Are you still excited about the Plan?" and Harry, amazed that Jack would even be thinking about this, said only, "Why? Are you?"

"Of course, bro, of course. And if I can't be there, you do it for me. Promise me that, okay?"

"Oh, Jack," said Harry. "I don't want to do it without you. And I can't do it *for* you, you know that."

"Bro. For me. Don't hold up the Departure," said Jack, and Harry, fearful that Jack might actually announce on an open broadcast channel that half the residents of Chenega Island were planning to make fools of themselves in a big way, said quickly, "All right, mon, all right, just don't talk so much, will you?"

When Harry had switched off the radio's button, he didn't feel a whole lot better. The hospital had told Jack that he would be able to leave in four or five days and he seemed, overall, to be amazingly cheerful, but the half-commitment that Harry had made to run away without him if Jack didn't get back in time canceled out any pleasure he might have taken in Jack's good spirits, since who knew when the weather would change? Then, when Harry emerged from Trent's office and into what was usually a pleasant maelstrom of confusion, he sensed a degree of open hostility unusual for Chenega. Phil had apparently left the building and Norm and Stan were in a corner of the room hitting Kennie Dugan repeatedly on the shoulder with the flats of their hands; Emory, who rarely lost his temper, was swearing like a Mexican bandit while Arnold stood bewildered behind him. Harry asked Emory what was going on.

"These shitheads, they think they can whack Arnold around," said Emory, his face dark with anger. "These fuckfaces, they think he knows something he shouldn't. Well, if their goddamn Plan were any more public, it would be in the Anchorage newspapers."

"Shut *up*," said Norm, turning viciously from his brutalizing of Kennie to glower at Emory and then turning back to shove Kennie some more.

"You say one *word* about this, and you're dead," he said to Kennie. "Dead. You understand?"

"You can't do this to me," squeaked Kennie. "My father says that on the Day of Judgment people like you are going to be taken apart and stored in small pieces in great big storage tanks and then—"

"Dead," said Norm again. "And you can keep your bullshit about the Day of Judgment to yourself, because there is no justice in this world or the next."

"But it seems to be Kennie that's getting hit, mon," said Harry to Emory, who had turned from swearing at Norm and Stan to reassuring Arnold, and Emory said, "Yeah, well, first they heard Jack say that about the escape plan on the phone, and they said it would be a chilly day in hell anyway before that son-of-a-white-bitch—sorry, Harry—would get to go with them, and then Kennie heard them and said he was going to tell, and so Arnold said *he* was going to tell, too, not understanding what was going on, but just to be friendly, you know, and so they started to beat up on them both—"

"Here's Trent," said Stan. And they all suddenly scattered to their desks.

Evolution had been the subject of discussion for almost a week now, and Harry found it pretty interesting. The fact that men had once been animals living in the ocean accorded nicely with his feelings about water and the magic kingdom he had visited beneath it, and the mystery in which the origin of the Aleuts was shrouded was made more explicable if you figured they had once been whales or porpoises. It seemed odd to him in a way, of course, that all this evolution had happened without so much as a by-your-leave on the part of those things that were evolving, that they had all been sucked along, willy-nilly, in some great natural plan—or, rather, *that* didn't seem odd, that seemed perfectly understandable, since the Aleuts believed that everything that existed was a small part of a great whole, and that only if you were sick could you believe yourself to be separate from the union of all things. No, what seemed odd was that on top of getting sucked along, willy-nilly, in this great scheme of evolution you were also expected to control yourself. Maybe the one belief was an Aleuts one, and the other belief was white; he would have to check it out with his father, if he ever got to see him again. In the meantime, perhaps he could bring it up with Trent. He waited for a lull in the lesson.

The lull came just after Cro-Magnon man had evolved into *Homo sapiens*. Their book, which seemed rather chauvinistic about modern man, commented about this event: "*Homo sapiens* Man was the triumph of evolution, the being for whom nature had been reaching," and there was something about this statement that gave them all pause, as they looked around the room at one another. Harry took the opportunity to raise his hand and when Trent nodded at him he said, "What I don't understand, mon, is how they expect us to act right. In nature, things are always beating each other up."

"Yeah," said Derell. "You ever see a fish feed? Whomp. One chomp. Little fish gone."

"What do you mean by right?" asked Trent.

"Right, you know," said Harry. "Right." But he felt more confused then ever.

An animated discussion followed, in which Harry took very little part. Trent pointed out that different cultures had different definitions of what was right, and that in some cultures it was okay to expose female babies on the hilltops, while in others you could be killed for doing that. Was there anything which was universally right, or did everything just depend? Were you ever justified in taking another life, or was that not your role in nature? At first, Harry tried hard to answer each of these questions in his own mind, but the more he thought about it, the more hopelessly entangled his thoughts became, since it seemed to him both that he had had very little control from the beginning about who he was and what happened to him and also that he really did have the power inside him to decide what he should do. He might not have been able to control whether or not he came to Chenega, for example, but surely he could decide for himself whether or not he wanted to escape. He didn't. But maybe he wasn't really deciding that for himself, maybe he was just a coward, had been born a coward, and would always make the cowardly decision. In that case, he *didn't* have a choice, not really, not in the end. His head began to ache as he tried to reconcile the paradox, and he was more relieved than he could say when the discussion ended at last.

Still in a state of mild depression, he made his way back to the bunkhouse. He had gotten a letter from his girlfriend when the last mail plane arrived, and he wanted to read it once more, and think about his home reserve. He wasn't as good friends with his girlfriend as Emory apparently was with his, but he liked her a lot—she was very smart—and she was proving unexpectedly loyal. She wrote him at least once every two weeks and sometimes once a week, and she always sealed her letters with a kiss, which she carefully drew on with lipstick. But while he was crossing the compound, Harry passed Linda, the Stovepipe, and the way she waved made her breasts and buttocks, small as they were, wiggle cheerfully, so at the last minute, inspired by the sight of genuine female flesh, he changed his direction and instead of going to get his girlfriend's letter he went to the outhouse, carefully bolted the door, and picked up a copy of *Playboy*.

15

■ IT WAS AMOLIA WHO had sighted the cabin. She had been paddling along, in the bow of the boat, her pants wet to the knees, wondering if they were all going to drown, as the sea slapped over the thwarts. She was tired of being wet—ever since they had set out from Whittier it had been raining on and off, and though the tent kept them dry at night, getting *into* the tent sometimes proved to be quite a project. Then, through the trees, when she put her paddle down for an instant, she had glimpsed a blister of white, an alien presence in that mottled green landscape, and as she studied it, it had turned into the white-painted door of a hut. Now, in the middle of the following afternoon, she was in that hut cooking; they had spent the morning on the beach doing target practice, and although there had been nothing obviously strenuous about that activity—at which Amolia, for a novice, had done extraordinarily well—they had all worked up quite an appetite, so now she was baking cookies. She spooned the last bit of batter onto the cookie sheet, looking past her chest and stomach to do so—since that fish-and-chip lunch in Anchorage she had gained at least four or five pounds.

But somehow, this did not disgust her, and she lifted a tea-cup from the cupboard above the sink. The china here was very fine; you could see light through it when you held it up to the window, and in that it seemed to her a lot like her own mind had been lately, porous, susceptible to the slightest impressions from the world beyond it. Her old methods of maintaining control were, in fact, almost entirely gone—she could no more have kept the mottled world she was now traveling through neatly straightened up than she could have cleared the sky of stars— but a new method seemed to have moved in to replace it, and that was to let power penetrate her from the outside, as the light penetrated the teacup. The power was almost all generated by Spike, but she found herself acting as a conduit for it, a conduit that increased both its strength and its directionality, so that whereas Spike, left to himself, had a tendency, she had discovered, to squander his energies, with her around to respond to them and absorb them the whole journey had a large sense of mission. While the last batch of cookies baked, she heated a kettle of water for tea, and then carried a tea tray to the porch where Spike and Wesley were cleaning the guns.

As she came out Wesley looked up, relieved.

"Ah, sweetheart," he said. "All these little parts, they are so, well, so *tiny* and hard, and I think, I really do think, Amolia, that if the world spirit had wanted me to be a gun cleaner it would have given me smaller fingers than these." Sadly, he held out his hands, puffed as if with air. "It's funny, too, that guns need so much . . . well, what I mean to say is that we haven't used these, really, not yet, or rather, you were excellent, Amolia, truly excellent at target practice, but . . ." He trailed off.

Amolia set the tray down on the broad porch railing.

"If you don't feel like helping, Wesley, you certainly don't have to. Would you like a cup of tea with sugar?" She poured and handed him a rose-garlanded cup, its handle absurdly small and overwrought to be held by those puffed fingers. But Wesley took it, pinched it between his thumb and forefinger, and bending forward, blew on the hot tea anxiously.

The sky was gray today, though it looked as if it might clear. The sea was gray, too, although at times it seemed as if it were lit by an invisible light source, somewhere below the surface of the water. Black whales frolicked two hundred yards offshore, and as Amolia watched a huge sea lion's head emerged sleepily for a second from below the surface and stared at her unwinking. Then it sank, slowly, leaving no bubbles behind it. Amolia was almost certain that she was the only one of them who had seen it and she liked the feeling. She poured a second cup of tea and said to Spike, "Cream and sugar?"

"Just cream, baby. You're my sugar," said Spike.

Lately he had been saying a lot of things like that, which Amolia found slightly annoying. The bond they had was more subtle, she thought, than the merely sexual could ever be; it was electrical in nature, like blue fire around a ship's mast. Whatever Spike wanted to do but was confused about, Amolia gave him the courage to proceed with, and in his actions, she saw her own past rewritten. Although Spike was, she had learned, a transparent liar, as well as something of a coward, it wouldn't matter as long as she was around. She would steer him straight. She saw in herself, for the first time in her life, the potential for greatness; it had never occurred to her that her extraordinary ability to deny physical necessity might be directed into channels other than denying herself food. She had begun, after all, as a superachiever; in school she had always gotten straight As, had always brought home all the prizes from the English contests and the science fairs. Only when it dawned on her, at about the age of fifteen, that Wesley did not care whether she got As or Fs, that he was simply a bottle bobbing on a crazy sea, had she begun to diet obsessively, and to discover in the quality of her obsession a power that few of her friends could match or understand. Now, why couldn't she simply take that willpower and turn it outward rather than in? Not right now, of course, not immediately. But soon. Sometime soon.

Pouring herself the third cup of tea, she sat down on the sun-dried boards. Spike, who had been shoving a rod up and down the barrel of his gun, removed it and discarded the white cloth patch, then stared zealously down the barrel, whistling between his teeth. Wesley, who had taken three sips of tea before he set his cup down with a sigh, said, "I really am surprised, you know, at how many *whales* we find swimming around in these waters. It's consoling, don't you think, to find so many."

"Good eating," said Spike.

"Have you ever eaten whale?" asked Wesley, wincing.

"Not in the flesh," Spike said. "But I met a guy who did once. The Eskimos used to hunt them all the time."

Even more distressed, Wesley said, "Aaaahhh?"

"In the old days they went out with just knives, in little boats," Spike went on. "It was dangerous, because whales eat people, swallow them whole. When they got guns it was better."

Amolia, who knew perfectly well that whales did not eat people, chose to disregard Spike's fabrication and let her father writhe on the tip of it.

"So many bushes here," said Wesley, in an attempt to change the subject. "So much *vegetable* matter, actually. It takes some getting used to."

Spike, who had picked up the rod again and was now viciously ramming it down the barrel of the second gun, cocked an eyebrow at this.

"Vegetable matter, eh?" he said. "Maybe you're right, maybe you're right. You're thinking we should move on?" He dropped his eyebrow, set down the gun and got up to pace the floor.

"Yeah, yeah. It's like this, Wesley, Mole. It's September, see, and the snow's gotta fall here by, oh, December at the latest, right? So we gotta get started on our own house. At the same time, things can go wrong when you're building a house, things are out of stock, tools break down, who knows. So you have to have something to fall back on, an alternate plan, right?"

No one answered him, but Wesley wiped invisible sweat from his eyebrows.

"So what I've been thinking is this. We keep traveling a while, check out all the empty cabins we can find. One of them's gotta be better insulated than this one. A cabin you could heat in the winter, understand? But the only way to find that cabin is to look for it. So what say we take off again, now?"

"I'd better check the cookies," said Amolia, and went back inside the cabin.

She couldn't quite understand who Spike thought he was fooling—nor, really, why he had to try it. She knew from the map in the CYTS office just where Chenega Island lay, and there was no doubt in her mind that although Spike wasn't much of a navigator, their path was bringing them steadily closer. Spike just didn't like to camp out at all, had vastly preferred to stay in this cabin when she had found it; now, he was simply paving the way for staying in more cabins soon. But eventually, in a few days, a week at the most—eventually, they'd land on Chenega. Outside on the porch, she heard the suddenly quickened motions of Spike packing up the guns; now that he had decided to leave, he would want to leave immediately.

And indeed he did. In a little while, just as she was packing the now-cooled cookies into bags, he came in with all three guns in his arms and started to stuff them into a duffel bag. While Wesley sat out on the porch staring at the ocean, Spike and Amolia packed up their things—and some things, too, that were just becoming theirs. Every so often Spike would interrupt Amolia, holding up some object for her approval. The first one was a chain saw he found in the hall closet.

"Hey, Mole," he said. "We need this, what do you think? Nice new chain saw for a housewarming present?"

Amolia shrugged and fixed Spike with her eye. He put the chain saw on the porch.

Quite a few housewarming presents collected this way in a pile. Every time Spike held something up she gave the same noncommittal response, and they got a machete that way, and a double-bitted ax, an extra canoe paddle, and some smaller tools. Spike even found some costume jewelry in the back room and gave it to her as a special gift, insisting that she put it on immediately. It looked rather strange with the camouflage outfit she was wearing—during target practice that morning Spike had insisted that they all dress up—but she tucked the necklace under her shirt, and slipped the rings in her pocket. Last of all, Spike found some gas and oil for the chain saw, as if he had actually convinced himself that he was going to need it—as if he actually thought he might build a house. When they left the cabin, Amolia closed the door fastidiously behind her, and, as a last gesture, swept the porch.

Four days later they were much closer to Chenega, and had stayed in three more cabins along the way. Each time they broke into one of these cabins—by now Spike had gotten very good at wielding the double-bitted ax against the heavy padlocks—they wore their camouflage outfits, except for Wesley, who thought he would look silly. He only wore the cap. None of the cabins had been insulated for the winter, which gave Spike a perfect excuse for "pushing on," but in each one they had gotten more housewarming presents, and in order to get everything into the canoe—a radio, a hair dryer, a down quilt, fishing tackle—they were forced to unload and leave behind a lot of the food from Anchorage. They put it under the porch of the fourth cabin, where Spike said they could come back and get it.

When they left the fourth cabin behind them, they were, Amolia thought, about five miles from Chenega. The water was rolling beneath them like a barrel-bellied horse, although there wasn't any wind, and she really feared they might sink, dangerously overloaded as they were. In the distance she could see a blue-white river of ice, riven with huge crevasses; in the foreground a small shoal and several seals playing around it.

"Spike," she said, over her shoulder. "Why did they put you in jail?"

"You really want to know?" asked Spike, suspending his paddle for a moment and letting the canoe veer wildly off course.

"Oh, well," interjected Wesley hurriedly. "Not if you don't feel like telling us. I think we would both agree, wouldn't we, Amolia, that that is really your own personal business. We each have our personal feelings, secrets, things that we don't want to share. In fact, well . . ."

"I shot a cop," said Spike.

"Did you kill him?" asked Amolia.

"No. Christ, all the fuss they made, you'd think I'd killed him twice, but I wasn't trying to kill him, of course; I aimed for his shooting arm. So he moved, and I winged him further in—purely accident, but they don't believe in accidents, do they?"

"Why was he chasing you?" she asked.

"Oh, now," said Spike. "That, Mole, is one long story." He banged his paddle against the side of the canoe, considering, then hastily thrust it back into the waves. "Let's just say that my pappy—he was a coal miner, you know—my pappy died in a cave-in and left my mother all alone, penniless and stuff, with eight young children. Well, I was the oldest one—I was seventeen at the time—and I couldn't find work, try as I would. So at last my mother begged me to get some money for food. She gave me my pappy's old service revolver. I was caught—naturally, I was green as skunk cabbage—and that was that."

Although she didn't doubt that almost every word of this account was a lie, Amolia had a forlorn hope that the cop-shooting part was true, and she was amazed to discover this hope in her, amazed to find that, mixed with the tiny little bit of repugnance, she felt a much larger measure of relish. She had never liked cops much herself, she realized now. Cops and doctors, nurses and lawyers, they promised you that they were keeping the world safe and then somehow they expected you to do their work for them, keep yourself safe, work hard, be responsible for everything. A fishing boat came around the point of land ahead of them, trolling slowly. The boat looked old, and was shaped oddly, with both ends built the same way, flat. Amolia stared at it as it moved out of sight behind an island. Then she said, "That's quite a story," and smiled quietly to herself.

By now, it was time to stop, and there weren't any cabins around. Several miles away, across an inlet, there was a large island with a number of buildings on it, eight, or maybe nine, but there was smoke rising from some of the stovepipes, and the flicker of movement on the beach. Just opposite where they were now paddling there was a big patch of land that was raised above the beach like a mesa, and covered with fine long grass.

The land faced south, and it shone now like copper in the westering sun. Amolia suggested they camp on that grassy little mesa, and Wesley, with great enthusiasm, agreed. Spike was more reluctant, but eventually he came around.

"Tomorrow," he said, "is another day."

After unloading, they pulled the canoe far up onto the grassy area where they could be sure the tides wouldn't get at it. They had almost lost the canoe that way one night; luckily, Amolia had not been able to sleep, and while walking along the beach she had seen it bobbing, afloat just off the shore. So now they were, at Amolia's suggestion, especially careful, because it looked as if the tides rose and fell fast in this channel—it was fairly narrow and there had been quite a current at the end, just as they pulled in.

While Amolia began to get dinner together and Spike attempted to set up the tent, Wesley gathered wood and made a fire; tonight he had apparently decided on a log-cabin design, since in a surprisingly short time he had a veritable burning building to cook dinner over. Amolia, who had been fetching water, was returning from the woods balancing two buckets carefully on either side of her body when she noticed that the roaring inferno Wesley had constructed had caught the edge of the dry grass, Wesley having failed to ring his fire with stones, and the flames were being urged rapidly forward through the grass by the wind.

"Wesley," she called out, "stamp on the fire!" And Wesley, who had been happily breaking sticks all the exact same length to use in the upper stories of his building, bobbed to his feet in alarm, and, a look of panic on his face, called back, "Oh, dearest! In my sneakers?"

Amolia hurried forward, the water sloshing against her legs. By now, Spike too had noticed the spreading flames and was running toward the fire, the tent still in his hands and dragging on the ground behind him. Clearly, he intended to fling the tent over the fire and smother it, and had the tent been made of canvas this might have been a good idea, but this particular

tent was made of rip-stop nylon and would melt before it smoth-
ered. Amolia had to decide whether to drop the water and get
to the fire in time to stop Spike from ruining the tent, or to
keep the water and save them all from the growing conflagra-
tion. She kept the water, trying to call out a warning as she ran,
but Spike, heedless, flung the tent heroically over the flames,
and instantly the tent collapsed, its main mass melting at his
feet, small puddles of flame shooting in all directions and starting three or four subsidiary fires. Wesley was wringing his hands,
acutely panicked, and Spike was rubbing furiously at a spot on
the front of his jacket where one of the small nylon bullets had
shot him with a patch of flame.

When Amolia arrived, the buckets were only half full, but
by dint of careful rationing she managed to put out all but the
leading edge of the fire. This she pursued on foot, stomping
the flames again and again until they disappeared. Her breath
was coming fast and her heart was beating noticeably, but she
felt, all things considered, surprisingly calm. The big danger had
been to the canoe, which lay cradled not ten feet from the
blackened ground; it was quite enough that they now had no
tent without having no boat either.

"Hey, Mole, hey," said Spike, who had torn his attention at
last from his jacket and came up to join her at the fire's edge.
"Pretty quick footwork for a foxy lady. Did you see what happened to that junky tent?"

When Amolia awoke, it was long after dawn, and Spike and
Wesley were already up. Wesley was making a fire, but, apparently because of the accident the night before, he was making
a fire in miniature—still a log-cabin design, this log cabin was
for mice. The tiny burning cabin stood in the middle of what
seemed, by comparison, a vast wilderness of blackened ground
and Amolia yawned with some amusement. Spike was packing
the canoe, eager to be off; Amolia rose and began to dress, once
more in her camouflage clothes. She had gotten as far as but-

toning her shirt when Spike came hurrying up to her in what seemed, for him, true excitement.

"Listen, Mole, Wesley, what do you say we pull out quickly? That's a real nice fire, but we don't need breakfast today, not really. They'll have something all nice and hot there, waiting for us, over at the camp." The minute the last words left his mouth, he clamped it shut, but it was too late. Amolia glanced past him over the ocean at the island she had seen the night before, the island with eight or nine buildings on it. So that was Chenega; they were here at last. Now things would start to happen. The island was still several miles away, but near enough, and—perhaps the event that had stirred Spike's excitement—a large boat seemed to be pulling out from its dock, heading northeast around the island. Amolia looked at Spike and said, "You've been there before, haven't you?"

For a moment Spike seemed almost murderous and then, thinking better of it, he said: "Well, Mole, well, you caught me. But it was years ago, a long time ago, you understand, and probably there's no one there I know anymore. Long gone."

"What were you there for, anyway?" asked Amolia.

This time it took Spike longer to answer. He seemed to be debating one of at least four or five different approaches, and couldn't settle on one for fully thirty seconds. Amolia stood in silence, looking directly at him and wondering once more, but with greater heartlessness this time, what on earth he thought he was accomplishing.

Finally he spoke.

"You know how I told you my pappy was a . . . a lumberjack, and he was killed by a falling tree, leaving me and my nine brothers and sisters penniless? Well, what I didn't tell you, my mother died not long afterwards and I was sent to this school for homeless children, lived there for almost a year. Fond memories, fond memories, Mole, but also, hard to admit you're an orphan."

An orphan. In the book of tall tales, that one would certainly win a prize, Amolia thought. She noticed that Spike's father had changed professions from coal miner to lumberjack and also that Spike had somehow acquired two more siblings, after poor pappy's death. So chaotic did all this seem to her that if she hadn't remembered clearly the moment when she first saw Spike in the CYTS office—the moment fixed forever like the snowfall in a paperweight—she would have allowed herself to feel contempt, for Spike and his pitiful deceptions. Instead, she nodded and said, "I see. And now you want to visit it?"

"That's it, Mole," said Spike in relief. "A quick visit, with breakfast."

Amolia was filled with a dangerous joy, as she pulled on and laced up her boots. Since they had arrived on the Sound, they had seen no people, except at a distance, when Wesley had waved happily at boats, and though each time they had broken into a new cabin she had gotten dressed to the teeth in camouflage clothing, there had never been anyone to be camouflaged from. Acting was not much fun without an audience, or dressing up without people to admire you, and it would be a refreshing change to have someone there when they landed with their clothes and their guns.

"Wesley," she called. "You can put out the fire. We're having breakfast out."

16

■ "... AND THEN," Kennie Dugan was saying lewdly, "I just slipped her those six inches and . . ."

Linda stood up at the front of the dining trailer. As usual, she had on blue jeans and a button-down man's shirt, and now, as she waited for the kids to quiet down, she put her hands behind her back, hooked her thumbs on her waistband, and thrummed on the seat of her pants with the palms of her hands.

Kennie, whose final remarks had faded into the commotion, now looked up at her, and, grinning, said, "Going to the movies tonight, Linda?" When she just stared back at him coolly, he added, a little disheartened, "Picking your seat early?"

She stared at him some more and he shut his mouth.

"Okay," she said. "As you all know, we're doing something different today, and I want you to listen up. I've thought for a long time that the only way to teach you guys about living in the world is to teach you to cooperate with one another, and now we're going to try just that. We're going to be playing the *trust games* today, trust games, if you can imagine what that might mean, and we're going to do it all the way on the other side of Bear Hill, in the big meadow. And I don't want any of you out of my sight, ever, while we're over there. *Ever.* Got it?"

"Got something in mind, Linda?" called out Derell, true to form, and, encouraged, all the other kids joined in with like remarks: "Uh-oh, think you can handle all of us at once?" and "We'll have a ball, you know what I mean?"

Linda again waited them out, then said, "You little hoodlums have far too good an opinion of yourselves. I'll be surprised if any of you ever get laid with your boots off." Astonished, they shut up like a tape being turned off. Some of them blushed, all of them looked abashed. Linda smiled to herself, amused.

"So let's move out," she added. "You'll be in charge of your *own* lunches. If it rains, you'd better have a raincoat. If it gets cold, you'll be expected to have a sweater. Is that all clear?"

It seemed to be clear. With a good deal of pushing and shoving, the boys began grabbing lunches off the table at the end of the kitchen and tying them into raincoats and sweaters, which they slung around their waists. A few of them—Norm, Derell, Stan, and Harry—had brought little backpacks, which they filled with both lunches and gear. Linda picked up some food for herself; from immediately behind her, Kennie Dugan said, "Hey, Linda, is this all clear?" and when she turned he was holding his forefinger straight out behind her head, just where it would be likely to jab her in the eye when she looked over her shoulder. Luckily, it missed her eye, grazing her cheekbone instead, but for a second she was filled with rage. She wanted to slam Kennie against the wall and punch him in the face a few times, but instead she said, "Try that once more, Kennie Dugan. Just once more."

Ian, who seemed to thrive on turmoil, was standing in the middle of it now with his binoculars, staring through them out the window in the direction of Mummy Island. He grabbed the first boy who bounded in front of him—it happened to be Emory—and said, "Emory, you're not going to believe this, but somebody burned up Mummy Island. Three people are walking around in the wreckage. What do you think? Maybe they need help," while Emory looked at him, puzzled, listened to him patiently, and then nodded and went on to get his lunch.

"And a canoe," Ian added, now in the general direction of Linda. "Who would take a canoe out on Prince William Sound?"

"Somebody lucky," said Lorne primly.

"Somebody crazy," said Linda. Normally she would have been more interested in the question of who on earth could be camping out on Mummy Island, but at the moment she was distracted by the fact that she was supposed to be running this operation almost alone—Phil and Gwen had gone up to Fairbanks to take their exams, Motor had already taken the big boat down to the lower dock to work on the engine, and Trent was staying in camp to look after Arnold, whom Linda thought it wise, for his own sake, to leave behind. So she had only Lorne and Ian coming with her. Yes, it was weird about the fire, but she couldn't be bothered with it now.

"You want to start rounding them up?" she said, and Ian put his binoculars away.

It took an hour or so to walk to Bear Hill Meadow. The camp rarely used it, for several reasons. The first was the swamp which bordered it. In the summer, the place was a breeding ground for the kind of mosquitoes for which Alaska was famous, mosquitoes that could pick up a bull moose and carry him away. Now, in mid-September, the mosquitoes had almost vanished. The second reason was simply the difficulty of keeping track of the boys on the trip there. No one had ever cut a really good trail to it, and the trail that had been cut, years before, was getting overgrown. Devil's club foot grew in that part of the bush, and it was, as a consequence, extremely dense and difficult to navigate; the only way you could get a group through at all was to let each person find a route for himself, and hope that they were all still there at the end.

As a result, Linda was almost alone before the group was twenty minutes from camp. Taking a pack of Marlboros from her shirt pocket, she flipped the top open, knocked the pack against her hand, and extracted a cigarette. Putting it between her lips, she stopped to strike a match against her fly zipper, and while she was touching the flame to the end of the tobacco, Harry Dance came up beside her.

"You really should stop smoking, you know, mon," he said, looking nervously around. "It's bad for your health."

"Yeah, I know," said Linda. "Just like life." But she looked at him curiously.

"Whew," he said, still just as nervous. "This is far from anywhere, eh?"

"Not so far," said Linda.

"I mean," he said vaguely, "far from *camp*." He grinned briefly, his smile slashing across his face in that half-menacing, half-charming grin he had, and then vanishing. "But nearer to where the boat is, the dock, mon, am I right?"

"Where it is *today*," Linda said. "So what?"

"Oh, nothing, nothing. Just . . . islands. One way on them, one way off. Boats," he concluded.

Taking a long drag on her cigarette, Linda stared at him hard, wondering whether he was trying to come on to her. She ground her cigarette out against a rock, punched him lightly on the arm, and said, "Come on, kiddo. We're falling behind."

When they came out of the woods, thirty minutes later, all the boys were in the meadow ahead of them. The whole time

they had been walking, Linda had sensed that Harry had something he wanted to say to her, but although she wondered, in
a way, what that something was, she did nothing to encourage
him to talk. Today, she didn't want any distractions. She felt,
for reasons she did not entirely understand, that this afternoon
was a crucial one for her future, and she was nervous, too,
about the trust games. The last time she had seen them done
she had been, what, about nineteen?

Nineteen, and a pretty cynical nineteen, she thought as she
looked back on it. It had been a gorgeous windy afternoon when
the Outward Bound course she was on had gathered in a pas-
ture on a Colorado mountainside for their first real effort as a
group, and she had gone into it with a chip on her shoulder
about as big as the mountain. She had had nothing but contempt for most of her fellow Outward Bounders, many of whom
were from wealthy families who had apparently paid for their
sojourn in the wilderness with cash money, and would have
paid just as readily for a little trip to France. Also, she had hated
contrivance, when life itself was quite challenging enough. And
indeed, the first few games had bored and irritated her, as had
the enthusiasm of her fellows, as had the windy day, and even
the clear blue sky. But gradually, the games had caught her up,
the sense of group accomplishment had made her, for the first
time that she could remember, lose her rather chilly stance, and
from that start she had progressed by leaps and bounds, until
she was offering suggestions and encouragement as wildly as
anyone, a regular shouting fool. And that sensation—feeling, in
the flesh, connected to the rest of mankind—had so delighted
her that it had, quite literally, changed her life, had led her, in
fact, to Chenega.

"Okay, okay, listen up," she called out to the assembled boys,
who were threatening each other, racing around in circles, lying
on the ground staring at the sky, and arm wrestling, producing
more activity in a small geographic space than she would have
thought ten boys capable of. "Listen up." At length they did,
at about the same time that Lorne, cursing audibly, straggled

into the meadow with a hole in his fine woolen shirt and a scratch across his cheek.

"First, we're going to play something called Mad Dogs and Englishmen," Linda said, surprised to find the name of this game passing her lips so easily, and, indeed, wondering whether she had gotten it quite right—it hardly sounded like a noncompetitive game. "I'll go around and whisper in each of your ears the name of the animal you're supposed to be. You make the growling sound, or whinnying, or whatever. Or you might be an Englishman, or a Frenchman, or something. Either an animal or a foreigner, you understand. Everyone will have a partner who's supposed to be making the same noise he is, and the person who finds his partner soonest wins. You get it?"

"You mean like oink oink oink is a pig?" asked Kennie Dugan, the first rational question Linda could ever remember him asking.

"Yeah. And somewhere in the crowd there's another oink oink oink and he's your partner."

Cheers, jeers, and catcalls greeted this.

"He sure *is*, Kennie D.," said Derell. "He *sure* is."

"You better watch it, Derell," said Kennie. "My old man says that when Judgment Day comes people like you are just going to rot in hell, rot in hell, some of them are going to burn, and some of them are going to freeze, and some of them are going to boil, and some of them are—"

"All right, Kennie. That's enough," said Linda. "We get your point. There's going to be a lot of cooking going on. Meanwhile, you're playing Mad Dogs and Englishmen and the other rule is this. You're divided into two teams and the whole team wins or loses. There's twelve of you altogether—yeah, that's right, counselors too, except me—and that means two teams of six, three pairs of partners. Whichever team has all three sets of partners together first wins. Get it?"

As she said this, it began to seem to Linda that the game was unduly complicated, at least a lot more complicated than she remembered it, and she wondered fleetingly what the point was of coming all the way out here to Bear Hill Meadow to play this stupid game when the kids could have rejected it just as rapidly back at camp, and then realized that this, indeed, was why they had come, because the kids were at their best—from the counselors' point of view—when they were separated from their most familiar surroundings. And if *she* couldn't quite make sense of the rules of the game, the boys seemed to have managed, since they were all now impatiently demanding that she tell them who or what they were going to be, so that they could get it over with. She told them to close their eyes tightly to make it harder to find their partner, and then went around and whispered in people's ears.

"Team One, rabbit," she said, too late remembering that rabbits usually don't make any noise, just wiggle their noses and hop, and adding—to Emory, who happened to be her first victim—"an angry rabbit," and then, while his tightly closed eyes unclosed and he gazed at her open-mouthed, went on to the next person and the next, telling them that they were, respectively, a sheep and a horse, and to the next, who were a whale and cat, and then to the next who were an Italian and an angry rabbit again, and so on to the end, hoping all the while that she had kept the teams straight. When all the participants had received their characters she told them to "make contact."

Astonishingly, they all kept their eyes shut, even Lorne and Ian, and while Linda watched, began to whinny and baa and mew, and say "It's good pizza" and "Mamma mia." The two to whom she had given the whale assignment did surprisingly well—Derell, who Linda would have imagined had never once opened his ears to information about the natural world, knew enough about whale language to let out a series of shrill little yips or peeps, and Stan, who certainly wouldn't have managed to do this first, followed his lead and soon was standing next to him yipping also. The Italians had no difficulties, nor did the horses and cats, and even the sheep—of which there were few in Alaska—were linked up in very short order. But the angry rabbits were in trouble, as Emory and Ian respectively made first little woofing noises, and then shrill beeps, not unlike the whales, and then followed these with the noises of almost every other animal they heard around them, threatening to confuse the real partners quite seriously, before moving on to their next desperate venture. Team Two won the day hands down, and they crowed while Ian and Emory complained bitterly that their assignment had been too hard—"too hard," thought Linda, was a picturesque way to describe the impossible—and she wondered again why this game was supposed to be noncompetitive, since Team Two was indulging in every form of elation known to victors through time.

"All right, good," said Linda, not at all sure that it was. "The next game is, let's see, everyone gets on that rock." There was a smallish boulder standing at one end of Bear Hill Meadow, a boulder that Linda supposed must have been deposited during the last ice age; it was perfect for her purposes, being clearly too small for all of them to stand on. Before she even had time to begin to explain the concept—the object of the game was to get everyone off the ground somehow, even though not everyone could plant his feet firmly on the granite—they had all, including Ian, taken off at a run for the boulder, each player determined to get up on it first.

"No, no!" Linda shouted, but she had to wait until five of them—Ian, Lorne, Norm, Stan, and Derell—had climbed aboard, shoving the competition out of their way, before she could get their attention once more, pull them down off the rock, and start fresh.

"You work *together*," she said. "You work together to make sure that all of you are off the ground. The ship leaves only when everyone is aboard." And this time they understood, and all started shouting at once as they discussed how best that could be accomplished.

"Twelve people on this rock? You must be kidding," said Eric.

"Just be glad Trent and Arnold aren't here, too, mon," Harry responded.

While they were arguing, Linda took out another cigarette. She also was glad that Trent wasn't there, not because he would have made things more difficult for the rock climbers—indeed, he was tall and skinny enough so that if anything, he might have served as a useful anchor—but because she wasn't sure she would have been able to concentrate, if he had been there, on what she was supposed to be doing. Ever since that conversation they had had on the beach, she had been thinking about him rather more than she should have, wondering what would happen next. In Linda's mind, a relationship in the developmental stages was a delicate sort of dance, and though by now—for heaven's sake, she would be twenty-nine on her next birthday—by now she should have known the steps of the dance cold, she felt that in this case, with Trent so, well, *shy*, she was going to have to learn it all over again.

By now, the boys had worked out a plan, and were in the final stages of carrying it out. With Lorne and Ian planted firmly in the middle of the rock, they were stacking bodies around them, heaviest ones closest in, lighter ones on the edge. Ian and Lorne had their arms outstretched so that other people could cling to them, like tree climbers clinging to branches, and the rock itself was a tangle of feet, sprouting out from and on top of one another. The lightest boys—Josh, Rudy, Eric, and Doug—were still on the ground, where they would stay until the last possible minute, and then, leaping up, they would attempt to place their feet somewhere against the stump of feet, using the stump as a lever. As the moment approached, the central mass of bodies was still swaying precariously back and forth and there were muttered recriminations and savage expletives, but they seemed to be getting it, they really did seem to; Linda's spirits rose. At last, with a desperate series of leaps, the smallest boys were up; they were grabbed by many arms that emerged from the central mass; they hung like leaves leaning against the wind; and Linda shouted, "Okay. We're off!"

Well, this was more like it, this was bringing the point home; the boys were pounding each other on the back. Or at least

most of them were; Linda noticed that Stan, Norman, and Derell were having a conference about something, talking in low
conspiratorial tones. After letting the boys congratulate themselves for a while, she gestured and shouted for silence, but just
as she got it, and the boys were standing around her in a re-
spectful attitude as if, though they would have preferred not to
have to admit it, they were finding actively working together
rather fun, all things considered—a sudden mechanical putter-
ing filled the meadow, a low put-put-putting that rapidly became the loud roaring of a boat engine being started up
somewhere remarkably near. Though Harry had reminded her
on the way down here how close Bear Hill Meadow lay to the
lower dock, where Motor was now working on *The Reach*, Linda had not really taken it in, and she, along with everyone else,
flinched at the sound.

17

■ SPIKE HEARD THE ENGINE start up, too, as he pulled
toward the Chenega dock. The tide was with them, and the
powerful ebbs that, Spike remembered, sometimes sucked the
channel almost into a river had not delayed them this morning.
What had delayed them, just for a moment, was that the big
boat, after pulling away from the main dock, had not made for
the north as it generally did, but had disappeared around the
southern tip of the bay. Spike recognized it as "the big boat,"
though it was about a third smaller than he remembered it, as
indeed was almost everything else about the Sound. The bald
eagles skimming and swooping, the sea lions staring and wink-
ing, the seals bobbing and ducking, all these were just as he
remembered them, but the land, the spaces, the sky, the buildings—these seemed to have shrunk with time. Spike set his
paddle aside for a moment and combed his hair back with his

hands, then, without thinking, stuck his left finger in his ear and held it there while he gazed toward the shore.

The camp didn't look at all the way he remembered it. In the first place, it looked deserted, and that was odd, because even when the big boat had left, in his day, few of the kids ever got to leave with it, and they were always milling around, or at least shouting from the schoolroom. No one was in evidence now, though, and that threw Spike off, because somehow he had been expecting, not just that everyone would be waiting at the dock to greet him, a kind of welcoming committee to pay tribute to his stature, but that Burke would be right at the front of the pack, where Spike could get a good clear shot at him immediately. Then, too, the buildings looked different. They were more than smaller, they seemed to have been moved, and there were several new ones, which ruffled his sense of place. Two of them were windowless—what they might be for he couldn't imagine, unless to imprison unruly boys—and one of them was a trailer, a big industrial model. For a moment Spike wondered whether this was still Chenega at all.

Then the canoe hit the wharf. Before settling itself against the half tires that had been nailed to the boards, it clanked and banged against the raw wood, making what Spike imagined to be quite a racket, and the noise, loud in the ocean stillness, appeared to him suddenly quite unaccountable, something that should not have happened. But while the unexpected arrival of the sound was burdensome to him, vexatious in the same way that physical objects could be vexatious, no one came, even though—just in case—he grabbed his rifle and swung it to his shoulder. Then he sprang from the canoe, and holding it by the stern rope, said to Amolia and Wesley in low tones, "Load your guns. But don't use them until I give the word." He noticed a curious sea otter that had followed them in, and although it was at least thirty feet away, he aimed a vicious kick in its direction.

Amolia climbed from the canoe, and Wesley lumbered after her, setting it sloshing around between its lines and hitting the dock with a rapid series of resounding clanks that seemed to echo all over the island. Wesley was wearing a huge jungle suit that made him look very much like a camouflaged puffball, since Amolia had insisted before they left the grassy island that he put on his special protective clothing. Spike stared a silent warning at him, then lifted out his gun and, cradling it loosely in his arms, made his way to the end of the dock. Behind him, he could hear Amolia speaking to her father softly, apparently giving him instructions on how to hold his gun, but Spike's attention was riveted on a tall man with a black case in his hand who had suddenly emerged from the door of the trailer and was now staring, presumably stunned, down at the wharf where Spike stood.

Presumably stunned. That was good. That was very good indeed. The vertigo which Spike had been trembling on the brink of just a moment before was suddenly gone, washed right away, and replaced by an eager truculence. In fact, Spike's whole body felt good, as the rush of adrenaline took it; his toes, his stomach, his hands, his face, they were all of them tingling and clean. It wasn't that that man, the tall man with the black case, was an enemy, not yet; it was that he was a potential enemy, which was in some ways even better. This was the best time, when you had them guessing, when they were still just scared out of their minds, and although, of course, to one extent or another you had them guessing the whole time, now— before they knew whether you were selling guns, or searching for them, or carrying a hand grenade, or about to blow the whole place up with TNT—they were always filled with a mixture of terrors that was like a palpable thing. The other guy's complete inability to figure out how this had happened to him, or why, was the energy that Spike lived on, and it made up, a little, for all those weeks and months when he was unable to figure out the same thing.

Finally, Spike started walking silently up the hill toward the trailer. He held his gun pointed directly in front of him, and he lifted his feet with precision, all to increase the effect of power, as Wesley and Amolia moved after him. His first line, which he would present when he was standing just four feet away from the man and could see the whites of his eyes, was going to be, "Don't move and no one will get hurt," and he rehearsed this line in his mind while he marched, holding his restlessness in check. But when he was still at least twenty feet away, the man with the case raised his hand, and giving a tentative kind of half-wave, called out:

"Hello? Can I help you?"

Spike did not respond. He was vexed that the man had spoken first, not prolonged the marvelous pause, and he lamented —not for the first time—that people never could follow the script. But all right, all right, so they'd move to the next stage, when Spike would fill space with enigmas.

"Who are you?" the tall man said now. "I mean, what are your names?"

"Oh, no," said Spike, smiling grimly. "I'm not going to tell you that." And he watched as, for the first time, the man's gaze left Spike's face and flicked down to the second and third figures in the line.

"I didn't mean that," the man returned, enunciating each word carefully. "I meant, what are you doing here? I meant, what do you want?"

The man had asked a good question, no doubt about it, but it was one that Spike could not answer. Now that the man had spoken, now that Spike was *here*, he was starting to get powerful rushes of memory; the outhouses perched up in the woods, the pile of logs close to the bunkhouse, the rattly clanging of the generator back in the bush, all of these poked at his head like tiny fingers, drawing back the little curtains that covered the scenes of his past, and strangely, instead of firming his resolve to get back at Burke, they seemed instead to weaken it. Whereas ten minutes before he had had no doubt at all that his whole purpose, his entire intention in coming back to Chenega, was to kill Burke and be done with it, now he felt the ragged edge of doubt. He saw himself, a young and wan fifteen, playing basketball in the wood lot; he saw himself, actually feeling important, trying to answer hard questions in school. The truth of it was, he had really been quite happy here, playing kung fu with his fellows, getting rewards for earning points. Sure, Burke had been a monster, with his great thick muscles and his nasty laugh, but Burke had not been the only counselor, and there was a lot about Chenega that had been fine. Spike remembered now, what he had forgotten in recent weeks, that when he had first conceived of making this trip it had been from nostalgia as much as from anger, and as long as he had lost sight of that somewhere along the way, he wanted to lose sight of it again. He hated confusion and not being quick at responding; and this power scene, it was one he was good at.

"Nothing to get upset about," he barked at last. "We're just here for a little robbery."

At this, Wesley suddenly let out a sound behind Spike, a sort of cross between a grunt and a moan, as if the word "robbery" were physically disturbing to him. The man with the case, on the other hand, seemed clearly to be relieved. He leaned forward a little and, bending at the knees, set the black case carefully on the ground, then, leaning forward some more and gesturing with his hands—his whole body freed, apparently, from a spell, at the simple word "robbery"—said hopefully, "This is a camp for juvenile delinquents. We don't keep anything valuable here. We can't. They'd steal it." He smiled slightly, as if to make sure they all got the joke.

But the smile made Spike angry—it seemed to reflect badly on his technique—and he put as much venom as he could into his voice as he tightened his finger on the trigger of his gun.

"That's all right," he said. "We don't want anything valuable. You make one false move and I'll blow you away."

"Oh, Micah," began Wesley behind him, and Spike spat at him without turning: "Shut up! Now," he said, addressing the tall man once more, "why don't we all go somewhere and get comfortable, have a little sit down, maybe a cup of coffee?" He felt very exposed out here, and not knowing where all the other counselors and boys were made him almost itchy.

"Don't try any tricks," he added—that was good—and gestured with his gun.

The tall man did not smile again, but turned and began walking carefully back toward the trailer. As they got near it, he said, in a tautly controlled voice, "This isn't a trick. But there's a boy in here. He's painting one of the walls."

They all filed in through an anteroom rife with boots and jackets. An elusive smell, the smell of boy, increased Spike's apprehension, and when he saw the child standing on the stepladder he felt almost as if he had been struck. From his position at the top of the ladder, the boy was staring at Spike in rapt astonishment, his tongue thrust between his teeth and his eyes bright and wondering. Someone had given him a paintbrush, and a wall to paint, and although some of the paint had landed on the wall, most of it seemed to have landed on him—his hair, his eyes, even the tips of his ears were covered with fine white dots.

"Arnold," the man said, in further explanation.

"Is it bad to eat paint?" asked Arnold after a moment, directing his question to the tall man. "I guess it is, but it was an accident, Trent."

"You *ate* some paint?" said Trent.

"It fell in my mouth," Arnold explained. He still had his brush poised high in the air above his head, preparatory to making another stroke with it.

"It's not too good," said Trent. "But at least it's latex." Then he turned to Spike and the Hannahs.

"This is Arnold," he said once more. "Arnold, these are ...?" and he looked questioningly at Spike. Before Spike could turn the question aside again, and take it, even, as an attempt at provocation, Wesley spoke from beside him.

"Arnold?" he asked, sounding very pleased. "My wife's brother's name was Arnold. Although actually, he didn't use it much, preferring to go by his nickname of Boots. Still, it's a very nice name, a very nice name indeed. And we . . . well, this is my daughter Amolia, Boots's niece. Amolia is the light of my life. And this is our friend, Micah Jones. Or Spike. Most people call him Spike, but I prefer Micah. Micah, as you probably know, was a prophet of the eighth century B.C. I am Wesley Hannah. Arnold and . . . Trent?"

"Yes."

"And Trent. Well, we're certainly very happy to make your acquaintance, very happy indeed. That is, we were just—"

But at this, Amolia interrupted him.

"We were just about to have some breakfast, I think," she said. "Are you two the only people on the island?"

"No," said Trent. "Though at the moment, we're the only ones in camp. The others are all out in the woods, in Bear Hill Meadow. They won't be back for a while."

"How many others are there?" said Amolia. "And how long is a while?"

"Well," said Trent. "I'd have to figure it out. There are twelve boys, minus one, and Arnold here, that's ten, and Linda, and the counselors, Ian and—"

Amolia cut him off.

"*About* how many?" she said.

"About . . ." Trent stared at the floor. "About . . . oh, fourteen, would you say?"

Arnold nodded and began painting the wall again.

This was not what Spike had hoped for from Fate, not what he had planned on at all. It was true that he had been a little uncertain about what he wanted to do on Chenega, thinking sometimes that he just wanted to drop by and pay it a visit, to show the place, if he could, how powerful he had become. But he was feeling more and more uneasy about the way things had started, with all the boys but this one missing, and now Amolia had cut off Trent before he even said Burke's name. Angrily, Spike started searching the kitchen cabinets, telling Amolia first to "guard the man," and although he didn't find anything in the cabinets that clarified his sense of purpose, he did find a lot of cans of food, and it occurred to him that he was hungry. He fished a can of pineapple juice down from a cupboard above the sink and, letting his gun dangle for a moment on its strap, punched large holes in it with a knife. Then he drank some juice straight from the can, rapidly, with loud harsh gulps. He set the can back on the counter, telling Amolia to keep an eye on the door as well, as he went back into the kitchen storeroom to see what else he could find. When he returned, he was carrying a loaf of Wonder Bread, a large can of tuna fish, a jar of blackberry jam, some peanut butter, and a couple of yellow onions.

"Let's have a peanut butter and onion sandwich," he said to Trent, setting the food down in a tumbled heap. "And for the others, make them whatever they want."

Amolia was still standing, ramrod straight, covering Trent with her gun, but Wesley had wandered off to the base of the ladder, where Arnold was spraying him with paint. At "peanut butter and onion," both Arnold and Wesley looked over, Wesley in mild astonishment, Arnold in sudden interest.

"Can I have one too, Trent? Peanut butter and onion, I mean?"

"Sure," said Trent. "Whatever you want."

Arnold climbed down from the ladder, still carrying his brush. Wesley made way for him, taking a few steps backward, and at the end of his retreat came up against the paint can. It tipped over, spilling paint on the floor and splashing his pants legs and, terribly concerned, he leaned over and picked the can up, then started brushing futilely at the pants with his fingers, murmuring apologies. Trent, before Spike could stop him, grabbed up a roll of paper towels from the kitchen and rushed to Wesley's side, where he knelt, mopping up the spreading puddle of white, and then Wesley knelt down too, and side by side they worked with the toweling, managing to get most of the paint.

"I'm terribly sorry," said Wesley. "Just terribly sorry. I had no idea . . . that is to say, I was backing up, and I didn't see the can, and then suddenly there it was, you understand and—"

"That's really all right," said Trent. "The floor's not in great shape anyway. Arnold," he added to the boy, who had wandered over toward Amolia, paintbrush still in hand, "why don't you put that brush down over there, and try to clean up a little before lunch?"

Obligingly, Arnold wandered back, set the brush neatly on top of the still-open can, and then smeared his sticky hands on his pants.

Spike, by now, was feeling just plain aggravated. The whole situation was clearly inimical to sensations of clarity and strength, and though nothing had strictly gone awry, there was nothing going smoothly either. Certainly Spike liked his victims to have a little starch, instead of freaking out and blithering all over the place—starch showed a little more respect, somehow, for authority than did limpness or total disintegration—but this man, Trent, was the first he'd encountered who could talk about latex at gunpoint. Amolia was Spike's ally, of course; Amolia could be counted on, but Wesley was a total loss, and this other one wasn't playing the game. He'd see about that; he'd make sure things changed; he knew a trick or two about terror. But meanwhile, he really did want a sandwich; and he had to find out about Burke.

"Come on," he barked. "Get on with it. I'm hungry and I want some lunch." Then he stuck his left finger in his ear, put his right hand on the trigger guard of his gun, and stood next to Trent while he sliced the onions, waiting for one false move.

18

■ WHEN THEY ALL sat down, ten minutes later, Trent felt close to hysteria. On the one hand, of course, he lived his life expecting daily disaster—deadly diseases, getting struck by lightning, even spontaneous combustion, were all real and present possibilities to him; on the other hand, these crazies seemed even crazier than any he had ever met in California, where the vast bulk of American crazies came off the assembly line, and it was very confusing, to say no more, that they should have dropped in on Chenega. Wesley seemed quite harmless, a fat man with an endearing, monochromatic quality of enthusiasm, but the skinny fellow, Spike, was certainly dangerous, and the woman even more so. There he had been, taking his clarinet back to the schoolhouse and hoping that Arnold wouldn't paint himself into the wall while he was gone, when suddenly he had looked up and seen these three strangers on the dock, dressed in army green and carrying guns; it had seemed to Trent at the time, in fact, that they were covered from head to foot in guns—the guns defined them, prepared them for any part, gave them stature on any ground. They stood on the island and they owned it. Suddenly, he had felt like an interloper, forced to explain his own presence here, and there was a pounding at the back of his head as if his heart had been trapped there and was trying frantically to get down into his chest again. When he had noticed that the third person in the line was a woman, all hope had left him for a moment. After his marriage to Rae, he certainly knew a lot about the merciless determination and competence of women, and suddenly the whole scene had looked to Trent like a collection of targets, each familiar object on the island set at a careful, measured distance from where Amolia stood. For that matter, there was still a targetlike quality to the setting around him. He covered his right eye with the palm of his hand, taking in the table set for five. "Bull's-Eye Brooding About Projectiles" he would call it. He picked up, but only picked at, his sandwich.

Wesley was eating happily, with Arnold at his side. He seemed to think that now that those first disagreeable moments were over—those moments when Spike had been, perhaps, just a trifle threatening—they had all settled down to a cordial relationship, with food at the center of its friendliness. Amolia was eating with surprising vigor for someone who had clearly spent most of her life starving herself—though she cut the crusts off her sandwich, she proceeded to eat them before she even started on the mutilated remains—but Spike was eating nothing at all, just drinking coffee in great gulps as if his body were a furnace that could only be stoked with black fuel. Wesley's gun kept bumping the edge of his plate as he leaned forward to pick up a sandwich or set a hunk of cheese on his bread. Looking down at the gun with distaste he said, "Goodness, these, these deadly items certainly get in the way, don't they? I wonder if anyone would mind ... that is to say, I think I'll just take this off for the time being, it seems to interfere, you know, with the digestion," and before Spike or Amolia could reprimand him, he lifted the strap over his head and set the gun on the floor behind him.

There was silence for a while, interrupted by chewing and clanks, and then Trent got shakily to his feet. He thought he might make some more coffee, for lack of anything better to do, and he asked permission from Spike, then pushed himself back from the table. He was surprised by the facility with which his legs took him over to the kitchen, but even more surprised by the way the kitchen looked when he came to it. Everything was in a jumble there; nothing looked the way it was supposed to. The forms and sizes of things seemed to have changed, as if they had been tossed to the bottom of the sea, and he couldn't quite remember, somehow, where everything was stored. At last he found a match, however, and lit the right front burner of the stove. Then he found the coffee can, and a spoon to measure the grounds with. But when he lifted the coffee pot forward over the flames, he found he had no idea if the pot already held one cup, two cups, or three. Though he stared at the dark liquid intently, and swirled it around in a circle, even the utmost concentration did not help him, and his hand trembled like someone else's. At last he dumped it all in the sink and filled the pot with fresh water.

While he waited for the water to boil, he tried to formulate a plan. The obvious thing to do—indeed, it was so obvious that he was certain even as he thought about it that there was no way on earth he would ever manage to do it—the obvious thing to do was to lure them all to the schoolhouse somehow, fling himself inside, bar the door behind him, and call the Coast Guard on the radio. If the boy at the table had been anyone other than Arnold, he might have counted on him for help in diverting the crazies long enough to accomplish at least the first part of this plan, but the boy *was* Arnold, unfortunately, and diverting though he might be, simply as a study in behavior—he was now wiping his plate off with his right elbow, his tongue clenched between his teeth as he concentrated on the task at hand—he was not likely to create a diversion which would look like one to your average lunatic. If Trent could find out *why* they were here; well, certainly that might help. He had not done too well with questions so far, but now he concentrated fiercely on his words, as if they were all that was left to him, and he felt, as he walked back toward Wesley and nodded encouragingly, that the sentence he finally put together was a triumph.

"You look familiar, somehow," he said. "Have we met, ever, do you think?"

Wesley paused in mid-bite, considering the question. He stared at Trent unwinkingly, his big sea lion's face loose and relaxed; he held his forefinger level with his eyes as if measuring Trent for a suit.

"No," he said at last. "That is, I don't think so. I generally remember the people I meet on my travels, unless I meet them at night. The quality of vision is so different at night from the quality of vision by day. And then, you know, you are so tall—you wouldn't be easy to forget. But I'm happy to meet you now, of course. And little Arnold, too, naturally." He nodded and returned to his bite.

It was hard to keep a grip on this; Trent thought he had a right to feel hysterical. Quicksand, it was all like quicksand, and when suddenly Spike got up from the table, pushing it so hard that it moved, Trent had another moment of stark, raging fear, something of the same sensation he had had once when his middle ear ruptured in an accident, a sense of disorientation that was physical, an endless falling sensation of loss, a desperate need to grab on to something and cling to it for dear life.

But Spike simply began to walk around the room again, restlessly disarranging it. He picked up a bowl and put it down, opened a drawer, then shut it. He appeared to be steeling himself for something; and, in the peculiarly slowed-down time Trent and the whole rest of the island seemed to have fallen into, that steeling went on and on. Trent returned to the coffee pot and watched the tiny bubbles start to rise at the edges of the water, and he was just about to add the coffee grounds when Spike went to the door, opened it, shut it, leaned on the doorpost, and then shook his rifle hard, saying to Trent, "You know what this is?"

Trent stared at the gun intently, as if he hadn't noticed it before.

"Well, it's some sort of automatic rifle," he answered, his hand arrested on its way to spoon the coffee grounds.

"It's an M-16," said Spike. "I got it in 'Nam."

The pounding started up again in Trent's head, just behind his left ear. It felt very much as if a bird had been trapped there and was trying frantically to escape, and he shook his head from side to side, trying to help it do so. When the war had been on he himself had been, of course, too young to be drafted into it, but his mother's students had been going. Every night she would turn on the news, sitting like a faulty caption in front of the television, feeling in some way responsible for the horror, and Trent too had watched, sharing in her sense of culpability. She was right; too young, he'd seen that no one is innocent, seen what the good guys could do to the bad. "Oh, you were in Vietnam?" he said.

"I was a sniper there. Not a Green Beret, you understand. I did recon work—reconnaissance they called it. They taught me how to kill over there. Never killed until they taught me. I was just a kid, seventeen, they put this gun into my hands. You know what this gun will do?" He shook it again, staring at Trent until he raised his eyebrows questioningly. "If I aimed it at that stove and pulled the trigger, it'd cut that stove in half. In half." He pointed it at the stove.

"Yes, I've seen it on TV," said Trent. "Amazing what those things will do." He might have been a speaker on the wonders of modern technology as somehow he forced his hand to move easily toward the coffee can and start spooning coffee into the pot. He felt the beginnings of something like fury at this man and at the woman who lurked behind him. Trent had come here to Alaska, after all, to get away from craziness and back to a place where things were simple, and where he might have a chance, for the first time in his life, to learn how to really cope, but now, now, these two were wrecking it. And what gave them that right? But before Trent could do anything with this feeling, Wesley stirred and spoke.

"Micah, you never told me that this object was quite so dangerous," he said, looking down at his gun with more than distaste this time, with something closer to horror. "If I had known, I don't see how I could even have carried it here. No, I really don't. The world spirit doesn't approve of that, of cutting things in half."

Spike, however, ignored him, and continued talking to Trent. "You wouldn't believe how some people have acted when they saw me," he said. "One woman, she saw me and fainted dead away on the floor. A man, he jumped me. As far away from me as you are, and he jumped me."

Trent shook his head reprovingly, feeling more and more actively murderous. He wished he could take that gun and physically bend it around Spike's neck, or—better yet—just take the neck itself and wring it between his hands.

"He must have been nuts," he said, though, with sympathy. "Why else would he do a thing like that?"

"Yeah," said Spike, with a gleam of excitement, "people are crazy. I know. You got a dude here name of Burke?"

"Lorne Burke, yes, why?"

"*Lorne* Burke?" Spike seemed confused. Sticking his finger in his ear, he brooded for an instant, and then an expression resembling fear passed across his face, and his eyes, which had been fixed unwaveringly on Trent's, moved away and drifted toward the window. But he screwed up his face and wrenched it back to its original expression, and there was an edge of ludicrous indignation in his voice as he said, brooking no possible disagreement, "First name, last name, what's the difference, it's gotta be the same guy. And man, you may not believe this to look at me, but I was once in the clutches of that son-of-a-bitch, fifteen years old and as clean as a baby's bottom, I was shipped off to this place to do time, and here was Mister Burke to help me through it. I ain't got nothing against you, man, not yet; it's Burke I came to do justice on."

"Golly," said Trent. "That's too bad. Lorne isn't . . . that is, he's in the hospital right now, everyone else is in Bear Hill Meadow, but Lorne got cut in the shoulder, badly, and he was shipped off to the hospital." In his relief at finding out at last what Spike was really here for, in his hurry to find acceptable business for Lorne somewhere off the island (unpleasant as he was, Trent didn't want to see him killed, particularly in a case of mistaken identity), and in his profound astonishment at learning that Spike himself had once been a student at Chenega—the most unsuccessful product, Trent sincerely hoped, that the camp had ever generated—he forgot that Arnold, too, was sitting listening to his excuse about the hospital.

"Lorne?" Arnold piped up, puzzled. "But Trent, you said ... I mean, it was Jack that was there, I hit him with the ax, you saw it, there was blood all over everything and—"

"Arnold," said Trent. "Be quiet now. We've got some serious talking to do, and your interruptions aren't helping much. Why don't you go paint the wall or something?" Arnold looked at him, bewildered, and then, without looking down, poured some salt into his left palm, and still staring idiotically at Trent, pushed his tongue into it and lifted it to his mouth, then licked his palm clean.

"But," Trent added, before Spike or anyone else could speak again, "there's a water taxi that runs out of Whittier. If we call the taxi, you can take the train into the city and have a talk with Lorne in the hospital. He's a son-of-a-bitch, no doubt about it. He could use a good talking to."

Spike studied Trent; so did Amolia. Trent tried to look unconcerned. The coffee water had boiled, a brown froth of magma erupting in the pot, and he turned off the flame and let it settle. Arnold, in the emergency which had descended on him when Trent told him to shut up, pulled out one of the several long pieces of string that he kept in his pocket and started to tie knots in it. Delighted, Wesley looked over; offering diffidently to show Arnold how to do cat's cradle, he took the string in his own pudgy fingers and started twisting and crossing while Arnold, pinching his thumb and forefinger tightly together, held the appropriate junctures. Amolia rose and stared out the window, sipping coffee. Finally, Spike spoke.

"Well, I don't know about that," he said. "That doesn't sound like such a good idea at all. But let's go get that phone, why don't we? I've got an idea of what we should do with it."

Although Spike's idea of what to do with it was undoubtedly to destroy it, Trent nevertheless felt a surge of hope. All he had wanted to do when he suggested they call a taxi was to remind these crazies that, isolated as it seemed, Chenega was part of the world. Now, the stasis into which they had all settled was rapidly dissolving around him. Wesley, at Amolia's admonishment, stopped playing string games with Arnold and picked up his gun from the floor—though he refused to sling it around his neck right side front and instead hung it down his back, where it drooped like a piece of firewood; Spike snapped his jacket up and took a last quick tour of the kitchen, and Amolia glided toward the door like a phantom in jungle boots. Whether or not this was going to help in the end Trent could not yet be sure, but as long as the others would just stay away there was a chance all might still be well.

But calling the Coast Guard was clearly impossible. Even if he did manage to get inside the schoolhouse before the others and bolt the door behind him, there were windows all around the south and west, and one right next to the radio. Perhaps he could lead them, instead, somewhere else, somewhere more easily defended. They didn't know, after all, where the radio was kept, and if he could reach, for example, the *gunhouse* and get inside—the gunhouse had no windows at all.

The air outside was very damp and salty, as if a storm were coming. Trent had almost forgotten there *was* an outside and the smell stopped him like a blow, but Spike shoved him in the back with his rifle and he started off toward the woods. He had a sick feeling, not unlike stage fright, and for a moment he confused the salt with fear, but then, with a sudden determination, he strode toward the gunhouse as if to meet a friend. Spike muttered, "They keep it up here?" when Trent veered off toward the tiny log building, but he said no more, just followed along, jumpy, it seemed, in the open. Amolia dropped back to cover the rear and Arnold and Wesley, now hand in hand, were off walking by themselves, talking happily and tripping over the few berry bushes and shrubs that grew in the compound.

At the door to the gunhouse Trent paused again, and fished his keys from his pocket. As he stood there trying to sort them out, still troubled by a certain confusion of the senses in that preternaturally silent compound, he was thrown back to a child-hood clubhouse, a hut that had looked much like this one. In and around it, some of the worst scenes of his youth had taken place. Tall, pale, and delicate of manner, fatherless in a time before that was very common, he had inevitably been made the butt of most of the cruel plots of his fellows—and yet he had stuck with it, with them, with their clubhouse; with trying to be one of the guys. They had constantly devised new and interesting ways to torment him; once they had tied him to a tree and stuck an entire pack of Winstons into his mouth, one by one, making him smoke them down to the filters until he was retching; once they had crept into his room at night while the family was at dinner and filled his bed with .22 shells; once they had pulled down his pants to jeer at the size of his penis. And he, hungry and hopeful kid that he was—he had always come back for more. Why hadn't he fought back *then*; why hadn't he vanquished the thugs? He found the key and turned it once in the padlock.

All right. Well, all right. Now was the moment. Putting it off wouldn't help. He had just time to notice that Spike's finger was, for an instant, away from the trigger and rooting around in his ear, when he flung himself headlong into the gunhouse, letting the padlock drop. There was a terrible pounding in his head, and a sense that his chest was being gripped in a vise, and then he was pitching himself into the velvet blackness behind the door, hurling it to right in Spike's face, and slamming the wooden bolt home. Finally, without even thinking, he cast himself down on the floor.

From outside, the sound of Spike's voice came, muffled but menacing through the wood.

"That was stupid, man. Very stupid. Don't go near that radio, or I shoot."

Trent lay where he was, trying not to breathe, his eyes adjusting slowly to the dimness. Above him, finally, he could see the gun rack with the shotgun and the rifle on it, the rifle's shoulder strap dangling in the air like a tiny leather stretcher.

Beside him was the leg of the desk where they kept the pistol and the ammunition, but the drawer itself was two feet above his head. Anyway, he had some dim idea that the shotgun would be a better weapon to try and shoot through walls with, though he couldn't remember just why. Indeed, he couldn't remember a great deal of the very little he had ever learned about guns and even now he didn't want to try. He heard Spike order Amolia to "fan out" and search the other buildings; he heard Amolia tell her father sharply to stop playing with Arnold; he heard Arnold ask curiously whether they were going to burn the schoolhouse down; but Trent just lay on the floor where he had fallen, breathing quietly in and out. Now that he had secured the gunhouse, he wished the others *would* come back.

19

◼ THE OTHERS, THOUGH, were still playing trust games, much to Harry's dismay. He had had some hopes that if the games were short enough, they would not provide Norm and Stan and Derell with sufficient time to get their nerve up for the break, but as the afternoon went on, Linda had managed to remember some better games than the one featuring the angry rabbits, and the better the games became the more underlying currents of excitement ruled them. They had just finished a game of "amoeba tag" and as Norm and Harry, arm in arm, whirled around in the muskeg like the tail end of a whip, Norm leaned toward Harry's ear and mumbled menacingly, "Better get ready, Harry. We're going for the boat as soon as Linda's back is turned."

"Aw, come on, mon," said Harry, softly, but as frantically as he could. "We should wait on this whole thing till Jack gets back, you know that. This isn't fair."

"Are you crazy?" said Norm. "I wouldn't wait for him if the

world was on fire," he added, just as Harry became accidentally detached from Norm's hand and went whirling off alone toward the edge of the trees, feeling very dizzy and sick.

"Okay," Linda called out, flushed and happy, her two cheeks round spots of color, her green eyes glittering in the reflected light of the greens of the meadow. "Now we're going to try a trust fall. Listen up, you guys, this is where you catch someone falling." Harry, still dizzy, made his way back to the center of the meadow, where Norm was now mumbling in Derell's ear as Derell nodded broadly and grinned.

"Okay," Linda went on. "So who wants to be the first trusting one? Remember, guys, you're going to have this person's life in your hands. He's going to plummet backward in space like a comet, and if you don't catch him he's going to break his spine. So you catch him and he won't. That's what makes it a trust fall."

It sounded horribly dangerous to Harry, and he tried to make himself unobtrusive as he was herded, with the others, toward the stump of a small tree. The surface of the stump was about two feet off the surface of the ground and therefore, according to Linda, absolutely the perfect height for the victim to fall backward from. Animatedly, she lined all the guys up in two lines on either side of the end of the stump, and placed Ian right at the end, where the head of the faller would land.

"All *right*, guys," she said then, rather impatiently. "It's not *that* dangerous. In fact, if your friends and buddies don't fuck around too much, it's not dangerous at all. Now who wants to fall first? You're all going to have to do it in the end, so you might as well get it over with. Rudy? Emory? Derell?"

"No, *sir*," said Derell vehemently. "Not when . . . not when it's so risky." Harry clenched his teeth in exasperation at the way Derell had almost let the cat out of the bag, feeling more annoyed than ever at these three idiots he was going to "run away" with. Ever since he had first heard about the escape plan he had feared the worst, and now the worst was about to happen. *The Reach*, as the sounds of its engine proved, was only the briefest hike away, and with all the other counselors either off island or otherwise engaged, the four boys would certainly have it in them to overpower Motor, take the boat, and sail away into the waiting arms of the police. If Harry hadn't made that promise to Jack on the phone, he would never be going with them, and just now that seemed like an awfully stupid reason, with the future so clearly a catastrophe. Meanwhile, they were standing there like three grinning dummies, drawing attention to themselves while Linda waited for a volunteer.

"I'll do it," Harry said suddenly. "But you guys better catch me."

He climbed up onto the stump, while the boys whistled and clapped. Even as he mounted it, noticing with peculiar acuity the whorled and uneven rings in the wood, rings which were said to mark the shape of the tree's life, he thought that this, this trust fall, was an odd thing for a coward to do. But he supposed it would be better to break his own back than to watch someone else break his, and at least it would give him a good excuse not to run—an excuse as good, really, as Jack's. Standing with his back to the group, he edged his toes to the very rim of the stump, so that his heels were actually balanced on the air behind him, and there he paused, wondering how to fall, and trying not to lose his pint of courage. While Linda gave her final instructions on how to hold their hands, the boys below him quieted and Harry took a deep breath. Then, holding it, he shoved himself backward hard, knowing as he did so that this was the end, the end of his life, not having the time, as he fell, to review how good that life had been, or how short, but having time for just one glimpse of the shifting, steely gray sky, and then he was down, held securely in eleven pairs of hands, each hand under his body a tender little pat of comfort and greeting, and he let out a sudden shout of delight and scrambled down while all of them, breathless with amazement, shouted also, and pounded each other's backs in sheer joy that they should have done this thing—that they should have saved someone's life.

After that, everyone fell in turn, and each time he was caught it was a new astonishment to them all, bringing the level of glee and elation to something like fever pitch. After they had quieted down, and Linda was able to regain their attention—wrenching it away, with difficulty, from the miracle of life—she said there was just one more game to play, and for this one they needed some props. In this one, they would all—even Lorne and Ian and she herself—be blindfolded; and then one of them would be picked to take his blindfold off and lead the group on a walk through the woods, as they all held hands and followed. The point of the game, she emphasized, was to trust the leader to take you on a route where you would be safe, and also to pay attention to the smells, the feels, the sounds of things in the woods—to tune in to the "other world" out there.

"And I've got the blindfolds," Linda finished, producing them from her rucksack. "Any questions about this one?"

"Yeah," said Derell. "How long does it last? How long do you get to be blindfolded?"

"Ten minutes," said Linda. "You'll find it's pretty long."

Ten minutes! That certainly *was* pretty long. And from the sneers and grimaces that Derell and Norm and Stan were producing, and from the way they gathered in a group as the blindfolds were being distributed, Harry was certain it was going to be just long enough. Now was the time when he had, at last, to make his final decision, and it was funny, but the trust fall had put him into such a good mood, had made him feel so high and giddy and elated, that what he felt now was, what the hell? Why not try it? Maybe he'd *like* running away.

"Blindfolds *on*," said Linda, and before he put his blindfold on, Harry saw his three partners in crime arranging themselves at the very end of the line, where it would be easiest to slip off without anyone noticing, except Emory, who was immediately in front of them, and was too honorable to tell. Now, it all depended on who the leader was. If it was a counselor, the plan wouldn't work even now.

But the leader was not a counselor. It was, of all people,

Kennie Dugan, whom Linda must have selected according to some arcane theory of child psychology. Even Kennie seemed astonished when she named him, and he looked down at his own chest, mouth ajar, when she pointed to it to emphasize her choice. Then he recovered himself and said, "Oh, boy, this is just the kind of thing that happens to people in the Good Book, the blind leading the blind, only I'm not going to be blind, but this is the way that God shows who his chosen people are, they can always be told because only if you put your faith in God will he repay you, and there can be no stubbed toes or rending wounds when the millennium arrives—"

Linda interrupted him. "I forgot to tell you," she said. "As the leader you can't talk."

So now they all lined up and put their blindfolds on, and a tug in the line told Harry that they were moving forward. He was standing just behind Stan and just in front of Norm, and two minutes later, when the whole line was inside the woods—already tripping slightly on the deadfall that littered this part of the bush that Kennie had chosen to lead them through—Norm and Derell and Stan detached themselves from the line and took off their blindfolds, and Harry did too, only to see, at the head of the line, Kennie's eyes grow huge with wonder and delight, as he said, "I see you guys, you can't do that, not while I'm the—"

He got out, however, only those first twelve words before Linda, who was directly behind him in line, kicked him in the leg and said, "Shut *up*, Dugan. How can they concentrate on the smell and sound of the woods?"

So here they were. Stan led the other three rapidly off to the north while the rest of the line went south at a crazy, creepy crawl. Although Stan had trouble with running in the normal course of events—had so much trouble that they had even, Harry remembered, taken him off the run chart—now he suddenly seemed to learn how, as he tore through the woods, leaping deadfall. Norm followed him more slowly; Norm's day pack, Harry noticed, looked heavier than it should, and he realized

with a sinking feeling—the elation had already worn off—that
of course Norm would have brought along his carving tools,
which Harry couldn't imagine why the counselors had ever let
him keep, and which meant that they were, essentially, armed,
since between the chisels and the knives they each had steel
and to spare. Well, all right, so they were armed, was that anything to be concerned about? Surely it was no worse than anything else that was happening and equally surely this was the
end for him, his father had been right, he was going to end up
in prison serving big time someday soon—and all because of
friendship and joy.

"Okay, guys, slow down," said Derell in a hiss. "I can see
the boat through the trees." Diving behind a rock, he peered
around it toward the water, and the other three boys landed
beside him.

Any second, Harry was expecting to hear an outcry from the
group, but they must all have been still wandering about blind.
Squinching down behind Derell, he studied the dock over his
shoulder, thinking how absurd this caution was. Motor would
certainly not suspect that anything was wrong if four of the
boys came down to the water; he would simply assume that
Linda had sent them over with a message, or that the boat was
needed back at camp. He thought of saying as much to Derell,
but decided not to. That wasn't what Derell wanted to hear.

"Here's what we do, guys," said Derell in a hoarse whisper.
"Stan and I will go first. We'll run straight for the boat and try
to sneak up behind Motor and take him by surprise. If we don't
manage it, at least we'll distract him and then Norm and Harry
can come up behind. We tell him we're taking the boat . . .
we'd better make him think we have weapons of some sort, I
guess . . ."

"We do have weapons," said Norm. "I brought my carving
tools." He squeezed out of his day pack and unloaded it onto
the ground.

Motor had been bending over the engine, making some delicate adjustments. Now, as Norm distributed his knives and

chisels to everyone, warning them not to cut themselves and above all not to drop or lose the tools, Motor straightened up and went to the cabin where he flipped a couple of levers and turned the key. The engine roared to life, a little louder than usual because the engine cover was unhitched and turned back on the deck, and then it settled down to a slightly uneven mumble. Motor left the cabin and returned to the engine, where he bent down again; this time the adjustments he made had the effect of quieting the engine and smoothing out the rough sounds. Norm handed Harry a small chisel, which he slipped reluctantly into his jacket pocket, wishing that he could wrap some moss around it so there would be less chance of getting killed accidentally if he tripped and fell.

"Okay," said Stan. "Let's go." And at a run he and Derell took off for the boat.

Before they had covered ten feet, Motor looked up and saw them. He waved one oil-coated hand, and turned to shut the engine off.

"Anything wrong, kids?" he called out, then. "Whoa, slow down, it's all right."

But Derell and Stan didn't slow down, they speeded up, and Harry saw that he had better put some steam on himself. Motor wasn't one of his favorite counselors, but the bewildered look on his face as he stood staring at Stan—a cannonball of angry energy who was now hurtling toward Motor with a large chisel in his hand—was enough to make Harry feel very sorry for him, and even as he and Norm, puffing, tried to catch up to Stan and Derell, Harry attempted to smile, so that he, at least, would be a reassuring sight. But Motor did not see the smile. Stan had reached the boat and, having leaped over the thwart with one hand on the gunwale to land on the engine deck with feet spread apart, was sticking the chisel against Motor's chest and saying, "Don't say anything, mister, and you won't get hurt."

Harry rolled his eyes. The line was "Don't make any sudden moves and you won't get hurt," or "Don't do anything stupid and you won't get hurt," but "Don't *say* anything and you won't get hurt"? What kind of a command was that? One that Motor, in any case, ignored completely.

"Are you kids playing some kind of a game?" he asked.

Stan glared at him.

"No game, man. We're comman . . . comman . . . we're taking this boat, and there's nothing you can do about it. So start the engine."

Motor looked incredulously at Stan and said, "Linda told us you were on the wrong diet. 'Meat and more meat, that's what Stan's up to,' she said. 'He's an Eskimo, for Christ's sake,' said Ian, and I said, 'How can any food be the wrong food?' Now I know what she meant."

"Just shut up and start the engine," growled Stan, and Harry—who was by this time standing beside him doing his best to look as if he weren't there at all—shrugged his shoulders apologetically when Motor looked over at him and said, "But you're an Eskimo, too!" as if that either explained everything or made the matter more murky still. Then he turned to start the engine. Had he been any other counselor on the island he would have at least *tried* to talk the kids out of it, warned them about the dire consequences they were letting themselves in for, both by running away and by stealing the boat—certainly a felony, no two ways about it, the boat must be worth twenty thousand dollars—but since he *was* Motor, Harry thought despairingly, he had a grip on mechanics and nothing else. Harry followed him over to the cabin, with half an idea of whispering to him to for God's sake sabotage the boat or something, but Derell came with them, and Harry couldn't find an opening.

He really could hardly believe that this was happening. Threatening a counselor with violence, forcing him at the point of a knife to help with an escape attempt—these actions went so counter to everything that not just he, but all of the guys were used to. Sure, they had all committed crimes before, but the crimes had always been against either property, or friends, or adults who were strangers, never against grownups they knew—never against people with authority over them.

The engine roared suddenly to life and the boys, except for Harry, cheered. The cheer was a tinny, rather pathetic sound, he thought, especially with the afternoon sea mists beginning to roll in and, swirling in the air, to make ghostly shapes and peculiar symbols that were really almost ominous. Stan commanded Motor to get out of the boat, and then ordered the other boys to untie the lines, while he positioned himself at the helm, putting himself in charge. After a few false starts—he ground the engine so that it sounded as if it had just been dropped from a great height onto a field of small boulders, and then he accidentally put the boat into reverse, so that they almost ended up on the beach—he managed to get them moving in the right direction, out to sea. Waving derisively to Motor, Derell shouted over the sound of the engine, "So long, motherfucker!" as Motor looked stolidly after them.

Once the boat had pulled around the first finger of land, though, Harry began to feel exhilarated again. There were no buildings in sight now, and the dock had disappeared into the mists behind them. The gray-wacky cliffs, plastered with sea gulls, and the wrinkled waves, fresh and sharp as tinfoil, all of these gave the scene a delightfully newborn look, as if this really were a beginning. There was nothing here, nothing but the sea and the sky and the four boys, moving at breathtaking speed through the water, which sliced away before them as they journeyed. The rapidity with which the wind pushed past them seemed to help it carry smells; salmonberry and seal, muskeg and whale, salt and earth, oil and sunshine, all of these seemed to be riding with them in the boat as it churned and slapped and fizzed its way forward. Derell and Norm and Stan were almost delirious with joy, whooping and hollering and throwing things—ropes, tackle, buckets, cans—overboard in an attempt to find expression for their feelings, and while Harry could not participate in this inchoate demonstration, he leaned his arms on the railing, and, bracing himself there to resist the motion of the boat, grinned and watched the pilot whales that gathered, curious and friendly, at some distance from the wake of the trawler.

Suddenly, the engine began to choke. Stan moved the controls backward and forward and Derell shouted, "Come on, fucker, come on!" but to no avail. After choking for a time, the engine died, and the boat, its forward momentum lost, immediately turned sideways to the waves, which started to slap and shove it with a force greater than Harry or any of the other boys could possibly have predicted. From a feeling of total control and utter happiness, the four passengers of *The Reach* passed immediately to a feeling of panic and despair; not only was the boat not moving away from Chenega and toward freedom any longer, it was moving sideways toward capsizing, and the sickening thud that rocked it every few moments as it climbed yet another trough, only to be met at the top of the climb with a rolling wave, was almost as jarring to hear as it was to feel. Harry joined in the general and confused attempt to get the engine going, ripping off its cover and staring at the mysterious and labyrinthine mechanism, while Stan fiddled with buttons and switches on the dashboard and Derell studied the gauges. It was Derell who finally drew a conclusion.

"Fuck," he said. "It looks like we're out of gas."

After the incredulity and the name calling had reached its zenith and begun to die, Derell pointed to first one and then the other gas gauge, demonstrating that both the main tank and the auxiliary tank were, in fact, absolutely empty.

"Just like Motor's head," said Stan, and they all agreed heartily with that, not liking to admit that it might have been their own and not Motor's head that was empty in relation to this tragedy.

Meanwhile, the boat was moving and at least it was moving toward land. That the land was Chenega was unfortunate, but it was better to be moving toward Chenega than toward the open ocean and if only the boat would edge its way to shore without actually capsizing, the whole event might have a better outcome than Harry had expected from the beginning. He got the single paddle from under the hooks that held it to the port side, and leaning gingerly over the gunwale, poked at the surface of the water. This didn't seem to do any perceptible harm, though it was doubtful that it was doing any good either, but Harry continued to jab at the water while the others sank down on their haunches in various attitudes of despair. The last thirty feet or so would certainly be the trickiest. There was a good chance that the boat would get stove in on underwater rocks and swamp, and that the boys, three of whom could not swim, would be left floundering in the grip of the shore wave—not surf, but still pretty strong.

The boat, however, adrift in waters that were, by lucky accident, unusually free of rocks and other underwater pitfalls, edged its way right to the beach without any mishap, and when it was in about three feet of water, Derell, the one swimmer among them, leaped over the side and grabbed the bow rope, guiding them all the way in. *The Reach* ground against the sand with an unpleasant noise, and as it turned entirely sideways to the waves the other three boys leaped out as well, getting up to their knees in water. They took their time and a good deal of care in securing the boat to the nearest strong tree, but since the tide was still coming in, this was not going to be a great help in an hour or so, when the hull would be adrift again and able to bang freely in any direction that the waters suggested. Harry was feeling slightly sick, whether from the rhythm of the sea or the situation that he found himself in he didn't know, and as the other three began to confer about their next course of action he went off by himself to sit on a log, and wish that Jack were with him. While he sat there, watching his three fellow *Homo sapiens*—the triumph of evolution—gesticulating wildly as they argued about which absurd and irrational plan to attempt next, he actually found himself blushing hotly, and he hid his head in his hands.

PART THREE

The Triumph
of Evolution

20

■ AMOLIA STOOD IN the center of the clearing, about twenty feet from Spike. Ten minutes had passed since Trent had thrown himself into the log cabin, and in that ten minutes Spike had done nothing at all except talk, intermittently, to the door. He had threatened the door with just about every atrocity imaginable, but the door had not responded, and now he seemed to be at a loss, unable to think or move. It wasn't as if he had never taken an ax to a door before, though of course he had just chopped padlocks, but something about being on this island seemed to be sapping his brain. So far, Amolia had not interfered with any of Spike's decisions, no matter how odd, but she was beginning to see that someone competent was going to have to take charge of things or they were all going to be in real trouble. Wherever all the other people who lived on Chenega were, they were not going to stay away forever, and when they came back they would come back together—fifteen or so against three. Obviously, either she and Spike and Wesley should be long gone by then, or they should be in a defensive position; they should not just be standing out here gaping and talking to locked doors.

Part of Amolia wanted very much to leave, before something worse happened to them all. No matter how absurd her father might be at times, no matter how much he could plague her, it seemed unfair to subject him to danger when he didn't even know what it was. But part of her wanted to take charge, to lead this operation like a guerrilla queen, and it was this part of her that was bigger, and stronger, and more intense. Although she felt frightened, she also felt stimulated; a clear wind was blowing in from the sea, the colors on the island were bright and clean, the pebbles at her feet seemed very much alive. Everything was waiting, crisp, around her, and all she had to do was to take charge. For some reason Spike wanted to kill the counselor named Lorne Burke. Well, she could probably arrange it. What would happen then she couldn't yet say.

At that moment, Wesley got up, and lumbering as always, approached her.

"Dearest," he said. "Light of my life. You know I would never question anything you do, indeed no, you know I trust you, but I do wonder, just a little . . . that is to say, adventures are nice, adventures are what the world spirit wants, but don't you think, perhaps, this is going a bit far?" He waved his arms in the air, the gun still slung down his back, and then, humbly, put his arms down. "Weapons, I mean? And locking people in?"

"He locked himself in," said Amolia. "Surely that was his own choice."

"Well, yes, when you put it that way," said Wesley. "But *why* did he, you see what I mean? He must . . . the truth is, he must not *like* us. We must seem to him like . . . like bad guys or something." Wesley ended by peering at her appealingly; without his glasses he could probably hardly see her.

"Bad guys," said Amolia. "Oh, I doubt that, Wesley. Besides, what do you want us to do?"

To that, Wesley had no ready answer. He bit his lower lip earnestly, looking at the ground, and then he raised his eyes and studied the gray sky overhead. While Amolia, amused, watched him thus engaged for a moment, she heard what she thought were voices, raised away to the south. But the sound faded quickly, and though she listened intently, putting her finger to her lips so that Wesley would not interrupt her, she could hear no more, except the slight rustle of the waves behind her, and farther away, the generator. Still, imagined or not, the voices stirred her to action.

"It's time we took cover, Spike," she said.

Spike did not respond. He walked up to the locked door of the cabin and gave it a furious kick, then howled as the pain from the blow shot into his toes and up through his foot. He lifted the injured leg, hopping on his good one, and in a sudden senseless fury aimed his gun at the cabin door and fired. Then he dropped his gun and picked up his foot instead. Wesley, shocked, began to wring his hands and moan, and Arnold hopped to his feet and called out, "Trent? Trent? Are you okay, Trent?" and suddenly Amolia heard voices again, this time for sure and much nearer, and she turned toward the sound to see, emerging from the woods, a gang of what appeared to be about twenty people, all of them running toward her.

Arnold was behind her, still calling "Trent," so, pointing her gun at the human pack—which had dissolved, for the moment, into a thick-looking man, about five or six teenage boys and a woman, the woman Amolia had met when she'd come about a teacher—Amolia backed rapidly toward the sound of his voice, reached one hand behind her, grabbed him, and held him in front of her body, under the gun. At the same time, she called out, "Wesley! Spike! Get into that building down there, and fast!" and then she stopped, waiting until they had done as she said, Spike limping a little as he ran, and Wesley still wringing his hands and moaning. When they were both safely in the doorway below her, and when Arnold had finally noticed that the grip with which she was holding his chest to hers could hardly be called a friendly hug, she started to drag him backward with her toward the building, all the while watching the group that was coming toward them.

Or that had been coming toward them. Now the woman was telling the boys to stop, and she herself was standing staring at Amolia with a look of the sheerest astonishment, one hand unconsciously raised to tug the end of a pigtail, the other slipped into her back pocket. Just as Amolia reached the door and was about to drag Arnold over the threshold with her, the woman—Linda, Amolia remembered her name was—gathered her wits enough to say "Wait! Stop!" but Amolia did not want to stop, and, viciously tugging at Arnold's arm, she wrenched him around until he was inside the building and then backed in after him and bolted the door. The woman now called out, "Let's talk!" much to Amolia's satisfaction.

Spike, by now, had gotten a grip on himself and was ready to take credit for what had happened. Looking at her thoughtfully, as if he were measuring her worth in some deep chamber of his cerebral cortex, he nodded approvingly and said, "Good work, Mole. Quick thinking and now we're snug as bugs. You're quite the terrorist, in fact, quite the little terrorist."

"We'd better secure the building," she said, ignoring his praise. "Spike, why don't you find out what's in that room? Wesley, you guard the windows on the west. I'll take the kid and guard the north. Is everyone's gun loaded?"

Spike looked at her for a minute, as if debating protest, then headed off toward the closed door. Amolia, without letting go of Arnold, examined the building, which was apparently a schoolroom. Desks and books and globes and posters were strewn about the place in considerable disarray, and in this, and in its size, it resembled the school Amolia had gone to as a child. That had been a one-room schoolhouse on the outskirts of Anchorage where the teacher had been, of all things, a man, a man with an enormous white cotton handkerchief, or several of them, into which he would blow his nose at least once an hour—each time in a different spot—and then peer into the newly used portion afterwards as if he were reading the secrets of creation there. The children had called it his snot rag, and had tempered their natural respect for male authority with an odd kind of contempt for its ever snotty nose. Amolia herself had loved school then, and had striven always to have the neatest and best projects, the ones that were pinned to the bulletin board as an example of the very best work the children in her school could do—and since, ninety percent of the time, she had succeeded in her attempt, she thought even Mr. O'Grady's snotty nose far from objectionable. Now, picking up a text that looked as if it had been designed for her and her cohorts at Crow Lake Elementary, although it was used, it seemed, by boys in their teens, she felt a wave of revulsion for her small self, so earnestly trying all the time to please, to pour her life onto paper. Still holding tightly to Arnold's arm, she dropped the book on the floor. It hit with a sound like a shot, scaring Wesley, whose shoulders heaved in surprise.

"Goodness," he said, recovering. "Amolia, this is so very . . . that is, I don't think your mother would have approved of all this." Forlorn, he stared at her as if, in fact, he did not think her mother would have even recognized her daughter.

"Probably not," said Amolia. "But she didn't stick around long enough to make her feelings known." She picked the book up and set it back on the table in defiance.

But the reminder of her mother had a bad effect on her mood. Suddenly, Amolia felt vulnerable; whereas a moment before she had felt that with a gun in her hands and a wall at her back she could hold out forever against those people who were constantly trying to shove her around—or, more precisely, to shove her down, and once she was down, to force-feed her with their roast-beef certainties and their baked-potato irrevocables—now she felt that she was in danger. She had to maintain a ceaseless vigilance against both hope and acceptance, and for a moment, in some peculiar alchemy, she had felt that she was allowed to hope as long as she was risking her life. How much she had liked that feeling she knew only when it was fleeing; desperate to recapture it, she looked around for something to do, and found Arnold in her arms. A pitiful-looking creature, just the sort her father would make friends with, but he might serve two purposes in this desperate transaction.

"Go on," she said to him, shoving him away. "Go sit in that chair. Spike, have we got anything like rope?"

Spike did not answer immediately. He had managed to break the lock on the closed door, and had discovered the radio phone beyond it. This he had set to work to destroy, and he was still furiously banging the instrument against the surface of the desk, tossing it against the wall, stamping on it with both feet, though it was now so thoroughly dismantled that pieces of it had popped off and shot through the air with enough force to land twenty feet from the scene of operations, where Amolia could see them—little pieces of copper wire and black transmitter, crushed red plastic. He did not stop until Amolia went to the small office and said, quietly, behind his back, "Spike." Then he turned around and looked at her, with an icy delight in his eyes.

"I think it would be a good idea to tie up the kid," she said.

Spike tilted his head judiciously to one side and, ever so slowly, jerked it. "Might at that, Mole," he said approvingly. "Might at that. You got any rope? You see any?"

"That's what I was asking you."

"You could rip something up," said Spike. "A curtain or a sheet."

"Or a shirt," she said, "which we have more of."

"And then," said Spike, slowly warming to the idea, "then we'd have him just where we wanted him, a hostage. We could trade him for anything—food, supplies, ammunition, even another hostage . . . like Burke. That's what you mean, Mole, Burke, isn't it? You don't believe he's not here, either, eh?"

Amolia had no feelings one way or the other, but she nodded in agreement with Spike's words. Actually, now that she thought about it, it did seem likely that Trent had been lying back in the trailer, when Spike was making a fool of himself pretending to be a Vietnam vet. But yes, there was that, too; they could certainly work a trade, if it came to that, though only if they made absolutely certain that Arnold did not escape first. She opened the drawers in the desk before her, and found nothing but paper and music books.

Well, the kid's own shirt would do. Now he was sitting in

the chair as she had instructed, looking remarkably happy still, with a goofy happiness that had, to Amolia's mind, an insectlike quality about it; thus would the giant bees look when they ruled the world in man's place. As Amolia approached him, Arnold looked up and said, "Trent's okay, isn't he? I mean, I didn't hear him answer when I called, but he would be all right, wouldn't he? He told me when I kneeled on a toad once that's why I have a little wart family on my knee."

"Take off your shirt," said Amolia. When Arnold just looked at her, she said again, "Take off your shirt." At that, Wesley left his post at the window, and, coming closer, said, "Amolia, do you really think—"

She interrupted him. "Wesley, we need you at your post by the window. Spike and I can take care of this together."

Wesley, still indecisive, dithering a little, sidled back toward the window as Spike approached him. And as Spike approached, Arnold turned to look at him rather than at Amolia. Spike came up until he was within two feet of Arnold, spread his legs apart, clasped his hands around his gun and said to Arnold, "You do what we say because we're in charge now. Understand?"

Arnold, struck dumb, nodded slowly and began to unbutton his shirt.

When he had it off and his pale, childish flesh was revealed beneath it, the two nipples little pink puckers in the expanse of hairless white, Amolia took it from his hands and tried to rip it up. But the material, a plain, tightly woven cotton with several cabbages on the front in shades of green, resisted her efforts to find a purchase on it, and after regarding this for a minute, Spike pulled out his knife and—telling her to hold the shirt taut in the air in front of her—slashed at it until it was ragged. The pieces were easy to detach from each other, and when she had a small pile of them Amolia knelt down behind Arnold's chair, grabbed his two small hands as they dangled unsuspectingly beside him, and wrenched them behind him and through the widely spaced spokes of the back of the chair, until one was on either side of the central spoke. Then she bound them together, pulling the cotton cloth cruelly tight by twisting it once it was in place around his wrists, willing him to whimper. But he did not, even though the flesh was bitten by the cotton, and Amolia tied it finally as it was. Then she tied each of his ankles to one of the front legs of the chair, and, somehow unsatisfied even with that, tied each of the knees also, so that the legs were held tightly all along their length. She tugged the bonds to make sure they were all secure. At last she stood up.

"Don't fall over," she said. "No one will pick you up again."

While she was tying Arnold, Spike had made a last check of the schoolroom, and was now standing looking out the windows on the west side. Amolia went to join him and saw that the new arrivals had gathered near the stone fireplace on the far side of the clearing. For a while, they had been shouting Trent's name and now they were all talking animatedly, and pointing in various directions as if disputing the next course of action; unwillingly fascinated, Amolia watched, wondering why Trent hadn't come out. Tired for a moment, she leaned against Spike, who put his arm around her shoulder and squeezed it.

To her astonishment, Amolia felt excited. It had been literally years since she had made love, since clearly anyone who refused to ingest food or drink through the central orifice of the face is unlikely to want to accept the corporeal world through any other orifice either. But now she felt a slight pressure in her vagina, a tiny heat, and such was her amazement that she turned to stare at Spike's face, beside her shoulder now, and smiling. No longer did he seem quite so bumbling and directionless as he had since they had arrived on Chenega, the essence of power diffused; instead he seemed the forceful man she had first seen back in Anchorage. She knew that this was craziness, but she did not resist it, and she slipped her arm around his waist and her hand into his back pocket. They stared together out on the crowd of people in the yard, still gesticulating and pointing, just as two teenagers at a movie might stare at the screen without really seeing it, while they explored each other's bodies with their hands and when Spike turned to Amolia and breathed heavily against her neck, she turned to meet his breath and planted the lightest, most delicate kiss on his top lip. His lips were moister than she would have suspected, and she kissed him again, with moisture on her own, and by now the slight pressure in her groin was more than slight—the heat that overtook her weakened her. But she didn't care, everything was melting, and after the second kiss she turned her face into Spike's shoulder, and kept it there while Spike ran his hand down her back, and while she, conspiratorial, pressed a small and hungry breast against his arm.

21

◼ OUTSIDE, IN THE CLEARING, Linda was staring at Ian with growing exasperation. Although she had her hands thrust into her back pockets and was thrumming her fingers furiously against her buttocks, this did not relieve her feelings as much as she might have wished; now, if ever, was a moment when she should have been knitting, taking her unleashed energy and weaving it into shape, but aside from the fact that it would have looked perfectly ridiculous under the circumstances for her to stand in the midst of the encampment with a pair of socks in her hands, she did not, at the moment, even know where she had put them. She couldn't think of everything at once.

This was really too much for one day. First, four of her kids had run away in the midst of—irony of ironies—a trust game, and just when Linda had thought that things were going very well, too, and that even Kennie Dugan, with his selection as line leader, had taken a tiny step forward in his growth; and then she and Ian had come back at a lope with the remaining six boys—Lorne, of course, had gotten lost on the way—to find that for some insane reason the secretary from the Anchorage office had decided to become a terrorist, and she and her two crazy partners had taken another boy hostage. Then it turned out that Trent was also missing and might or might not be in the school with Arnold. Finally, here was Ian, suggesting that Trent was probably strolling happily down the beach somewhere.

"No, no," said Linda. "That's what I'm trying to tell you. Trent would never have just gone for a walk and left Arnold alone here. What do you think he is, crazy? They must have *done* something to him."

"So what did they do? We heard a shot, right? Kill him?"

"*Kill* him? *You're* crazy. Kill him?" Inarticulate with rage at Ian for voicing this horrible possibility, Linda suddenly started to shout.

"Tre-e-e-ent! Tre-e-e-ent! Where are you?" and as she did, so did all six boys, who were still milling around them, and Ian, who tried to project his voice louder and farther than anyone else: "Tre-e-e-ent! Tre-e-e-ent! Tre-e-e-e-e-e-ent!" If he were anywhere within three miles of the camp, this he would surely have to hear.

Linda was turning round and round in circles now, trying to look everywhere at once. The truth of it was that—more than exasperated—she felt actively guilty; if it hadn't been for her and her trust games, none of this would ever have happened. Her feverish attempts to precipitate trust, all her nutty projects—what did they add up to now but the fact that this was her fault? And she was frightened. She cared about Trent— where *was* he?

"Tre-e-e-ent!" she called again. "Tre-e-e-ent!" And at last Trent appeared.

The gunhouse door had opened inward, and his figure filled the doorway. Looking slightly dazed by the sudden light, or by the events that had overtaken him, he moved forward into the clearing, while Linda went running to meet him. He had the Savage 30.06 with the scope slung over his right shoulder, the shotgun cradled at his left, and in his right hand was the revolver, pointing toward the ground. The front of his coveralls bulged with what were, apparently, several boxes of ammunition, so it was a metallic and rather bulky Trent whom Linda threw her arms around to hug.

"Thank God," she said. "Thank God you're all right." Trent grinned and kissed her on the lips.

By now the boys had joined them, and were shouting questions and comments. Ian had arrived, too, and he was shouting even louder than the boys, and Linda was forced to let go of Trent and step back out of the melee. Only then, as she stood on the edge of the circle, did she really understand about the guns. Although she had noticed the rifles the strangers were carrying—indeed, she had more than noticed them, she had *perceived* them, in their entirety, she had *known* them, somehow, from the moment she ran into the clearing—only when she saw Trent laden down like someone getting ready for the shootout at the O.K. Corral did she realize fully the gravity of the situation. And Trent. Trent. What did Trent know of guns? She would still have to be responsible.

"Okay," she said, in a voice loud enough to penetrate the roar. "Here's Trent and we know where Arnold is. Now, we probably should have checked on *The Reach* first thing, before we even came back to camp, but we didn't, and just in case they haven't taken the boat, we should send a runner down there to tell Motor to radio the police. A *responsible* runner. Emory, how about it? Then the rest of you boys should go back to the bunkhouse and stay there."

"And *stay* there," said Ian in agreement.

"The last thing this situation needs is any more loose JDs," she added.

"Or dead ones," said Ian grimly and with great satisfaction. This was just the kind of thing he loved, the kind of experience that he would later be able to transmute into a story for some other group of boys, prefacing his remarks with that traditional phrase, "You're not going to believe this, but . . ." Only in this case—at least so long as he told the story on Chenega—they *would* believe it, because undoubtedly it would become part of the great myth of the camp, the day the *real* criminals came to the island. That was another aspect of the situation she hadn't thought of, the fact that the boys would learn all the wrong lessons from it.

"What we mean, guys," she said more gently, "is that we know you'd help if you could, but you can't, so at the moment the biggest help you can be is to go and make yourselves scarce and safe. Get the fire going in the bunkhouse, lock the door, and settle in for the day. Come on, now. You can watch out the windows."

"These guys are pretty crazy," Trent added. "They shot at me through the door of the gunhouse."

"Through the door? Shot at you? Oh, bad, bad, mon. Very serious," but through the braggadocio in their voices—a braggadocio that seemed to have been earned merely by *hearing* about a dangerous event—Linda thought she could sense an undercurrent of fear, for which she was very glad.

"You really want me to go to the boat, mon?" asked Emory. "I should put on running shoes, first, then. But little Arnold, you think he'll be okay?"

"We'll get him back," said Linda.

Emory and the boys started trailing away now, with Ian saying "Step on it!" and Linda suggested that she and Trent walk back to the big stone fireplace, and there, behind the safety of its bulk, figure out what to do. The fireplace might have been made to be a barricade, because when they were settled on the ground behind it, there was still room for one or two more people to take cover if that should be necessary. Trent started setting the guns down onto the hard-packed dirt, neatly placing each one on the fire shelf and piling the ammunition beside it. As usual, he was wearing a chambray shirt, coveralls, and his perennial docksiders, and this uniform—which Linda would have imagined a peculiar contrast to the weapons—looked instead strikingly appropriate, as if it had been particularly selected to show them off. In fact, Linda thought that Trent had quite an air about him as he dealt with the guns, an air of sexuality that she had never really noticed in him before.

"Well," she said. "What do we do now? Does survival mean shooting these nuts?"

"No. I don't think so. They're not that dangerous. They just have to be handled correctly. Boy, was I glad to hear you guys shouting. Here, do you want the revolver?"

No, she didn't want the revolver. What she wanted was a formulated plan. Irrational as it might be, she still felt accountable for the situation that had developed, and she felt she should be responsible, too, for getting rid of it. The total failure of her trust games to achieve that happy spirit of cooperation which she had sought had set her back more than she had liked to admit at the time, but now she saw that, in a way, she still had an opportunity to triumph. Perhaps she had been a little premature in supposing that she could bypass force when dealing with JDs and other criminal elements; perhaps what they needed—as Trent had so clearly intuited when he brought out the guns—was not, actually, less reliance on corporeal expressions of power, but more familiarity with the physical laws of the universe, the laws of earth and water and force and counterforce. Maybe they didn't, in fact, need to learn to trust other people more—indeed, why should they, when you came right down to it?—but simply to trust their own bad instincts less. So what she needed—what they all needed—was a plan.

At that moment, Ian returned from shepherding the boys to the bunkhouse. He'd apparently just realized that unless the big boat was *not* gone, with the criminals in the schoolhouse there was no radio phone to be had, and the counselors were on their own; it was up to him and Linda and Trent to resolve the situation. He offered to sneak around and shoot the crooks through the window.

"Oh, for heaven's sake," said Linda. "What is this, a goddamn war?" But before she could pursue this line, the bunkhouse door, which had slammed closed when Ian came out, slammed open again and Emory emerged, in his running shorts, a ragged sweatshirt, and his beloved blue denim shoes.

"Well, mon," he called out to them. "I'm going. I'll be back as soon as I can," and without waiting for an answer he turned and began loping effortlessly down the trail through the trees until, in very short order, he had disappeared from view. Just before he did so, Trent, who had been staring at him in alarm, as if the mere sight of someone trying to act normally in this abnormal situation was enough to make him doubt his own sanity, murmured, "Where's he going, anyway?" but he said it, apparently, to himself, as the bottom of Emory's shoes kicked up the dust. Then he handed Linda the Savage 30.06.

As he passed it to her, Linda noticed once again how long and beautiful his hands were, and then, as he started to give Ian the shotgun, she interceded, and said, "No. The revolver's less accurate. Give that to Ian. I mean—he's probably a good shot." Actually, she meant just the opposite—that the revolver would be less dangerous in his hands than the shotgun if he should be insane enough to use it—but Ian took her words as a compliment.

All right, then. They were armed. The next thing, clearly, was to make contact. If the criminals were like normal criminals, they would probably shortly emerge with demands of some kind, demands for a boat, food, money, and immunity—in exchange for the hostage, Arnold. Linda seriously doubted that even his own mother would think Arnold was worth all of those things, but she would be happy to provide the criminals with the entire package just to get them off the island now.

"Okay, guys," she said to Trent and Ian. "Okay now, listen up. I'm going to call out to the nasties, try to get a bit closer to the window. I'll offer them terms—the big boat, food, immunity, etc. In exchange, we want Arnold and the radio phone."

"How can we give them immunity?" asked Trent.

"We don't *have* the big boat," said Ian. He knocked the cylinder out of the revolver, checked the bullets, and flipped it back in.

"We don't?" said Trent, puzzled. "What's going on around here, anyway?"

What was going on around here, anyway? Linda realized that of course Trent had probably thought that when she had said, "Just in case they haven't taken the boat," she was referring to the criminals, not to the boys, who he probably hadn't even noticed were missing. So, downplaying the irony of the trust-game escape as much as she could, she told him what had happened. Trent covered his right eye with the palm of his hand and looked mournfully off into space.

"Kennie Dugan," he said. "Oh, damn him."

In a way that was justified, though in a way it was not—she had actually kicked Kennie's leg to shut him up—but she did not explain the details, just looked down curiously at her rifle. She hadn't held a gun since she had worked for a time as a cook in a hunting camp on Kodiak Island, and one day she had seen a brown bear circling the camp when all the hunters were gone. She had hoped, briefly, that it would come close enough for her to shoot it—the irony had appealed to her—but the bear had ambled politely away when it discovered the evidence of humans. She had never liked guns much, actually, probably because she associated them with the silent reproach of her father's pistol, and even though it had been more than ten years since she had left the basement in Seattle, she had never acquired the fondness for firearms that was the sign of the true, naturalized Alaskan.

"Oh, well," she said after a while to Trent. "Kennie Dugan. Yeah. But to get back to the point, I'll try to talk terms, get them to send someone out."

"What if they don't want to talk terms?" asked Trent. "To tell you the truth, as far as I can tell, the only thing they want to do is to kill Lorne. Or at least the skinny guy does. He seems to think that Lorne is some guy called Burke he knew when he was here—as one of the kids."

"Jesus," said Ian, looking genuinely scared. "He came all the way back here for that?"

Linda, however, felt strangely relieved at this latest revelation. As long as she had imagined that the Anchorage office secretary had taken such a dislike to the organization she worked for that she had come out here to wipe it off the map, the whole situation had seemed bizarre almost beyond comprehension. But that one of the kids should grow up and still be one of the kids—well, it was too bad, but it was logical, it was what one had to expect. Still, there was no way to see this as actually *encouraging,* and a sagging feeling settled on them all.

Then voices echoed in the woods behind them, and Linda looked quickly over her shoulder, turning her head with such force that one braid whipped through the air in front of her like a riding crop. She saw a very sheepish-looking Motor and a sullen-looking Lorne emerging from the woods together. Lorne took a deep breath, fingering the rip in his right shirt sleeve—which, in his struggle with the woods, had grown considerably larger—but just as he was about to speak, both Trent and Ian hissed at him, "Shhh!" Trent added: "Get down on the ground, both of you. There's a couple of crazies in the schoolhouse with guns. They seem to want to kill someone."

Motor immediately threw himself on the ground, but Lorne stayed just where he was. He stared at them all as if they were huge green insects, and strangely enough, Linda—who in the past had not felt much for Lorne but dislike—felt pity for him at this moment. Trent, who had, after all, been the one to get this fact firsthand, was also the one to explain it.

"They want to kill *you,* in particular, Lorne," he said, sounding annoyed. "You can get down or not, whatever you want."

Lorne's hand came up to stroke his beard and he looked a little dazed. But as he slowly lowered himself to the ground, the dazed look was already giving way to one that was rather more peevish, and he seemed to think it was all too typical that he should be picked on in this way. Linda waited until he was well down, and then summarized the situation for them as they lay there. Already she was thinking about it in capital letters, The Situation, as if it were, like other proper nouns, something that could be bought, sold, traded, destroyed. Motor listened patiently and then said, curious, "But why did this happen the very same day those kids decided to run away? You know about that, don't you?"

"Of course they know about it," snapped Lorne. "That's what her trust stuff led to."

Normally, this would have pissed Linda off, but just now she felt obliged to take it, felt it was imperative that she get them out of this by staying calm and clear-headed. She was glad, though, when Motor, who didn't care a whole lot about the trust games and who was eager to give his account of the Great Escape, described the way the boys had roared off in *The Reach*, while Ian kept lifting up and dropping the revolver, taking quick beads on the windows of the school. After describing the trouble Stan had had even figuring out how to work the boat's controls, Motor got to what he clearly considered the best part of the story.

"But this is the catch. The boat was out of gas. It had maybe three gallons left, max."

Though it seemed to delight Ian and Trent and Motor, this news did not fill Linda with elation. Her plan—which was mainly to keep the crazies talking until help arrived from somewhere else—hinged on a functioning boat. She had been counting on the boys getting caught as soon as they reached the dock at Whittier or Valdez—plenty of fishermen and dock workers at both ports knew *The Reach* as the Chenega boat, and they would be distinctly suspicious if they saw it pull in without any adults on board. Then they would presumably send a police helicopter to make sure everything was all right on the island. Now, with *The Reach* sure to end up drifting idly around on the ocean, there was no certainty of rescue at any point in the foreseeable future, and while that might have been all right if they had indeed had a boat to trade with the crazies—as she thought all this out, she set her rifle vexedly against the fireplace and thrust her hands into her back pockets—it was not even slightly all right when the only thing she had in her hand was a bluff, and the crazies were stuck on the island. On top of that, it would be dangerous in a big way for the boys to be adrift without power. Without even realizing that she was going to do it, Linda let out a groan. Then, with very little difficulty, she convinced Lorne that he should get out of sight—his own hide being the most precious thing in the world to him, he was willing to comply for once with orders—and Motor volunteered to go with him to the bunkhouse, since emergencies were not his forte. Then she got to her feet, stomped around to the front of the fireplace, and shouted to the criminals in the school.

22

■ WESLEY STARTED AT Linda's shout and trundled over to the window. He wasn't used to standing up for so long at once—usually, if he wasn't sitting on a bench waiting for something to happen, he was sitting in a train or a bus, or, most recently, a canoe—and now, ever since they had left the dining room and that really quite delicious meal that the tall man—Trent?—had made for them, he had been continuously on his feet. Although he would have liked very much to sit down at one of the desks that were so conveniently scattered around the room, he knew perfectly well that Amolia wouldn't approve, and that she would tell him to get back up. His post by the west window was, she had said, the most important one of all, since he was looking out directly on the fireplace, behind which Trent and some of the others were now hiding. Wesley had seen them hide, and had seen the load of guns that Trent had produced for them, and he had seen, as well, two more men appear. He had chosen, however, not to report all this to Amolia, for a vaguely defined reason which he formulated in his own mind as not wanting to bother her with trivial details, but which he knew perfectly well deep down had more to do with what he feared might be her response. In fact, he had, without quite realizing it, even drifted away from his window.

Amolia had been acting strangely ever since they had reached this island—to what end Wesley couldn't imagine. Surely there was no need for all this fuss, all this defensiveness and animosity? Surely they could have worked everything out amicably together if they had tried? When Micah had begun to destroy the radio, stomping on it until its very heart was squished across the bare boards of the floor, Wesley had felt as if his own heart were being stomped on, and now, with Micah and Amolia leaning together and, well, fondling each other, he felt as if he were being choked again. He cleared his throat and shifted his legs to try and relieve them of their ache, then he resolutely turned his back on his daughter and peeped out the window to see where the shout had come from.

That woman was standing there, hands on her buttocks, glaring angrily in his direction.

"It's time to talk terms!" she shouted again, and Wesley, with abrupt decision, turned away from the window, and addressed a remark to his daughter. The voice he summoned up for this remark was sterner than any he had used in recent years—any, indeed, that he had used since the days when his wife was still alive, and then the voice had never been directed toward his wife or daughter but only toward those people who might possibly hurt them: cab drivers who came too close to the curb when they stopped to pick up the Hannahs, telephone repairmen who left treacherous loops of wire on the floor after they had installed a new phone in the Hannah living room. There had been a time, in fact, when he had used this voice often, a time when things had *mattered* to him, and when his voice, or the lack of it, could make a difference in the progress of events. Now, although he very much doubted that his voice could make an actual difference in the events that were brewing in the room, he thought perhaps he would use it anyway, out of sheer exasperation.

"Amolia," he said. "This annoys me. I have done my best

with you all my life, I have let you go your own way, trusting in your innate sense of goodness, and now . . . now you tie up innocent children!"

Slowly, Amolia separated herself from Micah. As far as Wesley could determine, she had been nibbling on his ear lobe, while his hand roamed around her chest. She looked at Wesley with some astonishment, and then she tried to speak, but all that would come out was "W-w-w-e-e—" Whether she was trying to pronounce his name, or ask him what he had meant, or whether she was about to swear at him, Wesley could not tell, but he didn't wait to find out as he spoke again, this time to Micah.

"And you," he said. "What kind of a way is that to behave to my daughter? And in front of a child, too? You may think you can get away with anything just because you have a gun, but let me tell you, they have guns too, and I'm sure they're prepared to use them."

Apparently the information he had just conveyed about the guns was far more important than the way he had conveyed it. Entirely ignoring Wesley, both Micah and Amolia rushed to the front window and peered out of it, first stationing themselves carefully one to either side of the sash, so that their heads popped out from the opaque safety of the wall only for a second, simultaneously, as they darted looks through the glass and then at one another. Apparently unable to believe their eyes, they went through the same routine again, and then leaned, as if exhausted, against the wall. The whole time they were engaging in this elaborate safety precaution, Wesley was standing in full view of the fireplace and the people behind it—and indeed the woman had not yet returned behind it, but was casting puzzled glances at Wesley and the popping heads while she chewed on the end of her braid.

"Well," said Wesley when Micah and Amolia had finished their inspection. "You see what I mean now?"

Micah gave him a nasty glare, then turned his attention to Amolia.

"They never had guns when I was here. I don't like this development at all. But Mole, we keep calm and nobody gets hurt. We keep calm and we *think*." He furrowed his brow and stuck his finger in his ear, but apparently no thought was forthcoming.

Then, "No," he went on, "they never had guns when I was here, but of course that doesn't mean they wouldn't have them now, of course it doesn't. The world's a tougher place, tougher and meaner every day, and everybody's getting guns, it only stands to reason. So here's what we do, here's what we do, Mole. We got to sneak up behind them, that's pretty clear, we don't want to get involved in a shootout. And I'm the man—I'll do the sneaking. You stay here and keep guard."

Impossible as it was for Wesley to see the sense of this plan—what was Micah going to *do*, for heaven's sake, after he had snuck up behind them?—at least it meant they would be getting rid of Micah for a while, and perhaps once he was gone Wesley would be able to talk to Amolia about the situation, talk to her as he probably should have talked to her years ago, when she had first begun to develop her skinniness. For, after all, wasn't it the same kind of thing, really, tying little children's legs and refusing to put bread into your mouth? They were both acts of—well, of meanness, that was the truth—of meanness, and an unwillingness to let things take their proper course, an aversion, really, to the promptings of the world spirit.

Meanwhile, Micah was saying goodbye, attached to Amolia once again. Wesley had been so wrapped up in his thoughts for a moment that he had not seen who initiated this latest bout of exploration, but he supposed it had been his daughter, since Micah seemed eager to be off. After one last kiss, he disentangled himself, checked his rifle, and then made his way to the window in the small office at the very back of the schoolroom, which looked out into the woods. This window he carefully raised. Then, with one leg on the sill, he said, "Okay, Mole, take care of things while I'm gone. Any luck, I'll be back in an hour." Then he dropped to the ground with a thump.

Well, that was certainly a relief. Yes, it certainly was. Wesley couldn't, now, remember why he had ever started traveling with Micah to begin with, that day when they had both been sitting in the Fairbanks trainyard, although he seemed to recall that he had taken a liking to Micah's little harmonica. His harmonica, for heaven's sake! And on that, spitty and dented, all this hung. Wesley saw in his mind's eye a group of people dangling from strings, hanging on a huge harmonica which arched across the heavens, white clouds darting round and about them. Micah, indeed! Wesley was certainly not a religious nut of any kind, but there had been a time, before he had understood about the world spirit, when he had read the Bible regularly, and in there the *real* Micah had said, "He hath showed thee, O Man, what is good! And what doth the Lord require of thee, but to do justly and to love mercy and to walk humbly with thy God!"

Amolia had gone over to the window to say goodbye, and now she turned back to Wesley. She looked puzzled, and a little hurt, at Micah's sudden departure, but more than that for the first time seemed uncertain about just what she should do next. Wesley couldn't help himself. He said, "That man is not a good influence."

But at this, most of Amolia's defiance returned. She stood very still, her arms hanging motionless at her sides, then looked at Wesley as if from a great distance. "I don't care what you think," she said.

"Amolia," Wesley returned forcefully, "I say the same to you. I am now going to untie this child, this Arnold," and in a move so bold it practically took away his breath, he pushed his glasses down off his eyes again, strode over to the chair where Arnold was bound, and kneeled behind him on large and cranky knees. He half suspected that his daughter would try to stop him, but she did nothing except stand there with her arms limp.

So far, so good. All right, what next? How could he untie these knots? He paused a moment to wipe imaginary sweat from his eyelids and then peered down at the tight tangle of shirt and at his hands, which reached out toward the tangle. These hands were hardly the ideal tool with which to approach such a knot, but he gripped a piece of cotton gamely and started tugging and pulling.

At this Arnold, who had not been gagged, and if he had wanted to, could have been chattering all along, suddenly leaped to life like a toy with a new battery and said, "That was my shirt, the one my mother sent me. It had little cabbages on the front and everything."

"I know," said Wesley soothingly. "I know. But we'll get you another shirt, just as soon as we possibly can." And as he struggled with the knot, finding first that his fingers did not work, and then that his fingernails did not work, and finally bending down like some enormous child bobbing for apples to place his teeth directly on the hard lump of cloth, his thoughts went back to a Halloween party that he and his wife had given for the neighborhood children when Amolia was a small child. He had bustled around the house for days beforehand—much slimmer then, and more elegant, he was nonetheless already capable of putting on a fine bustle at times—making sure that everything was perfect, that the donkey on which the tail was to be pinned looked like a real, though silly, donkey, that the witch's-hat candies were each bedecked with three distinct pieces of sugar ribbon, and that the spare bedroom, which they had turned into a house of horrors, had a new bulb in its nightlight so that the children would not get *really* scared by the skeleton that hung in one corner. Wesley wondered if Amolia still remembered that. He supposed she probably did not.

Finally, the cloth began to slacken, but not before Wesley's teeth hurt. He pulled the knot loose, revealing Arnold's little wrists, deeply bitten into by the bonds, the insides of the grooves pink and angry as the blood quickly rushed to fill them. Wesley rubbed the wrists vigorously, and then took them and lifted them back into Arnold's lap. Without getting up, he inched his way around from the back of the chair to the front, and there he began to attack the four leg knots, which Amolia had not managed to get quite as tight as the one on Arnold's wrists. Wesley, now an old hand at fifth-column activities, wrestled them quickly into nothingness.

But even when he was free, Arnold didn't get to his feet. He seemed to be in a state of shock. Wesley patted his knee and said, "There you are, you're all right now. I promise it won't happen again," and at that Arnold stirred, picking up one knee and then the other, and lifting his hands to hold them in front of his face. The child was still shirtless, and since the stove in the schoolroom had not been lit that day, the room was damp and chilly, so—apparently unconscious of his action—Arnold wrapped his arms about his chest and started bouncing in place, and then he rose to his feet and started hopping, and while he hopped he said to Wesley, "I don't understand all this, this is like a movie or something but I never thought I'd be in a movie, or that movies were so cold." His voice, because he was hopping, seemed to shoot up and down, back and forth, now squeaking, now rumbling, and his peregrinations took him over close to Amolia, who backed away with what Wesley could only hope was remorse. Wesley put down his gun, took off his shirt, and helped Arnold into it. It was so big on him that it hung below his knees, and the sleeves had to be rolled up to their midpoint before they cleared Arnold's wrists, but the child stopped hopping as soon as the shirt was on him, now a calm and goofy little tree. Wesley sighed happily, freed of many burdens, and prepared to light a nice fire.

23

■ BY THE TIME Spike started sneaking through the woods around the camp, the escape crew had begun the long trek back to the lower dock. With the senseless stubbornness that had dictated their movements from the very beginning, Stan and

Norm and Derell had still decided to run for it; they were going to steal a can of gas, take it back to the boat, start the engine up, and try to make it to Valdez. Vainly, Harry had attempted to argue them out of this scheme, pointing out that Motor would already be almost at camp, where the first thing he would do would be to call the police from the radio phone in the schoolroom. And even if Motor, for some unimaginable reason, was not able to get back to camp, five gallons of gas would never take them as far as Valdez; they would be adrift again on the ocean. But all this good sense had fallen on deaf ears, and Stan had told Harry at last to go ahead and be a coward if he wanted to.

Harry groaned inwardly as he struggled through the woods, thinking of what lay ahead. He *didn't* want to be a coward, had never wanted to be a coward, but by this time he was really beginning to feel like one. He dreaded getting back to camp, where Linda and Trent and Ian and Lorne would be waiting for an explanation of his temporary disappearance, but he dreaded *not* getting back just as much. He should have done one thing or the other, not both, stayed or really run for it; in his desire to provide for everyone's happiness, he'd been making stupid compromises all his life. In fact, he was in the midst of one right now. He had suggested that they take a shortcut inland—in his rush to get back to camp to face the music he didn't want to face—and not only had the shortcut proved almost impassable, but he was afraid that somehow they'd missed the lower dock, and that at any moment Stan and Norm would realize this and turn their murderous rage on him. Right now they were in a small, open meadow, full of marsh marigolds and marsh buttercups, where the layers of moss and peat were quaking beneath their feet like Jell-O and the apparently shallow pools of water that they tried to walk through were actually bottomless quagmires. Norm sank into one up to his waist before he grabbed a dead branch and hoisted himself out, cursing, and Derell fell flat on his face on top of an enormous skunk cabbage.

"Fuck this shit," he shouted when he got up. "Where the fuck are we, anyway?"

"Yeah," said Norm. "You got the answer, Harry? Where is the fucking dock?"

"It must be in back of us," said Stan, sitting down."You fuckhead." And they all, in turn, collapsed.

Trying to make himself look small, Harry sat down near a fair-sized rock. He was wet from the waist down; his sneakers were full of water; and the salt from his short dip in the sea had started to make his crotch itch. All that remained to make this day a complete misery was to be turned into a scapegoat by these three idiots, and placing his squishy shoes in front of him, and wrapping his arms around his knees, he wondered bleakly what he was going to do so this would never happen again. He was always going along with things that were . . . well, things that he didn't believe in; but he had no idea what he could do about that, when life was so complicated. He seemed to be able to see two sides to every question, or two paths of possibility, where all the other kids could see only one, and that was what had always made it hard, hard to know what to do. As he sat, keeping still in the hopes that the other boys would, in the throes of their own miseries, forget him, he became aware of a crashing in the bush, a crashing that moved first closer and then farther away, sometimes pausing for a minute and sometimes growing near hysterical in its fury and determination. Just as he had decided that it must be a bear, and that they should all make a rapid exit on the far side of the meadow, a man emerged about thirty feet away and stopped dead when he saw them. He was wearing army fatigues and dark glasses, although the mistiness of the afternoon, coupled with the darkness and the denseness of the woods, combined to produce a gloom so profound that it was surprising he could see through them, and it didn't take the gun hanging from his neck for Harry to iden- tify him immediately as another in the long line of psycho- pathic personalities who had surprised Harry for sixteen years with their sudden and dynamic appearances.

While the man fumbled with his gun, checked the action, and then swept the meadow with the barrel, Harry went through a rapid series of reactions. First, his heart started to beat very fast and his breath came in quick short puffs; then the world grew brighter for him, as if a flashbulb had gone off in the meadow; finally, his whole body felt smooth, smooth and light and fragile. At the end of all this, he forced himself to relax, and gave the man a casual smile.

In this, he did better than the other boys. Stan and Norm, who were sitting on marshy hummocks in brutal little piles of exhaustion, looked at the psychopath as if they had already been shot by him in the guts—their faces registering shock, horror, and terror in about equal amounts—and Derell, who had sprung to his feet when the crashing first sounded in the woods, actually let out a half-shriek, half-squeal when the gun crossed his part of the clearing. Then he started to run, his long legs and arms flapping out to the sides like a moose's limbs in deep snow, and—predictably—the crazy had barely had time to call out, "Stop, or I'll shoot!" when he tripped again, this time landing on his back. Obviously the other boys thought, some-how, that this man was the police, and that he had come in response to their Great Escape. As they saw it, that escape had miraculously been reported already and commandos had landed on the island to search the woods for them and destroy them where they stood, and this seemed to Harry so typical of their kind of ego—an ego that believed everything that happened in the world was a direct consequence of its own tortured exist-ence—that he could not help but be amazed, in addition to all his other feelings. Stan, Norm, Derell: they were the living, breathing embodiment of the guilty conscience. To Harry, it was inconceivable that they could not distinguish a criminal from a commando—and that they were equally scared of the latter.

Harry himself felt pretty scared; in fact, he felt terrified. But he knew this kind of scared, had felt it many times before, and he knew that it wasn't the kind of scared that you could run from, the way you might run from a bear. It was the kind of scared you feel when your best friend is counting on you to give him an airtight alibi and you're not sure, not quite, that you'll remember it correctly. It was the kind of scared you feel when someone is trying to make you angry, and you hate them so much that whatever happens, you don't want to give them the satisfaction. It was the kind of scared you feel when a whole roomful of people is looking at you. There was an element of delight at its bottom, delight in having such a challenge.

Derell, meanwhile, lay on his back, heaving like an upset turtle. When he dared at last to turn himself over, water dripping from his hair and his collar, he called out, "You got me! Don't shoot!" while Stan and Norm, side by side, had raised their hands over their heads and were now calling out sullenly, in alternation, "All right, so you got us," and "Fuck, they always get you in the end."

The man seemed obviously at a loss, though somewhat gratified by the attention. Now he said, "On your feet. Over by that rock," and pointed to the one near Harry. Harry, consequently, stayed where he was, while the others shambled over to join him, and he took the opportunity to empty out his shoes, and wring out the bottoms of his pants legs. He needed to find a good opening line, one that would calm the guy down and give himself a chance to figure out what to do next, and as he studied the false hellebore and dwarf hemlock that rimmed his little area of the meadow, his oldest line came into his head like a flash of sacred lightning.

"Hey, mon," he said. "How much that gun cost?" and while it finally seemed to dawn on the others that this man was not a cop, the man relaxed and said with real interest:

"Seventy-five dollars. Why?"

About half an hour later, Harry was leading the way to the boat. As he and Spike had talked, it had quickly become clear to Harry that Spike represented a real and active danger not just to the physical health and the mental happiness of the present inhabitants of Chenega, but more than that, a threat to the future, to the whole idea of the program. And since Harry liked Chenega as much as he had liked any place he'd ever been, and felt strongly, too, that this was a good program—better than vegging in prison—he had a double incentive to get Spike away before he did any damage. And that he could do real damage Harry had no doubt, because, although Harry had been around violence all his life, he had never before been in the presence of someone who emanated such clear, crazy hostility, whose physical aura was composed of so much that was unpredictable and dangerous.

But somehow, he didn't know how, he had convinced Spike to leave the island. He had told him that *The Reach* would hit sixty miles an hour, and that in it he and his friends—whom Spike had boasted of—could sail all the way to Seattle. He had said that it was essential that the other three boys go back to camp to make sure that nobody came down to the lower dock until Harry and Spike had managed to hit it up for gas, and, thin as this logic was, he had even managed to make the boys themselves believe it. Now he and Spike had just gotten through the densest part of the forest and were emerging into woods of Sitka spruce, and Harry was still balancing on a delicate tightrope as he managed to keep Spike talking. "I know, I know," he was saying now. "People can really be bastards."

"Yeah," Spike agreed with a gleam of excitement. "Even when I just walk into a town, go to a store, people aren't too happy about it. They look at me like I'm weird."

"Well, if you go into town in that outfit, mon," Harry said, purposely misunderstanding.

"No, no, even when I'm dressed regular. It's my face they don't like, I guess." He looked at Harry sideways as if daring him to say that he didn't like his face much himself.

"Hey," said Harry. "Faces. Look at mine." And he grinned, trying to look as cheerful as he could.

Spike almost smiled back. But instead a hard little twitch made itself evident at the corners of his mouth and then he said, "I think it's all those wanted posters that make them stare."

"Are you on wanted posters?" Harry asked flatteringly.

"Oh, yeah, shot a cop, they don't like that, don't like that at all. But I never asked for trouble. Just asked to be left alone. But they don't leave you alone, do they? Cops bust down my door, two months ago, shooting, made my wife lose her baby. I never asked for trouble. I don't like violence. Other people force it on me," and as he said this, through the spell that Harry was weaving he suddenly felt a shaft of the deepest sympathy penetrate, and he said to Spike softly, meaning it:

"I know. It's hard. Life's hard."

But as he struggled through the woods, talking, half his mind was still elsewhere. Spike's partners, he had gathered, held the schoolhouse, and that meant that they held the other radio—did it make sense, given that reality, to let Spike take *The Reach?* He didn't have much choice, that was the truth of it; if he could only get the big boat *going,* at least the danger would be gone. In the meantime, he *had* to keep this guy talking. Now what on earth could they talk about? Criminals? The ocean? School? Survival . . . that would do.

"I bet you're an expert on survival, mon," he said conversationally, as he tripped and stumbled his way through the worst tangle of devil's club foot they had yet encountered, slipping on the rocks that lay slick beneath it. "You look like a man who knows his way around the woods."

"You bet I do," Spike said, slipping also. "What do you want to know?"

What did he want to know? he thought. How to survive *Spike.* But he could hardly say that aloud, and since, obviously, this man knew no more about survival than he did about opening a charge account, it might be dangerous to ask him questions. Maybe he should tell him jokes, jokes from *"Call Me Joe."* When the Survival Expert had come, some of the other guys had had all sorts of questions they wanted answered, not about

SSST or whatever it was, or who blew his head off when, but about things like edible plants, and snares made from wire or string. But Harry couldn't remember any of that stuff; in fact, he couldn't remember much of anything except the story about the Indians. Maybe he should tell him that.

By now, they had gotten through the worst part of the woods and were within sight of the beach. Harry, as he told the joke— "So they fired off a round of three shots, and then they fired another round"—led the way through the last stretch of bush, impelled by a sense of urgency he didn't understand. Spike chose to ignore the question about survival at the end of the story, so Harry went on to say, repeating verbatim the Survival Expert's words so far as he could remember them, "Although, really, there *is* no expert on survival, right? You're the only expert on your own survival. 'Cause what's good for you isn't worth the powder to blow it to hell for me," and suddenly, with a surge of speed, he pushed his way out onto the pebbled beach, relief flooding him at the sight of the five-gallon gas can sitting brightly on the dock.

Once they had the can, it was a surprisingly short jaunt back to the boat, which was tied just where the boys had left it, though rather more unkemptly. The tide, which had continued to come inexorably in, had loosened the hull by lifting it forward, and the bow, as a consequence, was now swinging wildly back and forth on its line. But Harry and Spike managed to get the lines tight enough to pour the gas into the auxiliary tank— although they were delayed in this task for a moment when a helicopter flew overhead and Harry had to reassure Spike that it could have nothing to do with them. Then, as Spike stood at the wheel, Harry pushed the boat off into the sea, the smell and the moving freedom of the ocean making him feel exhilarated once again. When they were clear of the beach, he started the engine, and then, with the wind picking up, pulled out two yellow slickers, handing one to Spike. He was delighted to see that Spike too looked relaxed, happy to be out of the woods, and as they started moving back around the island, as if there were a purpose to their lives, Harry felt suddenly, he wasn't sure why, that he would never be a coward again.

24

■ WHEN SHE FIRST HEARD the clicking of the helicopter's blades, Amolia was sitting at a desk. After her father had untied Arnold, the two of them had gone off to the far end of the room, where they were sitting in front of the window that looked out on the fireplace, playing cat's cradle again with Arnold's piece of string. Ever since Spike had gone out the back window, Amolia had been expecting the people from the clearing to burst in the front door, and the fact that they hadn't yet done so seemed to her almost unpleasant, portending a long and mysterious wait for events to occur over which she—as the weakened partner—would have no control at all. Because she was weakened, there was no doubt about that, not so much by Spike's disappearance as by the love play they had engaged in before he departed. She had sworn long ago that she would never do anything of that kind again, and she had been right. All it had taken was one moment of weakness for the whole construct of her life to start trembling, shaking apart.

Suddenly, the *chut-chut-chut* of a helicopter sounded, very close, and Amolia got to her feet. She stood in indecision, holding the back of the wooden chair with her hands, her body taut and upright. Her father was standing by the window now, excitedly flapping his hands and gurgling to Arnold, and Arnold, a look of goofy interest on his face, was pointing in front of him with a hand still entangled in string. Stiffly, Amolia moved to join them; her heart was pounding and she had difficulty breathing, and although she could not imagine that this was the police—the radio phone lay in shreds on the floor, after all—she also could not imagine that it was not, and it seemed to her now that she had known all along that this was how it would end, how it must end, that she would be dragged off to prison, and her father, too, for no reason in the world. The helicopter was roaring as it hovered over the main part of the clearing, kicking up dust and small pieces of paper even though it was still thirty feet off the ground, and Amolia looked up to see, on its side, the large red cross that marked it as medical.

Like an elevator, it began to descend. Amolia felt as if it were pushing her toward the ground. She supposed that Trent had been telling the truth after all about Lorne Burke being in the hospital in Anchorage, since this was, presumably, the return of Burke, but although she was relieved that the helicopter was not the police, she did not see how that fact was going to help her much in the long run. The helicopter would certainly summon them unless she did something to prevent it. Maybe, after Burke was disgorged, she could take the pilot hostage, and demand that he fly her and Wesley and Spike to somewhere on the mainland, somewhere they could immediately lose themselves in large crowds of people and therefore escape from what seemed to her right now the inevitable result of the day. But how could she get close enough to the pilot to get him at gunpoint? And wouldn't those others all shout to him first?

The helicopter landed, thunk, but there was no cessation of its whirring. From her post at the window, Amolia could see the people behind the fireplace waving their hands frantically as the door pushed open and someone's legs emerged. The fireplace crew did not leap to their feet, however, probably because they did not want to risk getting shot, and the man climbing from the machine did not even see them as he turned and shouted something to the pilot, then jumped to the ground with a spurt of strength. Now the pilot would turn the engine off, the fireplace crowd would get together with the pilot, and she would be caught, and sent to prison, there to live out her days.

But, to her amazement, the pilot did not shut off the engine. Instead, he lifted off again into the sky, with no fuss or bother;

one minute he was perched on the ground, the next minute he was soaring delicately into the air again. Now the people at the fireplace were going crazy; one of them actually stood up, careless of any danger, and started whirling his arms around in enormous circles, as if he were trying to lift off too. But the helicopter just banked, turned, and chutted off into the west, banking and turning again as it cleared the edge of the island and then sailing off toward the mainland.

Suddenly, Amolia was in action. Without even knowing that she was going to do it, she grabbed Arnold, who stood beside her, and, shoving him along in front of her, almost ran toward the door of the schoolroom. The guy who'd just landed— Burke—was still standing in the middle of the clearing staring after the helicopter and then at the shouting gang behind the fireplace; he was only twenty feet from the school, and closer to Amolia than to the others. So, once outside, she did run, pausing only once to twist Arnold's arm when he stumbled in front of her and then running on until she had reached his side, where she stopped, one arm wrapped around Arnold's throat, the other holding the gun. This child Arnold was no good to anyone, but Burke—Burke would be a real prize for Spike when he got back.

He was staring at her in total amazement, which gave her great satisfaction, then he started to speak, but she said, "Shut up," and he actually closed his mouth again. From the fireplace she heard shouts and groans, and when she looked over she could see that the man doing the helicopter imitation had stopped it, and had sunk down onto his haunches again. She turned enough so that she could see both them and her new hostage and then she called out, "All right. I have a proposal."

That shut them up, all of them, and they waited in silence to hear more. Until she spoke, she didn't know what she was going to say, but when her mouth opened, the words simply came to fill it.

"I want to exchange hostages. This little wimp for that muscle man. That's the first point of the plan."

Even in her own ears, the words sounded ugly, and she wondered what had been happening to her. She had always been so delicate, so proud of the catlike grace with which she could move through life, disarranging little, straightening much, not committed to any course of action but denial. The house she had carried on her back as she went through the years was a diamond house, hard and glittering as a drill, and now, naked before the damp mists of day, she was standing simple and revealed. In a way, she felt frightened. In this wide clearing, dusty and littered with wood chips, she was a hundred times more visible than she had ever been before; her blood tingled, as if it were full of air.

"The second point," she went on, the words entering her mouth by express delivery from her unconscious, "is that when Spike gets back from wherever he is, you let him into the school, with no questions asked. Or I shoot the hostage, whichever one it is."

There was still silence, though it was a deeper, more horrified silence than it had been a minute or two before.

"And the third point of the plan," she went on, "is that you find us a boat. I don't care where you get it or how you get it, but you find us a boat and you don't tell anyone, the police or anyone, about what you need it for. You bring the boat back, fill it with gas, and then we all get in and leave. When we're a couple of hundred yards offshore, we'll let the hostage jump."

The man who had been spinning his arms called out to her, "How do we know you'll actually do that?"

"You don't," Amolia said. "But why would we want to keep him?"

From the fireplace she heard the voices, murmuring anxiously together. Amolia was staring now, however, at the muscle man. He looked very young, hardly a man at all, and it dawned on her as she studied him that Spike must have confused something somewhere, since clearly *this* Burke could hardly have been born fifteen years before, much less have been tormenting Spike. But what did that matter? He would do for her purpose.

He had a bandage on his shoulder—she could see it peeping out from the V in his shirt—and he had a hard, mean look on his face. Right now, he was actually glaring at her, in fact, as he made his hands into fists and held them clenched in front of his chest.

"Okay, lady," he said. "You better let that little guy go."

"I'll let him go when I've got you where I want you," said Amolia.

"Oh? And where would that be?" sneered the young man.

"In his place," said Amolia.

But from the woodpile there was another shout. This time it was Linda's voice.

"Don't do it," she called. "You might rip your shoulder open again. Don't do it. We'll think of something."

"Oh, yes?" said Amolia, tightening her grip on Arnold's throat until his hands went a little limp and he made soft choking noises beneath her arm.

"Okay, okay, here I am," said Burke. "Just let the little kid go."

Amolia dropped her arm, and Arnold slipped out from under it. Running, his legs banging as they struck the ground, he headed for the fireplace and disappeared behind it, making inarticulate noises of relief, as Amolia moved in to secure the other hostage. Spike wanted Burke dead, and although this man was almost certainly the wrong Burke, at least she would be able to show Spike, when he returned, that she had used her time alone to good advantage. But she realized that she really did not want to touch her new hostage, didn't want to take hold of him as she had taken hold of Arnold; it was fairly clear that with this kid she would have no muscular advantage, that he might even overpower her if she got right up close. So she just moved around behind him, poked the tip of her gun into the small of his back, and said, "All right, now, let's move."

With the man on her gun like a fish on a spear, she started to move cautiously toward the school again. Looking up, she caught sight of Wesley watching her through the window, a look of infinite and almost pitiful distress on his face. He was wringing his hands again—she was surprised that they were still firmly attached to his wrists, he had been wringing them so often lately—and, in an exaggerated pantomime, he was mouthing words at her from behind the glass, not making any sound, since surely she would have heard him if he had just spoken up a bit. She couldn't be bothered to try and make out what he was saying; she just shoved her hostage impatiently in the back and told him to get on with it.

But before they had gotten very far, she heard Linda calling out again. "Jack! Jack!" she said, and, almost unwillingly, the man on the tip of her rifle looked back, and said, gruffly, "What?" and though Linda launched then into speech, Amolia didn't hear her, she heard only the name, "Jack," so naturally used, so unselfconsciously responded to that she could not but be certain that Jack was in fact this man's—this boy's—name, and that therefore he was not a victory for her coolness in the face of tension, but simply an error, a pointless exchange of one person for another, the exchange, in fact, of a child who was as helpless as a caterpillar for a young man who looked quite capable of making intelligent trouble if she took her eyes off him for a second. Wildly wondering whether there was any way she could trade him back, she glanced over her shoulder at the fireplace, and at that moment, as she looked away from him, Jack twisted in front of her and got his right arm into throwing position, then tossed a punch directly at her chin. She turned back just in time to see it coming, but not in time to do anything specific about it, except to execute an evasive wiggle so that the blow, when it came, landed not directly on her chin but instead on her cheekbone. It didn't hurt at all—later she would discover with her hand that it had actually broken the skin and there was blood oozing onto her cheek—but it angered her excessively. A flash of heat not unlike the heat of lust swept through her body as she watched Jack double over with the pain of his own punch, almost crumple, in fact, before her eyes, and without thinking, without pausing for a minute to consider the consequences of her action, she took the stock of her gun, drew it back and smashed it into Jack's shoulder. The crumpling which he had already been engaged in when she hit him simply continued; he went down to the ground where he lay writhing, his legs folded beneath him.

There was a great silence in the yard. Amolia felt pale and empty. She realized that now that she had knocked her hostage down, there was absolutely nothing to stop one of those people behind the fireplace from putting a bullet through her chest, and yet she couldn't seem to move. Part of her wanted to lean over and finish what she had started, pounding this Jack's body with her gun until it was a bloody mass of pulp lying at her feet, a mass of oozing bone and flesh like the bloody mass of her mother's body, which—though she had never admitted it to anyone, not to her father, not to her friends, not even to the psychiatrists who had gotten their hands on her after she had stopped eating—she had *seen* that day when the earthquake had erupted around her, the whole world then not so much like a field of Jell-O as it was like a soup, bubbling and farting, full of legs and arms and animals and boulders, blood and granite and tar and bones, and she herself just a piece of the soup, a chunk of the viscous fluid of which the world was made and by which it fed its own inexorable and insatiable maw. Her mother's legs had both been severed by the first slab of granite that had sheared off from the front of J. C. Penney's like a bit of flaky pastry, and the blood had come out from the stumps of them like water from an old-fashioned pump. Her mother's head was twisted back on its neck, and Amolia was looking directly into her eyes, in which, though the light was fading fast, there was still a spark of life, of recognition, when the second piece of giant granite had descended, covering her mother like the cheese on top of onion soup, and that was the last she had ever seen of her.

But she did not hit Jack again, because the other part of her was sick. Sick at what she had done and sick at what she was capable of doing, sick of this day and this island and this world, just sick and tired and empty. She had tried everything she could think of, for years she had tried to sweep the sky clean of stars, to dust the ground clean of earth, to take away from the world the terrible power it had to jumble all things together until they were one and people were no more than conduits for its force—but she had failed. Still a conduit for its force, she was acting now in a way that was wrong, that she knew was wrong, and yet she could not seem to help herself. In a world as casually cruel as hers, why should she even try?

The silence went on and on. Even the generator seemed stilled. And into the silence, her father descended; she looked at him as he came to her side. He looked back at her as if he didn't know her, then, awkwardly, he knelt down in front of Jack almost as if he were praying at a shrine, and reached one tentative hand out to touch the blood that braided over Jack's shoulder, his hand as delicate as a flower. And his hand, his tenderness, and the look which he cast on Jack, a stranger, seemed to Amolia so heartbreakingly vulnerable that she thought she would split in two, the sick side of her and the angry side of her wanting to be joined, oh so badly, with the ineffable center that was the real Amolia, the center that was open to change and willing to love. But she could not move, and it was almost in a waking dream that she watched her father touch the young man's cheek with his fingers, then cup his hand along the pale, contorted face.

25

■ TRENT WAS SITTING on the ground with his arms around Arnold trying to make the child stop crying, when Amolia knocked Jack down. He had never imagined, even in his wildest dreams, that Arnold *could* cry, this boy who probably didn't have enough brain cells in his head to make a shirt for a canary, this boy who, more than a space cadet, had from the first seemed to Trent like the entire regiment. Now his whole body was shaking with sobs, and as he crouched against Trent, almost completely hidden beneath the large camouflage shirt that he had acquired, his face was literally streaming with tears, as if all the stored-up tears of a lifetime had decided to come rolling out at once. Over and over he tried to talk, breaking into tiny, gasping stutters, and then trying again, until at last he got out "Oh-oh-oh, Tre-trr-trent, they ripped up my shirt that my mo-mo-mother sent me, the one with the little ca-ca-cabbages on the front," and Trent passed his hand again and again over the boy's hair, which was damp with sweat—the sweat, he guessed, of fear—and leaning down, talking almost into Arnold's ear, he said, "Oh, shh, shhh, it's going to be all right, you're the *best* little guy, the *best* little guy, you were so brave back there, I don't know what we would have done without you," thinking to himself even as he did so that this was the way he had been accustomed to talking with Rae's dog, a big lumbering golden retriever with an earnest disposition and a set of feelings that were easily hurt, and thinking too that it made no difference, and that Arnold was still just a child. His white face, so languid at the best of times, seemed almost to be melting now, trying to paint on its limited canvas all the agony of the world.

"Shh, shhh," Trent kept murmuring, and gradually Arnold's sobs abated.

Arnold had come running straight to Trent the minute he was freed, and Trent had had no choice but to take him in his arms. As a consequence, he had missed most of what had gone on with Linda and Jack, and had looked up only at the gasps of horror that Ian and Linda exhaled, to see Jack crumpled at Amolia's feet. Then, it seemed to Trent that for the last three hours, ever since these crazies had surprised him outside the dining hall, he had been hedging his anger in with restraint, and now the hedge had been torn. He remembered the last time he had seen Jack lying thus on the ground, bloody, and how he had acted to help him—maybe to save his life—feeling empowered by the blood and pain to summon up his best. Then, there had been no one to blame; now there was, and all the power that had been turned, last time, to action, was now helpless to transform itself into anything but rage.

"You asshole!" he shouted at the top of his lungs. "You crazy bitch, don't touch him!"

But by now, Wesley had emerged from the school, and was remonstrating with Amolia himself. Ian—whether at Wesley's sudden appearance or at Trent's outburst, Trent couldn't tell— said, "Shit, shit, shit," and then, clarifying his perturbation, said to Trent, "Great! I had a nice clear shot until *he* came!"

This dangerous statement diverted Trent from his anger, and he looked at Ian with true alarm. But before he had a chance to question Ian about his meaning—surely he could not mean that he had intended to *shoot?*—Linda exploded by his side.

"Ian! What do you think this is, for Christ's sake? We don't want any nice clear shots, thank you. We just want a nice clear solution to the problem," and Trent, as he watched her say this, noticed as if for the first time the cracked green marble of her eyes, her high and generous cheekbones. In a way she was lovely—strong and honest, her face bold and alive. And her defiance, which had previously induced in Trent disapproval, now seemed to him admirable, the sign of a true survivor. Trent himself—Jesus, with his history, it seemed to him right now that he was lucky to still be here at all. Anyone as willing as he was to excuse the world was lucky the world hadn't crushed him.

At that moment, Wesley straightened up. "I'm very sorry," he said to the assembly behind the fireplace, "very, very sorry for what my daughter Amolia has done in her ... that is to say, I think that she is very very sorry herself, but she has been under pressure, great pressure, you understand, and I suspect that for a moment she simply didn't know what she was doing. I think we should get this young man to a bed somewhere,

where he can be taken care of properly, and then we can end all this ... this upset, and things can return to normal." He looked almost absurd as he stood there in his undershirt, his green glasses on their brown chain dangling in front of his chest, his useless and unwanted rifle hanging down his back; but there was an expression on his face of such sorrow that despite himself, Trent's heart went out. He got to his feet, gently pulling Arnold—who was still clinging to his leg—to one side, and said, "Well, that's the first sensible thing I've heard in hours." He was going to go on to say that the four of them could help Jack to the bunkhouse, where they could put him near the stove and see to the reopened wound in his shoulder, but just as he opened his mouth he heard shouting in the woods, and a long drawn-out shriek like a wolf howl.

Startled, he turned around. There were too many people *loose* on Chenega, the coincidence of the crazies arriving and the boys running away on the same day had created too much chaos. The shriek came again, but closer, and suddenly, running at top speed, Derell burst into the clearing, his face bright red from exertion, his pack hanging by one strap, his long hair matted to his head like a cap. He looked wildly around and then—without apparently even seeing Amolia and Wesley and Jack—flung himself to the ground beside the three counselors, so hard that he jammed his arm into the fireplace.

"They're after me," he gasped, as soon as he got his breath. "Stan and Norm, they want to kill me. They've got knives and they threw one, they were mad because they got so scared by that guy and then Harry managed to talk him into letting us go, but they're trying to take it out on me and—" He stopped, as the other two arrived.

Despairingly, Trent saw that Amolia had backed up against the schoolhouse wall when Derell arrived, and was now holding her gun in use position once more. Every time things seemed to regain a little of their sanity, something new and hopelessly unpredictable happened, and turned it all upside down again.

"Oh ho," said Stan scornfully. "Look at the baby, crying to his mommy." Norm nodded agreement, but said nothing.

"You guys are in enough hot water already," said Linda to them grimly. "And this isn't the time or place. We're having a little trouble here right now, in case you didn't notice, and I want all three of you to scram for the bunkhouse, *now*. You'll find Motor and Lorne there, waiting. I'm sure they'll be very glad to see you."

"Yeah," said Ian. "You guys got a lot to learn."

"But they—they were so *mean* to me," said Derell, whining. "Don't you even want to know what happened with that man with the gun?"

"Yeah, I guess we do," said Linda. "But we want to know it quickly, you understand?"

"Well, Harry took him to get *The Reach* and he's going to bring him around here to camp to pick his partners up, and then we ran into Emory in the woods, but he wouldn't believe us, he said he had to go see for himself, so he went on, and then, like I said, Norm and Stan were—"

"Okay. We got it. Now go," said Linda.

"But the boat was out of gas," said Derell, still whining, "and we left it way down around the other side of the island and that man was really crazy, and—"

"Go!" said Trent. "We've got things to do."

It wasn't that he wasn't concerned about Harry; he was, there was just no way he could help him now. But Jack he could still help, Jack there was a chance with, and Trent tried to pick up the conversation with Wesley where they had left it, saying "Shall we move him, then, into the bunkhouse?" But it was too late, the moment was gone. Amolia had regained her command of the situation, and she was obviously not going to let her new hostage go into the bunkhouse or anywhere else, as she backed against the wall and said, "Don't anybody else move. We're taking muscle man here back into the building with us. No," she said as Wesley, despairingly, flapped his arms and tried to interrupt her, "Wesley, stop acting like a goose. If Spike is coming up here in a boat, we need to have some way to cover our retreat. Now help me get him into the building. Take one arm and *you*"—she nodded coolly at Linda—"take the other."

Linda stood up and put her hands in her back pockets. She gazed at Amolia somberly. As Trent muttered, "Don't do it, that woman is a psycho," she began to thrum her fingers gently on her buttocks. "What are you going to do if I don't?" she said.

Amolia said nothing, just stared at Linda with her huge eyes, the irises lost somewhere in the midst of the white, and as they all stood there, a frozen tableau that, Trent couldn't help thinking, might have been labeled "Psychotics Stare at One Another in Alarm," he heard, somewhere in the distance and south of Whale Point, a boat, with an engine that sounded extraordinarily like the engine on *The Reach*. In a flash of something less than intuition he understood that Harry and Spike were now heading their way.

Amolia, too, Trent thought, had understood. She took her gaze off Linda and looked out toward the still empty sea. Linda stopped thrumming, Ian groaned either in pleasure or in pain at the confusion still to come, and Arnold, who had been huddled behind the fireplace still shivering a little, perked up at the sound, peered around the stone, and said, "Trent? Trent? That's *The Reach*, isn't it? Who do you think it is, Trent, are they coming this way, will they save us?"

"Shhh," said Trent to Arnold once again, but now with different inflections. "Shhh, shhh. We'll have to wait and see."

It was funny, he thought, that they all just stayed there, waiting as if for a mailgram. If he had had any sense he would have gotten them into the woods, or even into the bunkhouse, anywhere they might have had some true cover, now that Amolia, with her gaze riveted by the sound of the approaching boat, was no threat. But they all stood there, as if enchanted, under the empty sky.

About a minute later, *The Reach* pulled into sight. It looked the same as ever, unhurt by what it had been through, and at the wheel Harry stood, a yellow rain slicker whipping around him. When he saw them all standing in the compound staring at him, he waved, his hand a gay gesture of happiness blowing over his head, and Trent felt a rush of pride that Harry should still be so calm. Spike stood behind him, his legs spread, looking as if he had been bolted to the deck of the boat—looking, Trent thought, as if he had discovered the Nile. He gestured with his gun to Harry and Harry sharply cut the engine's power, so that as the boat pulled alongside the dock, the engine merely muttered a complaint. Executing a nearly perfect docking, Harry cut the power completely, and then leaped out to secure the bow line while Spike stood bolted still in place. Only when Harry had tied up the boat did he move, silhouetted like a tree on the skyline.

Trent had some trouble understanding what happened next. He was just thinking how easily the situation had gotten solved in the end—packing the crazies off, in his mind, on *The Reach*, sending some sandwiches with them—when he was aware of movement by the fireplace, and the clink of metal on metal. Linda turned to see what was happening, and—following the motion of her body—Trent turned too, but by that time Ian had already stood up beside them, arms outstretched in front of him, pistol pointing toward the sea. The shots that he fired seemed deafeningly loud three feet away, and Trent's hands went up to cover his ears even as he pitched toward the ground. Spike, at whom Ian had apparently been aiming, seemed quite untouched by any bullets as he leaped off the deck of the boat to the wharf, where he crouched along the port side of *The Reach*.

"Are you *crazy?*" Trent shouted to Ian as Spike, trying to hide in the shadow of the boat, pointed his gun uncertainly toward them. Linda stood stock still, staring in wonder at the scene around her, as if she had been waiting all her life to see something so strange and inexplicable—the sure and certain sign, perhaps, of a godless, meaningless universe—and he jerked her hand and pulled her down, so that she landed almost on top of him. Then, far above him and huge, a figure out of legend or folklore—Gretel in the forest, the princess fighting the dragon—he saw Amolia start running toward her father, who still stood beside Jack in the clearing, anxious and bewildered. She was running, she was running, reaching her arms out toward Wesley, to topple him to the ground. She was running, she was running, but Amolia never reached her father; before she could grab him and carry him downward, Spike's gun went off from the wharf. Once it went off, and then again, and though the sound of the shots was ridiculously small and tinny in comparison to the great harrowing booms of Ian's pistol—indeed, so plinky and ineffective did they sound that Trent began to breathe more freely, imagining they could do no harm—Amolia, at the sound of them, stopped in the middle of her headlong rush toward Wesley, tossed her head back like a horse about to whinny for sugar, and then, politely making way for a force more determined or volatile than herself, slid down to the ground. Trent didn't move, but instead of detaching Linda from where she lay half straddling his body, he held her close, his face in her breasts; they lay like the wreckage of a storm.

26

■ SPIKE STILL CROUCHED by the side of the boat, unable to believe his eyes. Things had been going badly ever since that Trent had tricked him, but he hadn't thought they'd get *this* bad, that he'd hurt Amolia by mistake. He was wet from getting the boat pushed off into the sea, and the trip back here in the cutting wind had chilled him to the bone, so that as he crouched, his mouth dry, he was shivering. And to think that he hadn't been aiming for Amolia at all, he had been aiming at that big monster up there by the fireplace, that lug with the high-powered revolver. Now Amolia was hurt, and she would probably hold it against him as if he had done it on purpose—women could be so irrational, he thought despairingly, they didn't understand that in combat you can't always plan every move.

Up there by the woodpile, no one was moving; most of them were down on the ground. Wesley was bending over Amolia, and that kid Arnold had crept out to be beside him, and otherwise not much was going on. Spike wanted to go up too and see how Amolia was doing, to try to apologize to her right away, before she had time to resent him. But he knew he couldn't do that; if that big lug had wanted to shoot him before, when he had been doing nothing at all, standing perfectly innocently on the bow of the boat, how much more would he want to shoot him now? Spike tried to melt into the curve of the boat.

Harry had simply ducked when the shooting started; now he got up and came over to Spike. Ever since Spike had first seen this kid, sitting on the ground in that clearing and asking him, "Hey, mon, how much that gun cost?" Spike had felt a certain interest in him, maybe even some fondness; certainly he had stood out head and shoulders above those other kids, idiots all, and even reminded Spike of himself when he was young. In fact, on the boat ride up here, Spike had actually told Harry something of his past—his real past, not his made-up past—and when he got to the way his father had abused him, Harry had replied, "I know where you're coming from, mon," as if he really did. Now Harry was saying in a low voice, "What a bad business, mon, a bad business."

"I didn't mean to shoot her," Spike said, and his voice, even in his own ears, sounded high and frightened, as if his voice box had been cut out while he crouched there and replaced by that of a much younger man, or one who was nearer death. He felt tired, that was the truth of it, very tired; he had been on the outside for almost eight weeks now, and it was taking its toll on him, this constant attempt to cope with changing situ-

ations, the way nothing was ever predictable or fixed. He had
come to Chenega, after all, with only one intention—to get a
little of his own back, to make that bastard Burke squirm. And
he hadn't been stupid about it, he'd been clever, going with
Amolia to the Action Center in Anchorage to make sure Burke
was still on staff. How was he to know that that wimp in the
office would mix everything all up, or that fate would be so
cruel to him as to hire a different Burke in the first place. Harry
had told him in the boat on the way up here that the Burke
who worked at Chenega now was new. And that meant that
the real Burke, the one who had ruined his life, would never
suffer for it at all, would never even know about Spike. He
thought perhaps his first mistake had been allowing himself to
become involved with Wesley that day in the trainyard in Fairbanks; it was always a mistake to load yourself down with other
people, to be responsible to other people. Things just went better, much better, when you played your hand alone. Although
if he'd been on his own, of course, he never would have had
the chance to meet Amolia, and Amolia—Mole—had been one
hell of a surprise. The way she looked at him with those eyes,
huge and almost shocked, as if she'd never seen a man before;
the way she stood with her arms dangling at her sides, as if she
had no need to *act* to be. But no, next time, next time he'd go
even farther away—across the sea, to someplace where there
weren't any people at all, and no temptation. Just barren rock,
and the surf thundering on the beaches.

Harry was talking gently at his side, and he wrenched his
attention back. "There's nothing you can do about the woman
now," he said. "Best leave her where she can get help, get to a
hospital. You've got the boat, we'll gas it up, then you can just
take off wherever you want. How does that sound, mon? Just
blow the whole scene?"

"Sounds good," said Spike. "Sounds good." But he said it
only because he felt he had to say something, not because it
really sounded good at all. In the first place, he'd never learned
to run a boat—it wasn't one of the skills they taught you when

you were doing time—and in the second place he was just so tired, he wondered how he could ever move again. He had always been puzzled by the way things looked and smelled and tasted, mystified by the laws of the physical world, and now, confronted with all this, he almost imagined that something had been left out of his brain, some essential part that everyone else on earth had. Well, and that was his excuse, yes, certainly, that was his excuse for making a mess of it; something, some little thing, had been *left out* of his brain. And that something, whatever it was—its absence left him desperate. But he couldn't pause, couldn't stop and think—he just had to keep on.

"What about the other guy?" Harry was saying. "Do you want to take him along?"

By now, Spike was so cold that his teeth were actually chattering, and he looked around him, half in a daze, wondering who the "other guy" was.

"The fat man," said Harry. "Shall I go get him?"

"Sure, sure," said Spike. "If he wants to come." He found himself hoping that Wesley would want to come; he wasn't ready to be totally alone just yet.

Harry got to his feet, saying something about the gas, and then climbed up onto the boat. Spike watched him while he unscrewed the caps to the two gas tanks, climbed back onto the dock, unwound the nozzle from the storage tank, and switched off the control lever. Then, looking as relaxed as if he were a gas-station attendant, he bent over until the tanks were full. When they were, he wound the hose again, and said, "Why don't you go on in the cabin?"

Making sure that Harry was between him and the fireplace, Spike climbed to his feet. The long crouching, wet and chilled as he was, had stiffened every muscle in his body, so that he felt he was almost creaking as he unraveled upward. Tired? He felt more than tired, he felt old, old and worn out. He let himself be urged into the boat's cabin, and Harry shut the door behind him.

Then he waited. He could see Harry climb the hill, see him

gesturing to the boat below him; he could see Wesley rise to his feet, and, shading his eyes, look down too. Then, gradually, they all got to their feet and shook their arms, loosening themselves up as if after a bout of hard training, and though all of this went on—as far as Spike was concerned—in absolute silence and therefore with an air about it that was almost comedic, the gestures, not exactly in slow motion but detached from their meanings, gave him no way of understanding the scene except as a kind of crazy salad of despair. As he watched, it occurred to him for the first time that Amolia might be dead, and that whether somebody was your partner or not, killing him was considered a crime; if she was dead, he had no choice, he really had to run for it.

At last Harry started back toward the boat, and at his side was Wesley. They had gone perhaps fifteen feet from the group, with Wesley looking back over his shoulder at every second step, his great whale's head seemingly fastened to the spot where Amolia lay, when suddenly Arnold came apart from the others, running after Wesley at a stumble. Wesley stopped, and so did Harry, and as Spike watched almost incredulously, Arnold began to struggle out of the great camouflage shirt that he was now wearing, and which came down to a spot somewhere below his knees. Wesley ceremoniously took off his gun and his glasses and set them carefully on the ground at his feet, then he pulled the shirt over his head and tucked it loosely in. He picked up his glasses and placed them on his nose, but he did not pick up the gun again, did not so much as look at it. He leaned over to give Arnold a hug. Then he started walking down the hill again, with Harry once more at his side, and to Spike it seemed that the lumbering, awkward old fat man had acquired from somewhere a new dignity; there was an elegance and even a grandeur about his walk that Spike had never before noticed.

When they got to the wharf, Spike opened the cabin door; then he couldn't think what to do next. He wanted to ask if Amolia was all right, if she was hurt badly, but the quality which—from the world behind glass—he had taken for dignity in the old man was really, he saw now, shock.

Wesley stared at Spike as if he were blind and Harry took Wesley's arm to help him onto the boat.

Wesley did not speak to Spike; he just went over and sat down on a bucket. His face appeared to be dripping with water, and after a moment Spike recognized that this water was coming from his eyes, in an eerie, silent stream. Now Harry, with a presence of mind that Spike recognized and admired even in his current state of weakness, was demonstrating the various steering mechanisms to him, and though Spike missed at least two thirds of what he was saying, he did grasp a few of the essentials. Then Harry flipped a switch and started up the engine, saying cheerily, "Well, mon, it's all yours!"

Spike looked at him, uncomprehending. Harry said again, "All set. You ready?" and this time he nodded briskly and said, "Right. So long," although he still felt entirely bemused, and Harry jumped down and untied the ropes that held the boat to the wharf, and suddenly they were drifting free, caught in the hand of the waves. For a long moment Spike didn't move, his hand hovering indecisively at the controls, the lever that would shoot them into action. There was something wrong with this, he knew that much, but just what was wrong he couldn't say. He still felt numb, dazed, and weary, but suspended in a kind of breathless fog-chill silence that made everything about him seem unreal. The very boat on which he stood seemed to him now unreal, fastened to the water by some mystery of attraction as strange as his own attraction to power. Suddenly, with a terrible jerk, he rammed the speed lever backward, and the boat came loose from where it was glued and carried him out toward the sea. Objects fell over on the deck—a bucket full of fishing rods, the empty metal gas can—and he felt that it was he himself who was acting as a counterweight to their sudden collapse; he and the boat were two ends of a swaying scale. Not at all understanding why he did so, he shoved the lever back into neutral and stalked over to these objects to toss them over the side. The gas can floated, but the fishing tackle sank at once into the grayish sea. When he started the boat moving again, much more slowly and calmly this time, he felt freed, as if the lightening of his burden by just a few ounces would save him, in the end, from his own inexplicable desires, and even, perhaps, from death.

They were four miles or so from Chenega before Wesley stirred. Spike thought that they had been heading, generally, south, but it was hard to tell since the heavy though patchy mist which had started gathering in mid-morning and which had been getting thicker all day long prevented any long-distance determinations, and the sun was now completely obscured by clouds. So far, Spike had been content just to keep moving, since he had no real plan of action outlined yet—no idea where, if anywhere, he wanted to go, or what, if anything, he wanted to do once he got there. But he was getting hungry again—the lunch in the trailer was hours behind them now—and that made him remember suddenly that he had failed to bring along any food. The motion of the boat was soothing, and it would have been nice to be able to rest, but he knew he should be making plans. Perhaps they should take to the woods. Or maybe—yes, there was an idea—they should go back, first, to that food cache. What a smart idea that had been after all, leaving some food for emergencies.

Now that he had some direction, he immediately felt better, and when Wesley at last rose from his bucket, Spike was almost his old self.

"Well, feeling better, feeling better, Wesley old man?" he asked, trying to maximize the jovial quality of his voice. "About time you sat up and took notice."

"I'm afraid my thoughts have been with my daughter, Amolia," said Wesley dully. "I can't understand why I left her behind. I think I must be losing my mental capacity, since I imagined, just for a moment there, that the world spirit was directing me to leave Chenega. But now I can't think why it would."

"Oh, sure it would, sure it would," said Spike, though he agreed completely with the old coot's assessment of his sanity. "Nothing you could do there, after all. She'll be well taken care of."

"I have to go back," said Wesley, apparently not even listening to him. "I think she may be dead, you know."

"Dead?" said Spike bluffly. "Not a chance. Don't give it another thought." But he was stunned by Wesley's suggestion that they turn around and go back.

Like a bumper car with a short circuit that couldn't quite be fixed, Wesley started to move about the deck. He would start and then stop, coming to rest in the most peculiar positions, one leg thrust forward, one arm behind him, static until suddenly released. Around and around the deck he went, backward and forward, never stopping to do anything in particular that Spike could see—he didn't wipe his foggy glasses, he didn't tuck in his trailing shirttails, he just stopped, sometimes looking toward the bow, sometimes looking toward the stern, sometimes looking over the port side, sometimes the starboard. Spike—after watching this behavior until it almost mesmerized him, the hypnotic quality of the disjointedness holding him as powerfully as one of those objects whose very existence he could not understand—tore his eyes, with difficulty, away, and started trying to remember where he had left the food cache. It was, he thought, at either the third or the fourth cabin they had stayed in—but where exactly had the cabin been?

Certainly not to the south, where he was heading. No way it had been to the south. No, if he wanted to recover the food from the cache before he took to the woods—and he thought that when he did take to the woods the time would be right for him to part with Wesley—he would have to turn around and head north again, try to retrace his trail almost to the port of Whittier. Without thinking to warn Wesley, he suddenly wrenched the steering wheel around, and Wesley, who had been in the stop position, jerked and fell to the deck. Without even glancing at Spike, he hauled himself up again and continued his bumper-car routine, still colliding with nothing visible. Viciously, angry at Wesley for reasons he did not understand, Spike wrenched the steering wheel again—though there was no reason now to change direction—and when Wesley once more fell and once more hauled himself to his feet without apparently noticing that Spike's action was in any way responsible for his mishap, Spike got even angrier, and slamming the speed lever forward into its maximum position of power, he hurtled northwest toward Whittier, looking for a chance to trip Wesley again.

27

■ FOUR MINUTES AFTER the boat had driven away, Linda was still standing by the fireplace like something that had been conjured there. The moment the last growls of the engine had been heard in the distance, all the kids who weren't already outside had erupted from the bunkhouse, and though Linda usually would have been quick to admonish them and order them back inside, this time she had no impulse to do so; she let them go where they would.

Trent and Ian were still working over Amolia, doing CPR. Ian was giving her mouth-to-mouth resuscitation—looking very wild, even frantic, as for once instead of popping words out into the air he popped breaths—and Trent was doing the cardiac massage, his long, sleek fingers splayed across that bony clavicle, which had been thrust into the air by the extension of Amolia's neck. So far their efforts had produced no results, and although Linda had volunteered, almost in a state of slow motion, to take over one or the other of their tasks, she did not think they had even heard, because they were both still bending down and popping up, bending down and popping up, like those birds that drink water in store windows. Perhaps they, like Linda, were impervious for the moment to the chaos around them—Arnold and Stan and Norm were trading stories, Lorne and Motor were calling for silence, Emory (who had just arrived back from his run to the lower dock) was plaintively asking what had happened, and Harry had assigned himself to Jack, who was still on the ground. Kneeling at his side, talking in a low voice, Harry was trying to help reposition his bandage, through which blood was visibly seeping.

Still Linda could not move. It seemed to her that she had spent her whole life in motion, dashing from one place to another, one plan to another, pushing herself to achieve and change things, moving through life in a headlong rush of will. Why she had thought in a million years that giving Ian the pistol would help matters she could not now imagine; how could she have felt that "talking terms" would achieve results when she knew perfectly well that these people were lunatics? If anyone was responsible for getting them off the island, it was Harry and his superhuman calm.

Now, though, Harry was no longer calm; he was excitedly talking to Jack. Linda saw that Jack had opened his eyes, and in the brief instant that he held them open, taking in the confusing scene around him, Linda imagined that he wanted nothing more than to be back in the Anchorage hospital again, or even in some facility for juvenile delinquents that was a lot more conventional and safe than this one—somewhere with lots of walls and guards and no one to hit you with a gun butt. Then he shut his eyes again, tightly, and only as Harry continued to implore him did he unwillingly open them again, groan, close them, groan, open them, and say, "Hey, bro, *what* is going on?"

"It's all over now," said Harry. "And you're okay. It's too bad about your shoulder, but we just got to get you warm and stuff. Hey Derell! Stan! Emory! Help me get Jack into the bunkhouse."

Linda knew that she should overcome her stupor; it was time for a grownup to take charge. It was obvious that Amolia was dead, nothing could change that, she had been shot in the head, the first thing Linda had noticed when she had been able to notice anything again. And she remembered—a grisly bit of information from her father—that when you're shot in the head with a .22, the bullet will often ricochet around inside the brain pan, doing irrevocable damage ten times over. There was no point in trying any further. But Ian and Trent did not seem to know that, and she could not seem to tell them, and as Jack stretched and groaned some more, she still stood in a daze of new awareness. She had thought, she guessed, that the world could be beaten into submission if only there were more people like her in it, people who knew what they wanted and acted resolutely to try and get it; now she saw that the world demanded a certain deference, and that events had to be coaxed, even coerced toward grace.

Motor had gone around to lift Jack's shoulders, and Harry had taken his feet. Cursing loudly, Jack protested that he could still walko, bro, for fuck's sake, but Emory and Stan moved in now to help with his right side and Linda took his left. Awkwardly, a five-pointed starfish, they waddled sideways toward the bunkhouse. Jack continued to protest until Harry said, "Shut up, mon," and they got him through the door. They settled him on Harry's bunk and then, without being told to do so, the other boys—who had, most of them, followed Jack's supine body from the clearing—began to build up the fire, check on the hot water, and—with lewd jests—cover Jack up with a blanket. Since the situation seemed to be well under control, Linda went back to the clearing, leaving Motor and Lorne to take care of the rebandaging.

There, Trent and Ian had finally stopped. They were both panting as hard as if they had just completed the afternoon run but Ian, at least, was very pale, and his pupils looked as large in his face as if he too had suffered a concussion. Amolia lay sprawled on the ground, her arms and legs squandered among the wood chips, her neck still bent back so that her clavicle saluted the sky. Linda said nothing, just knelt beside Trent, who covered his right eye with the palm of his hand and stared down at Amolia's body as if it were a sea creature that had, after playing merrily in the waves for hours, decided for mysterious reasons to crawl up on dry land and expire at his feet. Ian, on the other hand, seemed panicked, close to the edge of hysteria as he leaped to his feet and began to pace back and forth, starting four or five times to say something and stopping abruptly each time.

Finally, Linda spoke.

"I guess she's dead, eh? I think she was shot in the brain."

"The police," said Ian. "The police will have to come." Linda could not tell if he was terrified or glad at the prospect.

"I'll call," she said. "You guys rest."

Even before she got inside the school she had the feeling the phone was gone. There was an emptiness to the room, a sense that something in it had been misspent, wasted, or worn out. And when she saw the parts of the instrument scattered across the floor, tiny accidents as capriciously arranged as the events of life itself, she realized again but as if for the first time how dangerous those people had been. With two of them still loose on the Sound, and no way to call the police, this was turning into a very long trust game, and as she walked back to tell the men the news, she moved with the concentrated precision of excitement. A fog had continued to gather over the water and she felt for a moment an almost personal animosity toward the moisture, which might conceal anything. The Sound, which had always been so simple and safe, had become a setting for violence. The low bare mountains to which she had finally become accustomed were apparently made of papier-mâché. The trees, sharp and brittle, the water, soft and gray, the shingle, hard and crunchy—they had all the conviction of cardboard, and the sky was full of menace. And then she saw Amolia again and her fear receded. Surely the worst had already happened. Surely this poor woman was all that would be lost.

They decided to carry Amolia into the school and lay her across some desks there, and Linda, reaching to lift her legs, had a powerful sense of déjà vu. First had been Harry, in the trust fall in the woods, when he had fallen backward off the rock as straight as an arrow and as heavy as a stone, and all the others afterwards following; then there had been Jack, muscular and squirming, protesting their sidling starfish walk to the bunkhouse; and now it was Amolia, light almost as a quilt, as bony as if she'd been dead for weeks. Her eyes were shut, but beneath the lids Linda could imagine those huge pupils staring at her, purple irises set into the white. There was something judgmental about the eyes; they asked Linda how she would earn her own good fortune.

But Amolia's body, the first that Linda had seen, was comforting as well. So shrouded in secrecy was the process of human death that Linda had always imagined the body underwent a metamorphosis the moment that life departed from it, that it became strange or ugly, terrifying and stiff, even grotesque and mean. Now she saw that it did none of these things, and that it was, in death, just as it had been in life, only gentler and more serene. Amolia, Linda thought, had had a kind of radiant conflict about her, which emanated from her like a light, and now that conflict had vanished, leaving, still, something behind. What Linda was carrying in her hands right now—as she moved into the school and toward the neatest row of desks, Trent and Ian backing up before her—was neither ugly nor empty, but rather like a brandy glass that retained a few sweet drops.

Together, Linda and Trent held Amolia while Ian arranged the desks. Then they laid the body gently down, as reverent and restrained as if they moving around an altar already blessed, and when Ian and Trent stepped back from the desk, Linda settled Amolia's limbs. She drew the ankles together and then, disturbed by the jungle boots that had somehow been fastened to those frail and delicate feet, unlaced them and pulled them off, discovering that the feet, surprisingly, were encased in soft, cranberry-colored socks. Amolia's arms—with hands that had been drawn by hunger into fine violin strings—did not seem comfortable either, where they lay spidery and wan at her sides; experimentally Linda lifted them and folded them together on the chest. But that looked odd too, as if Amolia were praying, so she moved the hands apart; still flat on the chest, the right one was now higher than the left one, and that looked fine, as if Amolia had suddenly raised her hands to stop a pain, to press her heart into submission.

By now, it was past dinnertime, though Linda was certainly not hungry. When she and Trent and Ian reached the bunkhouse, though, they were greeted at the door with many shouts for food, as well as cheers and cries of joy, a burbling outpouring of elation and enthusiasm that seemed to hit them like a tidal wave. Jack was now sitting up in bed, propped on what appeared to be every pillow in the bunkhouse, and he had recovered enough, it seemed, to be able to tag every second word with *o*.

"No, bro," he was saying now, to Emory and Derell and Stan. "My shoulder wasn't quite its old selfo. Or I would have gotten her good."

Arnold, to Linda's amazement, had his own circle of listeners, among them Eric and Josh and Kennie Dugan.

"Well, *she* was very weird, I think, kind of spaced out and angry and calm all at once, but the man, Mr. Wesley, he was *really* nice, we played string games and round the round robin and he had very many things to say and—"

Harry, who should in Linda's opinion have been getting all the attention and more, was simply building up the fire in the stove again. He glanced up at Linda as she came over, grinned, and said, "What? Not smoking, Stovepipe?"

"Not now, kiddo. By the way, thanks for saving our lives."

"Oh." Harry looked abashed. "I've got an older brother, that's all."

"That's what your older brother's like?"

"Sort of. But not so easy to push around."

■　■　■

In the dining hall a little later, Linda still felt very quiet. She had decided to see to supper, after putting Trent in charge of organizing all-night watches of Amolia's body and of the beach, the first from a half-rational fear that some wild animal—a deer? an eagle? a rabbit?—might smell the death and come to investigate, the other from a nonrational intuition that Spike and Wesley might return under cover of darkness. Linda was more than happy to let Trent make those arrangements, felt indeed a sense of relief at being able to give up her prerogatives. She was so used to carrying the weight of the world on her shoulders; now she had managed to let it go before she was felled by that weight, crushed, finished. It passed through her mind that sometime soon, perhaps tomorrow, she would have to decide what, if anything, to do about the trust-games escape; it occurred to her, too, that the odd visitation might have a bad effect on her funding. But the whole earth looked so lovely to her now; the tangled salmonberries that stretched luxuriously along the ground, the beach grass, the wild rye that blew like a coverlet drying in the breeze. On her way down to the dining hall, she had plucked and eaten some stonecrop, and the tart crisp taste of the odd little plant was all the dinner she needed. Arnold and Emory and Kennie Dugan were behind her, and they hooted in hilarity, but she didn't care. She smiled at them, then set them on a bench while she made dinner all by herself.

"So," said Arnold, apparently picking up on a conversation that he had suspended in midstream, just as if no time at all had passed between his last word and this first one, "so then she said, we could rip up a shirt, or if there was a curtain, but there wasn't any curtain, and I was just sitting in the chair where she had told me to so she told me to take off my shirt, the one with the cabbages on it that my mother sent me, only—"

"Your mother takes drugs," said Kennie Dugan. "She can send you all the cabbage shirts she wants but unless she stops taking drugs her brain will rot and if her brain rots she'll never be able to say Yes to Christ. Christ is standing in a big operating room, twenty feet high, and gleaming with stuff, and all you have to do is go to the door and say, 'Take me, Lord,' and he whisks you in and sets you on this table and sticks his knife in you and then you're cured."

"Hey, mon," said Emory suddenly to Arnold. "What are you doing with just one shoe?"

Linda, who was halfway around the top of a huge can of cream of chicken soup, watching the edge crimping away and separating from the side like a round wrinkle of happiness, turned to look at Arnold, who had put on another shirt, aqua blue, after giving the camouflage outfit back to Wesley. He had gotten up from the bench he was sitting on and wandered over to the ladder that was still standing next to the wall he'd been painting when the crazies first arrived. Although his pants had slipped down so far over his hips that the cuffs were dragging on the floor, she could see that, yes, it was true, he had on only one shoe. Arnold looked back over his shoulder at Emory's words, a quizzical expression on his face and the tip of his tongue protruding thoughtfully from between his lips; then he reached down and pulled up a pants leg, studying his foot solemnly.

"I don't know," he said.

"Oh, mon," said Emory, getting to his feet. "What are we going to do with you? They might come back and you'd have to run. How you going to run with just one shoe?" And he started his litany about hiding places for shoes, while Linda upended the soup can into a pot.

Arnold, however, was not paying much attention to Emory. He had picked up the paint brush, and, studying the wall that he had left half-finished, was tentatively jabbing it here and there. Then, as he dipped the tip into the paint can and took a first, smooth stroke, he said, "I hope we have smashed potatoes for dinner. Can we, Linda?"

"No, kiddo. It would take too long. How does smashed soup sound instead?"

"Oooh, smashed soup!" said Arnold, as Emory said, "I bet

it's in the bunkhouse after all," and Kennie said, "They might come back. They might come back and then where would we be, running and screaming and moaning . . ."

Gently, Linda stirred the soup. It was such a beautiful color.

28

■ DARKNESS WAS BEGINNING to fall when Micah, to Wesley's great relief, finally located the island where he had left the food cache. They had been in the boat for some time by then and Micah, who had never seemed much good at navigating, seemed worse than ever now—Wesley felt quite sore from falling down, as well as slightly seasick from the smell of the gas and oil. But more than his physical injuries, which were, after all, slight, were his mental injuries; he could not believe that he had been persuaded, even for an instant, that he should leave his daughter Amolia. Oh, it was all very well to say he had been confused, even disoriented, by the sudden explosions practically in his ear and then by the way Amolia had acted, so fawn-like, running forward, seeming nimble-footed enough as she approached him almost to rise up into the sky like Peter Pan, and then, somehow, never reaching him, an optical illusion, maybe, the way she seemed to keep running and running and never getting any closer until finally she just fell out of the air in exhaustion, her feet still pedaling beneath her. Yes, he had been disoriented—who wouldn't be when so many confusing things were happening at once?—but to let himself be trundled off to the boat like a wheelbarrow just because a smooth-talking young fellow had said his daughter would be better taken care of in his absence; well, it was perfectly ridiculous, that was what it was, and he would have a thing or two to say to that young lad if he ever met him again. But meanwhile—meanwhile he was separated from his daughter at what might well be the most

crucial moment of her life, when she was hurt, probably unconscious, and she needed to have a familiar voice at her side calling her back to the world of the living.

Not that she was dead. No, he didn't believe that for a second. Yes, he had told Micah that he thought she might be dead,
but that was just as a way to get him to turn around; if he had
really thought she was dead he would never ever have left her
alone, no matter how many people tried to persuade him otherwise; if she was dead he would be there to help her spirit
cross over into the land of the dead, to prepare it for its journey
to the place where it would stay until it was time to be reborn
again—in some comfort, he hoped, but certainly less happy if
it had not been seen on its way by Wesley or some other loving
presence. Because the truth of it was—the truth of it was that
he didn't really believe in a regular heaven, certainly didn't believe in the heaven of the Christians; he thought it was perfectly ridiculous to imagine that one man born two thousand
years ago somewhere in the Middle East could possibly make
sure that everyone else for all time got to go to a happy hunting
ground. That would mean that people weren't responsible,
really, for figuring things out for themselves, that they weren't
actually in charge of their own lives. The only thing that made
sense to Wesley—and he had believed this, in fact, all his life,
even before his beloved wife, Cynthia, was killed—was that each
person came to the earth again and again and again, in a different form, a different body, sometimes fat, sometimes thin,
sometimes man and sometimes woman until they had each,
through suffering all the possible variations on human misery,
come to learn that what was important was transcending that
misery and ignoring that suffering and not inflicting misery on
others. You couldn't, realistically speaking, expect that all the
things you did wrong could just be erased, forgotten, by the
simple flick of a hand, the simple movement of a lip. You
couldn't expect that any more than you could expect that rats
could turn into coachmen. What you could believe was that
people could get better—not in one lifetime, of course, one

lifetime was far too short a time to expect a lot of real improve-ment—but in many lifetimes, over the course of centuries, of eons. So if Amolia had been killed—not that she had been—but if she had, she would be heading back to the waiting room and he should have seen her on her way.

But what could he do now? Micah was attempting, pain-fully, to dock the boat in the semidarkness, which, though misty, at least had the beginnings of a moon. He had approached it three times so far and three times had landed at least five feet from the edge of the dock and then been carried immediately even further away by the movement of the tides and the bur-ring of the engine. He had sworn a lot, and was now making a fourth attempt, but he hadn't yet spoken to Wesley, and so there was nothing Wesley could do except hope that this time it would work. It did work, although more violently than Wesley had anticipated; the fourth time in Micah managed to crash the boat practically head on into the wharf, and then to wrench it around so that it slammed brutally into place.

"Okay," he shouted to Wesley then. "Hop out and get us secured!"

Wesley tried to hop—he wanted to be cooperative, after all, since he felt, vaguely, that the more cooperative he was the sooner he would get to see Amolia again—but the best he could manage was a slow waddle, and he almost failed to get clear of the boat before it drifted toward the sea once more. For a mo-ment his legs were straddled precariously between the port side and the wharf, and then he managed to unstick the left leg and cross over to the dock. Micah threw him a rope and he wrapped it around a big wedge of wood that had been fastened to the wharf as a crosspiece. So they were here. Yes, they were here, and it brought back painful memories.

The last time Wesley had been here Amolia had been with him, making tea with sugar. He had been surprised at how many whales they had found swimming around in these waters, when he had understood that whales were vanishing from the face of the earth, and when he had mentioned that they seemed to be thriving—as indeed they did, even today he had seen at least ten of them—finding it in some way consoling that there were still so many around, at least to all appearances, Micah had said that whales made good eating, and Wesley had been appalled. The truth of it was, now that he thought about it, that he had been appalled by pretty much everything Micah had said or done, right from the beginning, and he couldn't for the life of him figure out why he had stuck with him. Why, there on that very porch—Micah had joined him on the wharf and they were now, in silence, making their way up the long ramp toward the shore—there on that very porch he had been forced to participate in helping clean those terrible guns, their parts all much too small for his fingers to handle anyway, their aura one of real unpleasantness. And now here he was, still trotting along, willing to do anything Micah said.

Well, no, he wasn't. He certainly wasn't. And he was ready to make that clear. Micah could do what he liked, stay here or go to the moon, but he, Wesley, was going back to the island where he had left his daughter, as soon as they had gotten the food they had come for. He didn't know how he was going to do it, but he was.

"This is it," said Micah. "This is it, all right. The food's under the porch."

Wesley maintained his silence, unwilling to converse with this man, but Micah didn't seem to notice, just strode dramatically to the food cache like a chararcter in a Shakespearean play. He looked at it critically, and said, "Well, here we got enough to keep us quite a while, quite a while on the run, old man."

Of all the habits that Micah had, the habit of calling Wesley "old man" was perhaps the most specifically annoying, since Wesley—at fifty-two—did not consider himself old. But this time, instead of trying to ignore the slight in silence, he found himself speaking aloud. "I am not old," he said, "though I am indisputably a man. And I don't know what you mean by quite a while, but I would say that there is food here for—maybe—three days. I, personally, am not hungry."

Micah stared at Wesley in a measuring silence, then apparently decided to ignore his comments.

"We need something to carry this in," he said.

The cabin was still unlocked—the padlock, which Micah had chopped off with an ax when they first arrived, had been entirely ruined and so when they had left Amolia had, after neatly sweeping the floor, simply pulled the door to behind her—and Micah just pushed his way in to secure a kerosene lamp. Most of the valuable or useful tools they had taken with them, of course, and all of those tools as well as all their other supplies were still in the canoe on Chenega. But Micah had left this lamp behind as unnecessary, and he found a match to light it now. The ceiling of the cabin sprang out at them, in a soft yellow glow that was both comforting and eerie, and as Wesley settled himself on the edge of a bunk bed, he felt awkward at being alone with Micah.

"Okay, Wesley, okay," Micah said then. "Here's what we do now. We got food for what . . . maybe three days? We got the boat, and we got the radio, so we have at least a day to get away. Now the way I see it—the way I see it, Wesley, you understand, and I want you to correct me if I'm wrong—we can't take the boat to one of the ports, where it'd be sure to be recognized. We could take it out to sea, I guess, into the Gulf and then down to Seattle, but that might be tricky, a little tricky, two people who don't know boats. So we ditch it somewhere where they won't expect it. Then we take to the woods, make it to the train line—and hop a freight for Anchorage."

Wesley did not move, just sighed a mournful sigh. Micah seemed to him more and more bizarre. Certainly it would be a long time before Wesley trusted people's names again; the Micah *he* had been expecting would never think that Wesley could "hop a freight train," and would question whether he would want to. But Micah never looked beyond himself. Maybe he couldn't help it—yes, there was that to consider. But if he couldn't help it, who could?

Micah was now searching the cabin for a suitcase, or, failing that, a sack for the food. So far as it went, it did not seem a bad idea to take their food with them when they left—Wesley had, after all a profound respect for food, at least the vegetable kind of it, and although he was not hungry now, he was well accustomed to preparing for hunger to come. But while he thought it a good idea, he could not bring himself to participate in the search—could not, perhaps, because he felt that from now on anything he did to aid Micah, no matter how indirectly, was in some way a betrayal of his daughter, who had fallen, after all, at Micah's hands. In fact—in fact, as he watched Micah in the glowing lamplight, his taut, rather feral face straining ahead of him into the darkened corners as if he were looking for something that was not to be found, quite, within the confines of this world, Wesley had the feeling that he was watching an animal, an animal with little but a sense of smell to guide him. When a wind came up; when a stronger smell interfered; when he had a cold that blocked the passages of his instincts, he was lost, just lost, overpoweringly vulnerable. Wesley raised himself up from the edge of the bunk and went out onto the porch to wait.

Presently Micah emerged with a blanket, slightly mouse-eaten, slightly musty.

"We toss the food in this," he said, "and tie it up at the corners. Pretty good, eh? We have all the food we need. But the problem as I see it, the problem, Wesley, is this; if we take to the woods, what do we do for tools?"

"Tools?" said Wesley, forgetting for an instant his resolve to stay uninvolved. "Why would we need to have tools? That is to say, Micah, a few tools, of course, matches and—" He stopped, unable to think further.

"And an ax," said Micah. "And a tarp to sleep under. And

sleeping bags and plastic and pots and pans and cups. And everything, in fact, that we left in the canoe, back on Chenega Island."

Micah said no more as they piled the food into the blanket, but Wesley had the sense that he was thinking. Wesley himself, though he knew that he should be making plans, clever plans about what to do when they got back in the boat, did not want to think. At the moment he wanted to study the food. There were several cans of beans, and several cans of fruit, and at least five cans of evaporated milk, and two *large* cans of tomato juice—and then there was soup, and crackers in a can, and Gatorade, and packets of jerky.

To Wesley, there was something infinitely reassuring in all this terribly prosaic matter, the graceful white letters on the red tomato-soup cans, the noodle *o*s that sang across the paper. The large tomato-juice can had a particular attraction for him, he could not figure out quite why; perhaps because, even in her skinniest days, tomato juice was the one thing Amolia would sometimes deign to take into her mouth, perhaps because it was *so* large, *so* heavy, it seemed an item to which nothing could stand up for long; even a wicked dictator, intent on destroying the world through war, would have to bow down in recognition of the superior power of this juice.

Together, Micah and Wesley carried the blanket along the wharf to the boat. They slung it over the side and let it land with a thump on the deck and then with one accord they both climbed after it. It was now almost completely dark, but there was a good bright moon climbing rapidly into the eastern sky, and in whatever ways Wesley disagreed with Micah, he too felt that there was some urgency in the air now, and that they should get where they were going. He had the peculiar feeling that any moment Micah would suggest they head for Chenega—his talk about the tools and the gear they had left in the canoe implied as much—and bizarre as he found Micah's logical processes, he could only be happy about this one. Because this one would take him back to Amolia, where he had known for hours he should be. As Micah started the engine, Wesley clung to the side of the boat. The engine putted a few times before it caught fire and started to roar, and as it did so Micah threw the boat into reverse so hard that they shot back into the sea like a battering ram. Then he spun the wheel around and with a nasty wrench of the steering column started them back the way they had come. This time, Wesley did not fall down.

It was minutes, though, before he regained his equilibrium; by then Micah was evolving his latest—and expected—plan.

"Okay, Wesley, old man, okay. The way I see it is this. We don't want to get those Chenega Islanders on our case again, we've all had enough excitement for one day, what do you think? But they've got our stuff, all our tools and supplies, and we got to recover those goods. So how do we do both those little things, how do we manage that? We wait for the dead of night, that's how, and we creep in under cover of the dark. The canoe should still be there; we unload it into this boat; and then, before they know we've been there, we're gone and on our way."

"All right," said Wesley. "Would you like some beans now? You said that you were hungry."

"Yeah, beans," said Micah, and Wesley got out a can of beans and proceeded to pry open the top with one of the many implements attached to the knife Micah handed him. His mind, he noted with amazement, was almost racing. It appeared that he had been correct all along in thinking—ever since they reached Prince William Sound—that Micah really had no plan, no idea what he wanted to do. At first he had claimed he wanted to build a cabin; then he had said he wanted to kill that man Burke; and now, for reasons that were hardly good enough, he wanted to return to Chenega. And it seemed to Wesley, though he could not have said exactly why, that if Micah were allowed to return to Chenega tonight inevitably something more would go wrong. It occurred to him that if he could get Micah's attention occupied elsewhere for a few minutes then he, Wesley, could use the radio phone that was bolted to the dashboard in the cabin and call the police—or anyone else—to come to humanity's rescue. But the cabin was small, and there seemed no way to assure that Micah's attention would remain fixed for any length of time on whatever diversion Wesley could come up with—unless he hit him over the head and knocked him out for the duration.

Knocked him out? No! With what? He'd never hurt anyone in his life. And if he did, it would have to be accidentally, or at least not with a weapon. No, the only way he'd ever hit someone would be with a . . . a giant squash, maybe, something natural, organic, part of the order of life. Or maybe, well, it wasn't exactly a squash, but maybe a can of . . . tomato juice. He finished tearing the lid of the beans open, and while Micah was spearing the beans with the tip of another knife, stoking the furnace of his mouth as if with tiny morsels of coal, Wesley casually picked up the tomato juice and set it carefully to one side. It was a handsome can, that much was certain—and very, very strong.

But still, he did not know if he could do it. The boat was moving rapidly now through waters that were getting familiar, and every minute that passed in indecision brought them nearer to the island. They were both inside the cabin looking out when Micah suddenly extinguished the running lights, and instead of slowing down, as he should have, actually speeded up. The moon was still bright, and they could clearly see the ocean, calm around them, but the darkness nonetheless seemed eerie, and Wesley felt very strange. As Micah stood at the wheel revving the engine, making the boat go faster and faster, more and more furiously, Wesley had a kind of vision, perhaps a hallucination, perhaps merely a waking dream. As he bent down to pick up the tomato-juice can, his heart pounding wildly in his chest and his breath so short that it sounded in his own ears like a small child's sobbing, he had the oddest illusion that all around them on the ocean, other boats were riding at anchor. Their lights, blue and green, were bobbing crazily in a rising sea, and as he watched, incredulous, the water was sucked back from the arm of the bay like an ebb tide, only quicker, quick as things can be only in nightmares, and "A tidal wave!" the skippers were shouting, "Pull up the anchors, cut loose!" For a moment there was no sea, the ships were sitting on the bottom with the thrashing fishes, and then the front of the wave hit, a wave that could drown the earth. All around him in the moonlight boats were going down, people were shouting, screaming, half the fleet of the world was vanishing as the tidal wave advanced, and then, as they came hard on the island, riding that wave, that dangerous wave, the ghost fleets around him vanished, the sea was calm again beneath the moon, and Wesley felt that the boat was standing still, while the rest of the world tore under it.

29

■ IT WAS ALMOST THREE in the morning when *The Reach* crashed into Chenega, and Trent was on beach watch. At first, so tired was he, he thought a thunderstorm had begun—just in time to wake him from the light doze he was thinking of falling into—but then the prolonged grinding and squeaking of the engine as the shaft got driven into the sand gave him time to come fully awake and realize what was happening. In his dream—because to tell the truth he really *had* been asleep, though just for a second—he had imagined that the buzzing of the boat's engine as it approached the island was the buzzing of a huge bumble bee in a meadow with flowers, exaggeratedly bright, that actually nodded their heads as if they were jointed on their stems, and they were nodding, it seemed, their agreement with an observation he had made about Life. Already the dream was gone so completely that he couldn't remember what that observation had been—though it seemed to him to have had something to do with capriciousness—and as he started running disjointedly and stiffly toward the site of the crash, he felt simultaneously disappointed that so profound an observation had been lost and devastated that the new, tough man whom he had discovered himself to be could possibly fall asleep when danger threatened.

Today had been so peculiar from the start. He had been astonished to find that—despite some of its more unpleasant moments, such as the first second, when he had thought the crazies were terrorists—there had been a thrill to the whole experience, a thrill he hadn't felt since Rae. Or rather, that he hadn't felt since breaking up with Rae; the agony of that had been so acute that he had felt fully alive for the first time in his twenty-nine-odd years. He had thought that the thrill, the sense of being fully alive, had been directly connected to Rae— that it was *she* whom he could not live without, *she* who had been able to make clear the essence of existence—but he was now convinced that any woman would have done, it was the being left that was important. It had opened up whole realms to him, realms of agony unimaginable, as he endured fantastic separation from everything that gave him satisfaction—working with students, playing the clarinet, talking to other people, just being alive in the world—and it had seemed, too, to make him want desperately to hold on, to hang on to life and what it brought him. Well, in a different way, that was exactly what had happened to him today. When he had woken up this morning, he had had no more thought of his own mortality than he had of when the next solar eclipse would be, and then, bang, into his life had walked these gun-carrying crazies and he had suddenly been fighting once again. And although at first, when they had all been eating in the dining room, he had not gotten a grip as complete as he might have, had not figured out what to do as quickly as he would have liked, he had nonetheless felt, from the moment he had flung himself to the floor of the gun room, that he *would* be in charge of his destiny.

Thinking of this, he slowed down abruptly, before he got close to the boat. He had heard some shouts from the direction of the compound moments before, and probably the others were on their way to join him, but for the moment he was alone, and he didn't know what lay ahead in *The Reach*. With any luck, it would be empty, its passengers having jumped overboard when they saw their collision course with the island, but there was also a chance—just a chance—that they were aboard, alive and kicking. From slowing down, Trent stopped, then moved sideways toward the trees. There, he dropped down so that he sat on one heel, with the other knee up and his rifle held loosely in the crook of an elbow. He worked the lever on the rifle, half opening it, and looked down to see if there was a cartridge in the chamber. The moonlit brass gleamed dully in the half-opened action and his heartbeat quickened and grew louder. Tentatively, he pointed his rifle toward the wreck of *The Reach*.

But as he lifted it toward his shoulder, he knew that he would never use it—that no matter how far he'd come today, he hadn't come that far. Besides, what if this wasn't the crazies at all? What if it was some totally innocent people, who'd somehow ended up on *The Reach?* Ridiculous, perhaps. But wild and ridiculous things happened. Anorexic women got shot on islands in the middle of nowhere, for no very good reason; the smartest boy in the whole camp ran away like the biggest fool.

Linda appeared now with Lorne and Motor, all of them crouching low. Quickly, Trent lowered the rifle and called out softly from the trees. At the sound, they all started, and Motor, who had the pistol—Ian had been relegated to the bunkhouse—raised it slightly in Trent's direction before he identified the voice. Then they all started talking at once, in low fierce whispers, and it was some time before Trent could outline his plan, which was for him to go aboard while they backed him up.

As far as he could tell, all was quiet on the boat now. As the sea moved, the timbers creaked, and there was still a slight whirring in the engine as if some blower or belt had been set in motion too rapidly to stop entirely, but of human noises Trent could not distinguish any; perhaps they really had jumped. But if they had, then wouldn't he be hearing splashes and cries from the sea, instead of just the slight moaning of the wind as it brushed the water and the sand? Moonlight glinted off the metal parts of the boat's cabin, but the bow had come quite far onto the shore, and had been forced up at an angle that obscured much of the craft from view.

When he was still ten feet from the wreck, Trent stopped short at a sound. A low moaning, not unlike the moaning of the wind, it seemed to start and stop rather more regularly than the wind did, and it was interrupted by a slight clicking noise. Moan, click, moan, click, and the first thought that crossed Trent's mind was that the click was like the click of a bolt being drawn back and forth on a rifle. Not that this was precisely what it sounded like, it sounded more like . . . well, he couldn't say. But he certainly wasn't going to figure it out standing there, so, at infinitely slow speed, he crept forward again, rifle in hand, coming up on the boat on its blindest side, and then, working his way inch by inch down along the rail until he could peer over the starboard gunwale, he looked into the belly of the trawler.

What he saw there completely surprised him. A picture of prostrated misery, Wesley sat on the deck weeping, lugubrious tears on his cheeks, Spike's head cradled between his hands. As white as a shell in the moonlight, and almost as smooth, Spike's face gleamed beneath the hands, his eyes closed, his hair wet, and blood spreading across his forehead like a little netted cap. All the antagonism was gone from Spike, all the restless chafing, the impetuous truculence; now he radiated repose. But Wesley was moaning, a long drawn-out moaning that stopped just for a minute as he reached out to hit a large can of tomato juice that lay against the railing, beating it with the handle of a knife, and then he resumed his moaning once more, until it was time to hit the can again. So absorbed was he in the process in which he was engaged that he did not appear to notice Trent's eyes peeping over the gunwale.

Trent cleared his throat, feeling awkward interrupting such intimacy. At the sound, Wesley moved and his eyelids came apart. His eyes, when he turned them toward Trent, were stricken eyes, not wincing or flinching now, without fretting or dismay in them, but full of bottomless regret, a deep, unexaggerated sorrow. He opened his mouth to speak, but the tears running down his face had collected on his upper lip and he paused to wipe them away before he said, "I hit him on the brains."

Without pausing to consider, without stopping for a moment, Trent climbed into the boat. He had to walk into the sea and clamber to the top of a rock in order to get enough of a grip on the rail to hoist himself up and over. Wesley moaned again, and hit the tomato can with the knife; as he finished the latter action Trent gently took the knife from him and hefted the tomato-juice can.

"With this?" he asked. There was a small dent along one side of one rim; it looked like a can with a history.

"With that," said Wesley, the tears running afresh. "I'll never be able to eat tomatoes again. And—" here, he was overcome with a bout of fresh sobbing, choked by the force of the words that were trying to escape from him—"and I *love* tomatoes, my grandfather, a Polish pup-peasant, used to eat them when everyone still thought they were pup-pup-pup-poisonous!" This last recollection completely undid him, and his tears literally poured down onto Spike's face, where they joined with the netted cap of blood, making it bigger and looser. Trent knelt down at his side and took Wesley's head in *his* hands, so that anyone watching them would have thought they were playing some kind of complicated game, with everyone holding some-one else's head.

Gradually, Wesley's sobs abated. He wiped his eyes with his forefingers, letting go of Spike—who still lay quite unmoving—and then he wiped his ears as well, knuckling them with enormous folded hands. He seemed to be trying to conjure something out of them—rabbits, perhaps, or just tiny lace handkerchiefs with which he could do the job more adequately. Finally, he took a huge breath, and turned to Trent.

"Please excuse me," he said, "for getting so upset. I've never, up to now, hurt anyone in the world, but I thought that in this case the world spirit would forgive me, because otherwise Micah might have killed someone. Or, rather, someone else, because I'm pretty sure, on thinking it over, that he killed my daughter. Didn't he?"

To that, Trent could only nod.

"I should like to see her body," said Wesley. "And perhaps Micah should be taken inside somewhere."

Trent nodded again, and then stood up and called out to the others, "It's okay. Somebody better go get some kids, though. We need a stretcher team for Spike." Then he made his way forward to the still functioning radio to call, at last, for help. He saw Wesley ease himself out from under Spike, laying Spike's head gently on the deck, then pick up the tomato-juice can and hurl it into the sea.

He couldn't seem to raise the Coast Guard, so he called the Whittier police. He had some trouble convincing the man who answered that he was not just a practical joker—a fisherman, perhaps, sailing with the morning tide and bored with the sameness of shrimp—but at last the message seemed to get through and there was a minute of stunned silence.

"Dead? Armed robbers? *The Reach* totally wrecked?"

"Yes," said Trent. "Yes, yes, yes."

The Coast Guard would certainly be called in. A boat would be there as soon as possible. Such a thing hadn't happened on the Sound for oh . . . as long as he could remember.

"Thank you," said Trent, and hung up.

He went to rejoin Wesley and help him over the side of the boat—which, with the tide receding now, was dryer and more stable all the time. Linda had gone to collect the stretcher team herself, so Motor waded out into the water to help receive him on the lower end, while Lorne, who had never been good for much of anything, remained true to form even now. Trent had thought Wesley too heavy to do more than trundle from place to place like a wheeled supply truck, but in actuality he had a surprising nimbleness about him, and though he was still slightly soggy with tears, and got soggier still as he descended into the sea, he did not seem to Trent—who had him by the arm—as earthbound as anyone might have thought. They had all three safely reached the shore and were heading back toward camp when Linda appeared again on the beach, followed by Emory, Derell, Stan, Norm, Eric, and Rudy. Linda was carrying the wire stretcher.

In the growing darkness—although dawn was not far away now, the moon had just begun to sink behind the western horizon—there was, it seemed to Trent, an air of ritual about this sudden gathering on the shore. Motor and Trent and Wesley, all wet with the salt of the sea, stood together in a group, forming a perfect triad with Wesley at its head; the six boys and Linda, a seven, were thrust forward toward the boat like a lance; and in that boat there lay a man, unconscious, his white face turned to the sky. Over all there was a hush, a hush that survived the sound of the wind and the lapping of the waves that seemed to grow beneath it like mushrooms beneath the muscles of the earth, and although he didn't know where it was coming from, Trent felt there was a power present. Not a power over anything, not a power that ruled, but a power that surged, a power that forced, a power that brought peace.

"Okay, kiddos, let's get aboard," said Linda. "And *carefully*," she added.

Like a lozenge melting into the sea, the moon disappeared just as the stretcher team clambered aboard the boat. Wesley turned and started walking toward the camp, and Trent followed him, leaving Motor and Lorne behind to help Linda if she needed them. He hoped someone was still standing guard over Amolia's body, but he wanted to get there before Wesley did in any case, just to be sure all was well. When he had last looked in, Amolia's face had changed; it had darkened, gotten slightly purpler around the ears and slightly yellower in the face, as if the blood, tugged by the force of gravity, had drained out of her face on both sides, and Trent was very much afraid that by the time Wesley saw her her spirit would have flown. Trent

was not certain why he even thought that—her spirit flown—
and yet it was true, when she had been freshly dead she had
emanated energy still, a field of force that, though muted, was
not unlike the field of force her life engendered. Then, as her
face grew yellow, the field grew weaker. Now, it was probably
gone.

Ahead of him on the path, Wesley stumbled a little, but he
caught himself before he fell forward headlong.

"Oh, dear," he said. "Pardon me," he added—apparently to
the rock that he had tripped on.

At the door to the school Trent stopped him, saying, "I'll
just check on how things are first," and Wesley obediently
waited.

Inside the school, everything was fine; the candles were fresh
and burning brightly, the stove in the corner was throwing heat,
and someone had cleaned up all the parts of the radio that had
been strewn across the floor. Kennie Dugan was on body watch,
and not asleep; the expression on his face as Trent surprised it
was one of a profound uneasiness and wonder, and Trent
thought fleetingly that this one night had probably taught most
of the boys more about reality than nine months of reality therapy would ever do. Trent told Kennie he could go back to bed
and—for once quite speechless—Kennie left. Going to the door,
Trent spoke quietly to Wesley. He did not follow him back in.

But after a while, his curiosity overcame him, and he went
silently up to the north window. He didn't know what he expected to see; nothing more than Wesley sitting quietly in a
chair, perhaps holding his daughter's hand, or, at most, kneeling
by her side praying. But Wesley was not doing either of those
things. He was moving around the desks on which Amolia's
body lay, moving around them counterclockwise, and he seemed
to be mumbling, or chanting, to himself, with a small, tender
smile on his face.

When the stretcher crew arrived, they decided to put Spike in
the dining hall. He was still unconscious, but he had moved

several times on the trip up from the beach, and once he had made a moaning sound, so—to be safe—they tied his wrists and ankles, and they left two counselors on guard. Lorne and Motor volunteered; Motor so that he would have the pleasure of telling Spike what he thought of him for wrecking *The Reach* when he woke up and Lorne so that he would have the pleasure of smirking.

By now, Trent felt stunned with exhaustion. He had not stayed up all night like this since he was in college, and he had forgotten that it had the effect of making one simultaneously very gloomy and ready to try anything in the world. He and Linda left the dining hall and stood staring at each other in the first light of dawn, their duties, for the moment, discharged. The sweet smell of woodsmoke was in the air, and the higher layer of clouds was breaking away. What the hell, Trent thought, what the hell. He couldn't live in the past forever.

"Can I ask you a question?" he said, leaning forward toward Linda.

"Sure," she said. "What?"

"Do you want to come back to my cabin?"

For a moment, Linda just looked at him, her tiny, lithe body braced backward as she strained to see his face, her hands tucked into her back jeans pockets. Then she stood on tiptoe and linked her hands behind his back, raising the tip of her chin so she could kiss him on the lips; he lifted her right braid as he kissed her, and then dropped the braid and put his hands on her shoulders. All of those things that he had once found vaguely unappealing about Linda—the straight lines of her face, the lack of curves in buttocks and breasts, the veins that stood out harshly on the backs of her hands—all these seemed charming in the early dusk of dawn, electric with possibility. Even the slight redness around the sides of her nostrils—which he could not see in this light but nonetheless knew was there—was now a blush rather than a flaw, and though he felt a little like the statue of an Egyptian pharaoh as he moved to put his arm around her and guide her toward his cabin, the truth of it was that he always seemed to end up with short women; he could make her a little bench, if she liked, to stand on when they kissed.

30

■ THE COAST GUARD did not arrive soon, whatever they had promised. Although Harry had made a mighty effort to stay awake all night so he could see this thing through from start to finish, he had been unable to keep his resolve much beyond five o'clock, and now he was in the midst of a restless sleep. Along with all his other fears—of psychopaths, of physical injury, of blushing, of the great natural plan—Harry was scared of heights, and so his sleep, in Jack's bunk fifty inches off the floor, was troubled by his feet, which kept protruding over the empty air and sensing the void beneath them. In his dreams, his feet kept protesting, telling him they were sick and tired of being forced to walk the plank, although of course they used more irritating language, with their fondness for fancy swearwords. "You humongous homunculus," they told him, "do you think we *like* this voracious vacuum?" "Come on, feet," he said back. "Just do what I tell you and shut up." But his feet, two spatulated fronds that danced across a sandy desert, sweat dripping from their five little faces, refused, and, jeering at him one last time, climbed over a dune and vanished.

At that, Harry woke up. So strong had been the feeling of helplessness when his feet had disappeared that he felt panicked and unhappy for a moment, but then, as the events of the preceding day gradually came back to him, the unhappiness disappeared completely and was replaced with satisfaction that fit him like a piece of clothing. It reminded him of the way he had felt when, as a child, he had visited the other world beneath the lake, the paradisal kingdom, and on the return trip, that long ascent through the whirlpool in the lake, had brought with him peace. There was still the lingering music from the escape attempt to be faced—perhaps that was what his foot dream had been all about—but he had the feeling that no one was going to play that music very loud, especially not to him. Spike, who could have wrecked Chenega, was securely under lock and key, and Harry's best friend Jack had returned and was going to be just fine. From below him, Jack's disembodied and slightly woozy voice called out now, "Hey, Harry!" and he wiggled over to the edge of the bunk and peered around it at Jack.

"What am I doing in your bunk, bro?" Jack asked. "And what are you doing in mine?"

"You don't remember, mon?"

"Oh, I remember all right, I remember, bro. That little bitcho, just wait until I—"

"She's dead," said Harry. "Didn't anyone tell you?"

At that, Jack looked rather shocked, and all the other kids began to talk at once. They talked about Spike, and Amolia, and their own part in the great events—however small that was—and for once there were no smartass remarks, no wiseacre pronouncements; no one was trying to pretend that this slice of life was less important, interesting, or puzzling than it was. But to Harry, bathed as he was in a sense of remoteness, a sense of perspective much more acute than usual, there seemed to be something unhealthy about the respect with which the boys were discussing the death; they were beginning to mythologize the crazies, it seemed to him, just because they *were* crazies, and for no more vital reason. Even Norm seemed to have lost a bit of his sullenness, as he said with something like awe, "Do you really think they'll get him for murder?"

And Derell responded, quite earnestly and not at all as if Norm had tried to stab him with a chisel just the day before, "Well, I don't know, but what else could it be, do you think? He killed her, didn't he?"

Arnold, who had one sock on his right foot and one sock on his right hand, looked up wonderingly and asked, "Do you think she's in heaven?" and at that, of course, Kennie Dugan started in.

"Well, she *could* be, because if you repent of your sins, that's the nice thing about Christianity, you can do any old thing you want to, at least as long as you have time to say, 'I'm sorry, God,' before you get shot in the head. But what I think is, well, she's probably *not* in heaven, because she didn't have time . . ."

Twenty-four hours before, Harry would have gone along with all this; twenty-four hours before he wouldn't have tried to change it. But twenty-four hours before he had been convinced that he was doomed to become a murderer himself and spend the rest of his life in jail, and twenty-four hours before he had thought he was a coward. Now he knew differently. He knew he had a talent. What he particularly liked—there was no getting around it, odd as it seemed—what he particularly liked was talking crazies like Spike down, making sure they didn't do anything violent. He had a talent for that; he didn't know what it was called, but he did know that he had always had it, and in fact—if he were honest with himself—one of the reasons he was here on Chenega right now was because he had tried to keep some friends out of trouble. He had known from the start, of course, that it was hopeless, because that was the other part of his talent; he seemed to be able to sense quite clearly who could be changed, and who merely stopped. Spike there was no longer any hope for. But Jack . . . Jack there was. He would take Jack to see the body. While he slid down from the upper bunk, the other kids managed to shut Kennie up, and in the lull that followed the cessation of his monologue, Jack said, confirming the necessity, "Good. So she's dead. The little bitch. That's what she gets for slugging me." But Harry managed to get his attention, and told him he had something to show him. Jack dragged his feet a little, complaining that he felt "pretty horribillo, bro," but Harry got him out of the bunkhouse and up to the school, and when they paused in the doorway there and Jack saw Amolia's body, he stopped short, his face going round and slack.

Wesley, sitting by Amolia's side, looked up as the boys came in. He managed to give them a smile, and Harry smiled back, and then by the force of his own example urged Jack right up to the body.

"Good morning," Wesley said to Jack. "You're the young man whom my daughter hit, aren't you, the one who came back in the helicopter? I hope you know how sorry she was, how very, very sorry. She was just . . . that is to say, she had been under pressure, great pressure, you understand, and I don't think she knew at all what she was doing. The world spirit left her, I suppose, for a little while. But now she has joined it, and you *do* forgive her, I hope?"

Jack, who had been staring at Amolia's face, now entirely yellow and with a waxen sheen to it that seemed to emphasize the emaciation of her flesh, wrenched his eyes away and mumbled, "Sure. Of course. Whatever."

"I am so glad, so very glad," said Wesley, wiping invisible sweat from his eyelids with his forefingers. "We all do things we regret, of course, and the only thing to do is to learn to go on. I, for example, have recently done something that I regret very much, very much indeed. That is to say, if it had been a vegetable marrow, or a very large turnip . . . something *organic*, you understand. But a can of tomato juice—"

Jack seemed hardly to hear this speech, so mesmerized was he by Amolia. He appeared to be staring particularly—as far as Harry could judge—at one part of her right ear, where a small birthmark was revealed, and he looked as if he'd been ordered to eat it and was having trouble phrasing his refusal. Around them, the paraphernalia of the school seemed strangely appropriate, the books and maps, the charts and pencils, the knowledge still to be acquired. Finally, Jack—who was traveling in regions of his own, where maps would be no help—opened his mouth and said, "Do all dead people look like this one? Kind of yellow and *dead*, you know what I mean?"

"I imagine," said Harry. "Makes you want to live, huh?"

"Does it *ever*," said Jack fervently. "Does it *ever*."

"I should add," said Wesley, reaching out to pat Amolia's

knobby shoulder, "that my daughter was never like this before she met Micah. You know you always hear about, well, the power of bad companions, and how they can lead you astray, but I never believed that, bad. But bad . . . well, it just means ill, I think, don't you?"

Ill. Yes, that could describe it. Harry looked around the school, at the potbellied stove squatting blackly in the corner, at the clutter of learning, and he saw, in a kind of visionary trance, all the bad guys he had ever known, the thieves and bullies, the hoods and killers, sitting at the desks, crouched forward with their chins in their palms. There was the Asian who'd called him Charlie, resting for a moment from attacking small boys; there was the chain-saw murderer, too, his sanity testament idle in his hands. There was Harry's own brother Tom, his eyes—the most clearly non-Aleut part of him—gazing at the four food groups. And there too was Spike, his legs thrust uncomfortably under the desk, his rifle pointing toward the sunrise. Finally, there was Amolia, resurrected for a moment from the dead and standing gazing out the window, her hands dangling loosely at her sides. There they all were, like patients in a doctor's waiting room, a cancer in the body of the world. It seemed that Life—a great roaring engine of vitality, catapulting through time—approved of life, but like the body of any of its creatures, it was subject to disease. And here they were, the diseases, and you couldn't blame them for being what they were any more than you could blame a cancer for not getting cured, for bringing down the body of its host. You couldn't blame them, you could only try to cure them. You could only hope that they would cure themselves. Harry nodded.

"I see what you mean, mon," he said. And all the cells winked out.

Outside, there was a lot of noise as the Coast Guard cutter at last arrived. Looking out the window, Harry saw that the boat—a big boat if he had ever seen one, it filled the wharf from front to back—had tied up and men in uniforms were swarming off it. Three were now talking to Lorne and Ian, who had emerged from the bunkhouse, and soon they detached themselves and headed up to the school. The one in the lead was a great bull of a man, with huge thighs, black hair, and an expression of what appeared to be permanent surprise on his face; as he came through the door he said, "This here's the corpse, I'm correct in assuming?" When he had verified that it was indeed the corpse, he turned to his two companions and said, "Okay. Bring along the stretcher."

"Let's get out of here, bro," said Jack, and Harry, after saying goodbye to Wesley—who had gotten to his feet and was fussing about the body—followed him into the sunshine. The day had turned beautifully clear, and though a low-lying mist was still hanging over the water, it would burn off before long. The ocean was calm; seals were playing in the bay and in the distance, about a mile off the point, a pod of killer whales was just now passing, the black and white, black and white of their fins and backs looking like some sort of strange conveyor belt. One of the whales lagged a little behind the others and while Harry watched, it suddenly shot forward, dived, and then rose halfway out of the water, the great blunt ram of its nose a monolith of ebullience.

The men with the stretcher emerged from the schoolroom, Wesley walking behind them. Amolia had been covered with a gray blanket, tucked in behind her head but not around her feet, so Wesley kept reaching out to touch her foot, then sheepishly withdrawing his hand. In the distance the *chut-chut-chut* of a helicopter made itself heard, and then the whirlybird itself appeared, pale green and yellow, buglike against the blue sky. It landed in a scurry of dust and this time it was shut off and the long drawn-out moaning of the engine as it died sounded like someone in great sorrow or pain. Just as it was finally silent, and—as consequence or accident—everyone else on the island was silent too, Trent and Linda appeared on the path that led down from Trent's cabin, both of them flushed and relaxed-looking, sleepy around the eyes. At their appearance, Harry instantly got an erection, and had to turn and walk awkwardly to the corner of a shed where he could shake his leg to try and dislodge it, but, despite the discomfort their new relationship was causing him, he was happy for Trent and Linda. They were met with whistles and cheers from all the other boys, who nevertheless somehow refrained from actually *saying* anything dirty.

By the time Harry had eased his penis into his pants leg and managed to return to the group, Amolia's body had been loaded onto the helicopter and Spike was being brought outside. He looked sick; his face was very pale, and he had an awkward, lopsided bandage around his head; there was no blood, but the bandage was wet. His hands were tied behind him. He staggered a little as he walked down the steps from the dining hall and though he tried to look up defiantly to meet everyone's eyes at once, he couldn't quite manage it, and he was actually inside the helicopter before he turned and said to all the boys, "Don't look so goddamned happy. You're just like me. You just ain't got to my point yet, that's all." He repeated the last words with great satisfaction—"just ain't got to my point yet, that's all"—and the surprised-looking Coast Guard officer looked more surprised than ever as he closed the helicopter door.

When the chopper had disappeared around the southern tip of Chenega, the Coast Guard began to take statements. This looked to be a long and laborious process—particularly because each of the boys, most vocally Kennie Dugan, insisted that his own statement was both important and unique—and Linda suggested that perhaps they should go ahead and start to make breakfast, that she was sure everyone must be starving and that she herself was especially hungry, she didn't know quite why. Trent grinned at her when she said this, and she blushed as thoroughly as Harry ever had, and to Harry's great surprise not only was this not greeted by dirty remarks on the part of the other boys but it wasn't even greeted by whoops and cheers. Instead, a bashful silence ruled.

Harry was on breakfast crew this morning, according to the charts, and Arnold was once again with him, so he secured

Arnold and headed for the dining hall as the Coast Guard began to untangle their forms. Wesley, who would be leaving with the cutter—the helicopter had not had room for him, given his size and weight—appeared to be at something of a loss now that his daughter and Spike were gone, and he followed them over to the dining hall. While Arnold stood dopily by the counter and cracked eggs into a bowl—or mostly into a bowl; one of them landed on the floor right at his feet so that the yolk, as he said, jumped up and started to chew on his sneakers, and one of them slid to the counter, from which he scraped it into the bowl with his forefinger—Harry thought about Kennie Dugan, who believed there was some big guy in the sky with all the answers. Harry didn't think so. He thought probably whatever answers there *were* were right there inside you all the time. Some people managed to read the answers wrong, and everyone asked the wrong questions a lot of the time, but eventually, if you tried hard enough, you could probably help evolution along. Harry made Tang while Wesley took bread and encouraged it into the toaster.

By the next morning a light rain was falling, a drizzle that looked as if it had settled in for good. Fog moved majestically over the ocean. King crabs clicked their way along the bottom of the sea, and a sand shark swam past Naked Island just at dawn. Three deer were browsing in Granite Bay; a Kodiak brown bear was fishing for salmon nearby. Two icebergs calved into the sea almost simultaneously and the birds flying above them started upward at the sound of the impact, which was like that of a kiss, magnified a thousand times. Spike was relaxing in the Anchorage jail, safe again, and Amolia was lying in a freezer in the morgue, a little tag on her left toe. Trent was awake, pondering the future. He wanted to pay a visit to the Survival Place. Linda, naked at his side, was admiring his undeveloped pectorals. A young otter in Kake Cove awoke from a night sleeping anchored to a bed of kelp, and made his first successful independent dive, coming up afterwards to float on his back, careless and triumphant. A green glass float from Japan washed up on Perry Island. In Anchorage, Wesley—who had been released, he wasn't sure for how long, after testifying tearfully that the tomato-juice can with which he'd "done it" was now floating south toward California—was beginning to plan a fine funeral. But Harry Dance, who had the brightest future of them all— who would change the world, who might, who knew? someday save it—slept on. He slept when the bald eagle, hunting over the ocean, folded its sharp wings and dropped, then rose with a fish in its talons. He slept when the humpback whale in Knight Island Passage shot into the air, easily flipping her great body over and then smashing it back into the sea. She jumped three times. Her body as it left the water was moving at the speed of an express train.

A NOTE ON THE TYPE

The text of this book was set in Electra, a type
face designed by William Addison Dwiggins
(1880–1956) for the Mergenthaler Linotype Company
and first made available in 1935. Electra cannot be
classified as either "modern" or "old style." It is
not based on any historical model and hence does
not echo any particular period or style of type
design. It avoids the extreme contrast between
thick and thin elements that marks most modern
faces, and it is without eccentricities that catch
the eye and interfere with reading. In general,
Electra is a simple, readable type face that attempts
to give a feeling of fluidity, power, and speed.
W. A. Dwiggins began an association with the
Mergenthaler Linotype Company in 1929, and
over the next 27 years designed a number of
book types, including Metro, Electra, Caledonia,
Eldorado, and Falcon.

Composed by Creative Graphics, Inc.,
Allentown, Pennsylvania

Printed by Fairfield Graphics,
Fairfield, Pennsylvania

Designed by Marysarah Quinn